Evolving Threat

Travis Hunter

Book 3

Toby Neighbors

Evolving Threat: Travis Hurts #3

Copyright © 2023 by Toby Neighbors

ISBN: 978-1-952260-68-1 ebook

978-1-952260-69-8 print

Mythic Adventure Publishing, LLC

Idaho, USA

Also by Toby Neighbors

End Times

The Four Horsemen

Surviving Wormwood

Wizard Rising

Magic Awakening

Hidden Fire

Crying Havoc

Fierce Loyalty

Evil Tide

Wizard Falling

Chaos Descending

Into Chaos

Chaos Reigning

Chaos Raging

Controlling Chaos

Killing Chaos

Elder Wizard

Lorik

Lorik the Protector

Lorik the Defender

We Are The Wolf

Welcome To The Wolfpack

Embracing Oblivion

Joined In Battle

The Abyss Of Savagery

The Vault Of Mysteries

Lords Of Ascension

The Elusive Executioner

Gryphon Warriors

Regulators Revealed

Avondale

Draggah

Balestone

Arcanius

Avondale V

Third Prince

Royal Destiny

The Other Side

The New World

Luck Holds

Zompocalypse

Spartan Company

Spartan Valor

Spartan Guile

Dragon Team Seven

Uncommon Loyalty

Total Allegiance

Kestrel Class

Jump Point

Gravity Flux

Modulus Echo

Zero Friction

Planet Fall

Charter

Jack & Roxie

My Lady Sorceress

The Man With No Hands

ARC Angel

Battle ARC

Broken Crucible

Hidden Kingdom

War INC

Carthage Prime

Cronus Team

Skandia Seven

Mercurial

Magnificus Prime

Incursio

Merlin Appears

Runners

Survivors

Infiltrators

Resistance

Conquest

Occupation

Extraction

The Signal

Battle Orders

Base Of Fire

Hard Site

Recall

Evade

Assault

Space Fever

Staying Alive

Fractal Cut

Blast Zone

Action Zone

Covert Infil

Armor Brigade

Havoc Squad

Thunderbird

Ghost Tactics

Quantum Combat

Infinite Threat

Shadow Threat

With Pete Garcia

Apocalypse One Percenters

Chapter1

"Toe the line!" the guard shouted.

Augustine Ward and sixteen other prisoners bound for the penal colony on Lucerine lined up with their feet touching the yellow line on the flight deck of the Transit Authority's prisoner transport. They all had leg irons; the loose chain rattled against the metal deck plates.

"You will board the shuttle one at a time," the guard continued in a loud voice. "From this point out there are no second chances. All prisoner resistance will be met with lethal force, and for those of you too stupid to know what I'm saying, I will make it clear. You step out of line, even just a little, and we can legally kill you dead, on the spot. Is that absolutely clear?"

The prisoners nodded and mumbled. Some probably thinking that death would be better than spending the rest of their natural lives on Lucerine. It was a hot world. Surface exposure during the day cycle would cook a person. Temperatures rose to well over the boiling point for water, which meant there was no liquid on the surface. It was an unforgiving world with a dried, cracked surface. The penal colonies, six in total, were situated in the cracks, usually several hundred meters below the surface, where the temperatures were tolerable, and consequently, where valuable minerals could be mined.

Augustine Ward was a gunslinger. He had expected to die in a fight, not on a sweltering, toxic planet surrounded by the very lowest and meanest people in the galaxy. He wasn't a tough guy, certainly not the type to dirty his hands with any real work. Guns were his thing, shooting, spinning, showing off, that was what he did best. And he was fast too. He liked fine clothing, and pretty girls, a good poker game, and best of all, an audience when he got into a showdown. Just the thought of going down to the prison camp was terrifying, and if not for the mysterious visitor who came to see him in Los Mesa as he awaited transport to the penal colony, he would have gladly stepped out of line and let the guards shoot him dead. But the woman had given him something to cling to, and he faced his future with a mix of trepidation and a sliver of hope. It was enough to keep him from doing anything rash.

"Next!" the guard shouted from the shuttle when it was Augustine's turn to board.

He shuffled forward, was pulled up into the shuttle's passenger cabin, and locked into a hard, metal seat by a metal bar that was pushed down onto his shoulders. It reminded Augustine of the restraints on a roller coaster, only the bar wasn't padded, and it was locked down so tight across his chest and stomach that he had trouble breathing.

When all the prisoners were on board, the guards sent word to the pilot, who started the launch process. The shuttle was moved into the drop position, the transport's outer doors were opened, and jets of compressed air flung the ship straight down toward the planet. For a full minute they were in zero gravity, then the shuttle hit the upper atmosphere. Gravity took hold and the prisoners were left hanging upside down as the ship rotated toward the planet's surface.

Augustine preferred traveling in first class when he had to use public transportation. And he had been in choppy air before. It was never comfortable when an aircraft trembled, shook, and occasionally dropped without warning. But those experiences were nothing compared to entering Lucerine's atmosphere. It felt to Augustine like the shuttle had been picked up in the mouth of a giant dog, who hoped to kill everyone on board by shaking them hard. His head was flung forward and back, crashing into the metal support he was strapped to. And it didn't take long before someone was sick. Augustine didn't see who it was. He had his eyes closed, and his hands clenched onto the metal restraint. People were screaming, crying, some passed out, others threw up. It was, by far, the worst experience of Augustine Ward's life, but it didn't last. Eventually, the ship dropped down into one of the massive cracks in the surface of the planet where everything calmed down.

The ship landed on a platform, the guards rousted everyone from the seats, and soon the befouled prisoners were marched into the intake room, where their clothes were cut from their bodies and the group was hosed down while still in their shackles. The water pressure was so high that it stung Augustine's skin. Nor was it a cool, refreshing experience, as the water was at least as warm as they were. Humiliated and drenched, the crowd of prisoners was taken into a room one at a time. Their shackles were removed, their bodies were shocked with a laser strobe that removed all hair, including eyebrows, that was meant to obliterate communicable diseases and vermin. The process left the prisoners with a mild sunburn. They were given lightweight jumpsuits only after a barcode was tattooed onto the back of their necks. Finally, they were taken into a small room with no seats, and ordered to sit on the floor. A safety video was projected onto one wall. It described all the ways an inmate could die on Lucerine, and reinforced the idea that death was expected. At one point the warden narrating the video actually said that he hoped they died sooner rather than later. There was no inquiry if a prisoner died, either by toxic exposure, or accident, or violence from other inmates. The bodies of the dead were merely collected and removed to a special facility on the surface where their remains would be cremated. It was a dreadful display, and left the prisoners utterly without hope.

"Welcome to hell, boys," a guard said as he opened the door to the small room where the video had played. "On your feet and line up. We're going straight down."

There were no elevators, and very few safety measures. The guards all wore harnesses that were attached to environmental suits to keep them cool and hydrated. On the harness hung an oversized laser pistol with a biometric scanner that only the guard could use. They started down a set of metal stairs with only one guardrail. The stairs hung out over the open crevice the prison was built into, so that with one wrong step a person could fall to their death. The guard hooked a safety tether from his harness to the guardrail, the prisoners were forced to just hold on. They had gone down about forty feet when the first of the prisoners gave up and stepped off the stairs into the void. He fell without a sound, his body disappearing in the darkness below.

"That's one less mouth to feed," the guard shouted from behind the group. "And one less person you have to keep an eye on every minute of the day. This is the Devil's Playground, and you are all his playthings. Now keep moving or I'll pitch you all off the stairs."

Another prisoner slipped and fell, but caught himself before going over the side to his death. He had to limp down the rest of the way, but made it. At the bottom of the stairs was a large open cavern that reached back several hundred feet into the rocky cliff face. There were men loitering about, all in small clusters. At the back was an automated ore machine, and a couple of prisoners with canvas sacks were emptying their haul from the mines into the machine.

"Life here in hell is pretty simple," the guard said as he marched the group through a gate that closed off the metal stairs. "You are all on your own down here. You want to eat, you work. The mines are full of mineral ore, but mercury is the primary. It's also poisonous. Contact with mercury will make you sick and kill you. Trust me, it's not pretty. You start getting a metallic taste in your mouth, followed by nausea and vomiting, well ... You can always save yourself the trouble and take the leap.

"There are mining suits to protect you, complete with breathing filters. You will need rock hammers to chisel out the ore. I don't have to tell you the kind of damage a rock hammer will cause to the human body. So be careful. You make enemies down here and you'll soon be meeting your maker face to face. Once you've mined ore, you carry it up here and deposit it into the machine at the back of this level. It will scan your code and assign the appropriate amount of food credit to your account. Food dispensers are your only source of nourishment, so take care of them. If you have questions, your new bunkmates will answer them. If you have a problem, solve it yourself, or die trying. Good luck, dirtbags. You're gonna need it."

The guard stepped back onto the stairway landing and closed the door. It was made of sturdy metal, with multiple locks, which were protected by live current. Anyone who tried to pry them open would be electrocuted. The group of new inmates stood just a few paces inside the large cavern. Some were sizing up their new home environment. Others were looking for any type of friendly face.

"Ward!" the guard barked.

Augustine turned around, and the guard on the other side of the metal cage at the bottom of the stairs motioned him closer. Augustine, half in shock, obeyed. He was completely out of his element, and despite the reassurances of the woman on Los Mesa, he was terrified. It was hot in the cavern. The stench of sweat, unwashed bodies, and human excrement was potent. There were several narrow passages on either side of the cavern. Occasionally, someone in a mining suit came out of one. It was the worst environment that Augustine Ward had ever experienced.

"I passed on word that you were coming," the guard said softly.

"Leon leads a little faction he calls The Family. You've got one week to convince him that your offer is legit."

"My offer?" Ward asked.

"That's what I was told," the guard said. "Once a week we come down here to collect the bodies. I'll select you and Leon to help. When we get to the surface you'll both get uniforms and a ride out with the outgoing shuttle. After that, the Incendius people take over."

"Sounds easy enough?" Ward said nervously.

"Oh, it's simple," the guard said. "The difficult part will be keeping Leon from killing you before that."

The guard's smile was sadistic, and left Augustine feeling hollow inside. He had stood face to face with killers many times, but always with his pistols. He felt naked without them, not just exposed, but crippled. He wasn't built for hand-to-hand combat. If he crossed the wrong person in the penal colony he doubted he would last a week.

"I don't even know what he looks like," Ward said.

"Big guy, scar on his chin, crooked nose," the guard said, holding up a data slate with Leon Ward's picture on it. "Good luck."

Augustine Ward watched the guard head back up the metal stairs. When he turned around, there were dozens of inmates converging on the group of fresh fish. Ward told himself he could endure anything for a week. But deep down inside, he felt as if he had already died and really was in hell. Right at that moment he vowed if he ever did get off Lucerine, he would find the bastard responsible for having him sent there. The bounty hunter would rue the day he crossed paths with Augustine Ward. He let his fury build for a moment as he thought about the bounty hunter who had taken him captive on Pergamum Prime. Then he went to face the horrors he presently found himself in.

1

"Scye Primary, this is the *Purgatory* requesting permission for atmospheric entry," Ava said.

The orbital control gave their consent. She pressed the icons on the dashboard touchscreen that activated the jet engines and shut down the Holstead dual Faster Than Light drive engines.

"Here we go," she announced to Travis Hurts, who stood behind the other pilot's seat, which had a protective child carrier carefully strapped in to make sure one week old Kaylee was secure during the entry to Scye Primary.

"I'm braced," Travis said.

He had his boots spread between the pilot's seat, and the bulkhead behind him. His left hand held onto a bar that was built into the roof of the cockpit for that reason. His right arm was on the mend, but the cut in his right shoulder from the assassin named Soto's knife, was deep. Raising his arm was still painful, and he kept it in a sling most of the time.

The ship rotated, entering the atmosphere upside down with

the ship's artificial gravity dialed just low enough to keep Travis from flying around inside the cockpit. They dove toward the planet, which was one of the top textile manufacturing centers in the galaxy. All the big fashion brands had offices on Scye Primary. As did the companies with patents on synthetic fabrics. Some of the best tailors in the galaxy lived and worked on Scye Primary, and some of the most expensive. Travis was there to visit Eduardo Hernandez who operated a little shop in the city of Capree. It was a small town located on an island surrounded by incredibly blue water, with the tip of Azaledia, one of the eight continents on SP, to the north, and wide-open tropical oceans to the south. It was a little off the beaten path, and one of the few places where a person could get garments with laser absorbing fibers sewn into the fabric.

They landed at an airfield just outside Capree, and after securing the ship, took a hovercab through the city to Eduardo's shop. It was on a small hill that overlooked the town and the ocean beyond. The building was all glass and solar panels soaking up the sunlight. They went inside and found Eduardo waiting for them.

"Back again?" Eduardo said. "I'll be honest, most men in your profession do not live long enough to need my services more than once."

"I almost didn't," Travis said. "Eduardo, this is Ava Lynn Baxter. She's my partner."

"It is a pleasure, madame. And who is this lovely angel?"

"This is Kaylee," Ava said. "She's one week old today."

"Such a tiny thing," Eduardo said. "And beautiful. You are truly blessed."

"Yes, thank you," Ava replied.

"I need a new coat and shirt," Travis said.

"What happened to the ones I made for you before?" Eduardo asked.

"They did what they were made to do," Travis said.

"And you brought them with you, yes? I can learn much from them."

2

"Yeah, we've got those," Travis said.

"You tell me the story, then we will talk business."

He let them out onto a wide veranda with comfortable seating and a magnificent view of the ocean. He served a sweet, chilled drink made of a local fruit that was blended with ice. Travis and Ava told Eduardo the story of what happened on Expanse.

"You are lucky to be alive," Eduardo said.

"Don't I know it."

"So you are more than partners," Eduardo said. "You are a family."

"We're still figuring all that out," Travis said. "But I have a favor to ask."

"I am listening," Eduardo said.

"I need a coat, and I'd like to get Ava one too. Something appropriate that she can wear if needed."

"Something big enough I can wrap the baby in too," Ava said.

"The clothing is not armor, as you well know, Travis. It lessens the effects, but doesn't offer full protection."

"That's right," Travis said. "We're aware, but we need to be as careful as we can."

"The assassin, he lived?"

"Yes," Travis said. "And escaped from Expanse."

"Then he will come after you again," Eduardo said. "I will do all I can for you, of course."

"Will you let me pay you installments?" Travis said. "I've only got forty thousand credits at the moment."

"Ah, hence the favor," Eduardo said. "We will spend more than this amount on the fabric. And the tailoring is laborious, as you know. Two coats, a new shirt, a dress, and a wrap for the baby. Two hundred and fifty-thousand credits. I cannot do it for less."

"Not less, just not all up front," Travis said.

"I can do it for half now," Eduardo said. "You are good for the rest, but I cannot take such a risk. It would ruin me, should you be killed and unable to pay the remainder."

"I can't do half," Travis said.

"Yes we can," Ava spoke up. "We'll pay one hundred and forty up front, the remainder as soon as we bring in our next fugitive."

"I'm not asking you to do that, Ava," Travis said.

"What else would I use the money for?" she replied.

"I like knowing you have options," he told her.

"And I like knowing you're safe. Will that work for you, Eduardo?"

"Yes, of course. Let me get your measurements. I'll get started right away."

He took their measurements and they transferred the money to the tailor's account. When he had all he needed from them, he sent them away. The couple decided to take a walk on the beach and enjoy their time on the island. It was warm, but the breeze off the ocean was cool and refreshing. They walked hand in hand, little Kaylee held snug to her mother in a baby wrap.

"You shouldn't have given up that money," Travis said.

"I have all I need on the *Purgatory*."

"A hundred thousand would get you a good start on any world you like," Travis argued. "You could rent a villa here and spend your days soaking up the sunshine. Tell me that wouldn't be better than living in a cramped little spaceship."

"I've been thinking about that," she said. "I even did some research. Have you heard of a Drysen Extension?"

"The thing you connect to your ship to make it bigger?"

"Yes. It's not hybrid, the extension has to stay in orbit. But you just fly up to it, and it basically doubles the space of your vessel. You can use it for anything, extra cabins, a full kitchen, even another bathroom."

"How much do they cost?" Travis asked.

"One for our ship would be about half a million," she said.

"We could sell the *Purgatory* and buy a bigger ship for that much," Travis said.

"Maybe," she replied. "I'm just saying, there are options."

Travis suddenly wished he hadn't lost Grant Stevenson. The wanted man's reward was three quarters of a million credits. With that much money he could have purchased whatever they needed. But just getting the gear they needed was putting him over a hundred thousand credits in debt.

"Options are good," Travis said. "That's why I liked you having that money."

"All the money in the world is worthless if you're dead."

"True, but we're back to where we always end up," he told her. "This is kind of crazy. I don't like putting you in harm's way."

"But I can help you," she replied. "Right?"

"Yes, you've saved my life," Travis said. "There's no doubt. And I love being with you. But I feel guilty, Ava."

"Just stop," she told him. "I made my choice. This is what I want. Kaylee and I aren't being put out by living in the *Purgatory*. So, stop worrying about it. The decision has been made. We just need to find a system that works good for us."

"I'll do whatever it takes," he said.

"So will I," she agreed.

That evening they took Travis' coat and shirt to Eduardo. He studied the scorch marks and looked at the threat counts under a microscope.

"Do you know what type of weapon was used?" the tailor asked.

"A Ripper," Travis said. "Morgan Black has custom weapons, but the standard issue is a six-inch barrel with a Xenon 11 power cell."

"That's a powerful weapon," Eduardo said. "Not what you usually see a shootist using. And you had on armor underneath?"

"A Kingsman Armored Vest," Travis said.

"Solid plate or interlocking tiles?"

"Interlocking tiles," Travis said. "Very expensive."

"Custom made?"

"Probably," Travis said. "I took it off a very wealthy criminal."

"May I see what the effect was on your body, Travis?"

"Sure, it's healing up pretty good now."

"We saw a doctor right after," Ava said. "He got fixed up right after I had the baby."

Travis pulled off his shirt. The burn was on his chest, right above his heart, a nasty point of impact with ancillary burns snaking off on all sides, like lightning shooting out of a star.

"It did this through your coat, shirt, and the armor?" Eduardo asked.

"Point blank, from twenty feet away," Travis said. "My coat wasn't buttoned."

"You're lucky to be alive. That much energy, right over your heart, it could have caused a cardiac arrest."

"Yeah, or he could have shot me in the face," Travis said. "No protection there, and he's known for doing that."

Travis put his shirt back on and Eduardo made more notes. "I'm going to try something different with this garment, the shirt and the dress both," he explained. "Normally, I weave the energy absorbing fibers into the garment going only one direction, but I think I might put them in both ways. It will make your clothing a little less flexible, but I doubt it will be enough to notice, and it might give you added protection."

"We'll take all the protection we can get," Ava said.

"Just so long as it doesn't show," Travis said. "I have to get close to these outlaws, and armor would be a dead giveaway that I'm law enforcement."

"Yes, we'll make it look right," Eduardo said. "You can count on it. I wish you had the weapon that cut your shoulder. Did you see what it was made of?"

"A metal alloy," Travis said. "That's all I know."

"It should not have penetrated so easily."

"The energy absorbing fibers also stop punctures?" Ava asked.

"Not always," Eduardo told her. "But I use a special type. It's actually more of a wire than a thread, burns up when it absorbs energy, but it should also stop a blade. That is the point, no pun intended. We don't want Travis getting a knife in his back."

"Maybe the fibers broke down over time," Travis suggested.

"I thought of that too," Eduardo said. "But I looked at those around the cut. They are not diminished. Some specialty alloys hold a very keen edge, right down to the molecule in some instances. I can't help but wonder ..."

"What?" Travis asked.

"I read an article about a metallurgist who perfected a hydrogen metal alloy decades ago. It's what your Slinger is made of, incredibly lightweight. The man sold his patent, made himself a tidy fortune. I looked up the article while you were away. The metallurgist's name was Sanada Soto."

"You think it's the same guy?" Ava asked.

"I think that's the type of person who could forge a blade that would cut my fabric," Eduardo said. "He had no presence on social media that I could find. No news articles about him either. He sold his patents a little over thirty years ago, while he was still in his early twenties, and just disappeared."

"I'll run the name through the law enforcement database," Travis said.

"Are you going to report him?" Ava asked.

"He's a ghost," Travis said. "Even if I did, there's no evidence of a crime, other than my word against his. But I like to know who I'm dealing with."

"Whoever it is, if that cut is any indication, he is not someone you want to tackle on your own," Eduardo said.

"He's not on his own," Ava said. "Not anymore."

"Good," Eduardo said. "Everyone needs someone they can count on. Life is short enough as it is. You should make the most of every minute you have."

"Agreed," Travis said.

"Well said," Ava agreed.

Travis could tell that Ava was thinking of her late husband. She of all people knew how quickly life could turn against you. He decided then and there not to question her decision to stay with him. If that's what she wanted to do, he would give her his full support.

2

The Luxor was a massive domed complex built on a Tridenex super foundation. It looked like a tropical snow globe floating in space near a spectacular gas giant with a series of vertical rings that glowed like gold in the light from the yellow star. With a wide lake at the center of the complex, Luxor was essentially a ring, and a masterwork of engineering with a distinctly Egyptian theme. There were temples, grand plazas, massive statues of men and beasts that could move, and of course there were pyramids. The lake was made of salt water with exotic fish, and an extensive coral reef. It was surrounded by white sand beaches, where people could lounge in padded chairs with their feet in the sand, while a host of stewards and stewardesses attended to their every need.

Sanada Soto could have lived at the resort. He had the money, and no other demands that were not self-imposed. And Soto enjoyed a certain amount of luxury. Gourmet food, for instance, and fine wine, rich tobacco, the highest quality silk. But all these things he allowed himself only in small doses. He was a man of moderation in all things, and one who valued physical discipline as one of his most sacred tenets. Which was why he avoided places like the Luxor resort and casino unless his pursuit of a target led him there.

After docking his space yacht, he dressed in a fine, tailor-made suit, and checked into a VIP suite in the Khafa Pyramid. The lower levels were rowdy places, with theaters full of spectators taking in simulcast and live shows of all kinds. There were restaurants and night clubs with throbbing music. Bars served patrons throughout the complex. Nothing was off limits on Luxor short of violence. Service was done with a mix of human and android workers. Nor was it a family friendly atmosphere.

Soto was whisked up to the VIP level which had a much more subdued environment. He checked in and then inspected his suite. It was a series of three rooms, a small foyer opened up into a lavish salon with a bar, leather sofas, a top-of-the-line holographic entertainment system, and a transparent outer wall with a sublime view of space and the edge of the gas giant Ramses.

The bedroom was in the corner of the pyramid, with a view of space and the resort. It had a massive bed with silk sheets and thick posts at all four corners. The bathroom had a large, two headed shower, a two-person tub with jets, and a floor-to-ceiling mirror. The tile floors were heated, and all the fixtures were polished gold.

Soto had little interest in the luxurious suite. He wasn't there for a vacation and he could be arrogant about people who sought such comforts. Everything he did, from the diet he observed to the bed he slept in, was designed to make him more efficient at ridding the universe of evil. He would sleep in the giant bed if he was forced to stay overnight. The fact that he was spending forty-thousand credits a night on the suite meant nothing to him. His fortune was large and diversified, earning more money than he spent year after year. It was, to Soto, just another tool at his disposal. He would, however, enjoy the variety of foods that the high-end resort offered. He knew the foundation was actually an enormous city where thousands of workers lived. They were the face of the resort, and the behind-the-scenes wizards who made sure everything worked according to plan. There were entertainers, and droid engineers, wrench spinners and animal handlers. The resort had its own cattle, poultry, and even seafood on hand, so that their guests could partake in the freshest gourmet foods. Soto didn't care to think about the conditions under the resort level, but he knew it was dark, crowded, and unpleasant. Behind, or in this case under, every beautiful place designed to make guests feel comfortable was an equally large space where people worked tirelessly in far less auspicious conditions.

Soto went down to the VIP restaurant, where he ordered a tasting menu from the sushi chef. He was given a private table on the balcony overlooking the VIP lounge. Below him people were enjoying drinks, fine hand-rolled cigars, a variety of recreational drugs, and making plans with the concierge. Some of the wealthy guests liked to mix with the rowdy crowds on the lower levels, others preferred to have everything catered exclusively to them. Soto settled in for a long, lavish meal, but he would people watch while he ate. It was both his custom, and a necessary part of his routine. He was there to find LeSean Mason, one of the shot callers and wealthy beneficiaries of the money laundering scheme on Las Brazzas. Like the others in the upper echelon of the corrupt plan, LeSean had the financial means to disappear, avoiding the consequences of his shameful actions, while living the rest of his life in pampered luxury instead of a hard labor penal colony.

The meal came in courses, each plate had no more than three bites. The fish was bright and salty, and the various rolls were a playful combination of flavors. Soto enjoyed his meal, but didn't spot his target. After eating, he made his way to the cigar lounge and purchased himself a fine Santiago cigar. Everything was billed to his room, Soto had only to sign a touch-sensitive tablet. He enjoyed the rich smoke, and the quiet comfort of a thickly padded and tufted leather chair. The lounge was contained so that the cigar smoke didn't permeate the larger VIP concourse. Soto sat near a transparent wall, watching and waiting. His was the perfect, posh camouflage. He was a predator amid a herd of prey, waiting for his target to appear.

It wasn't that Soto judged the wealthy patrons for their vices. In his beliefs everyone, no matter how good, had a bit of evil in them. Every person had a vice, if not several. A weakness, a desire for something that wasn't good. Many were excellent at hiding their evil, and some fought against it, but others, especially the wealthy, had no qualms about flaunting their dark side. It came from a feeling of superiority, and the knowledge that their wealth insulated them from the consequences that the average person faced. Ultimately, it was why Sanada Soto did what he did, balancing the scales, holding back the darkness that if left unchecked would sweep across the galaxy like a horde of the Hash Gore.

The aliens hadn't been seen or heard of in civilized space for decades, but there was no doubt in Soto's mind that they were still around, just biding their time. And if not the Hash Gore, the universe would send some other punishment upon mankind if they let themselves go too far into the darkness. But other people could worry about militant aliens, just as others would go after the criminals caught up in the corruption on Las Brazzas. His mind went to Travis Hurts. He and Soto had almost killed one another. And in the same night they had both fought the greatest of evil together. Not that Soto believed murder to be evil, but the taking of innocent life was evil. Killing a violent man, or a person who through their actions hurt others, was not in his belief a crime but a necessary duty. It was a chore no different than removing garbage from a person's dwelling. Was not the galaxy the dwelling of mankind? Who would choose to live in a home with venomous snakes and deadly spiders? No, first a person removed those threats and then they could live in peace. But peace should be guarded with vigilance, and those entrusted with that task had long ago embraced a reactionary role in their duty to protect and serve. Law enforcement reacted to crime; it didn't proactively prevent lawlessness.

Likewise, the justice system was far too lenient, favoring the criminal over the victim. All of which left the work of removing evil from society in the hands of a warrior dedicated to the art of death, which Soto had become.

Soto was just finishing up his cigar when his target strolled by. LeSean Mason was tall, with very dark skin and a thick, well-manicured beard. He wore baggy slacks over boots made from alligator skin. And his shirt was unbuttoned to the top of his stomach, revealing a cascade of gold chains with diamonds that glittered in the light. He was accompanied by two female escorts, and when he passed by, Soto could see the handle of a pistol tucked into a concealed holster at the back of his pants. Mason had done nothing to change his appearance, or to hide his identity. The man thought he was safe, and it was a grave error on his part.

Soto left the stub of his cigar in a thick marble ashtray and left the lounge. LeSean Mason had gone into a dispensary, but didn't linger over the options. He bought the drugs he wanted and immediately popped some into his mouth. His escorts did the same, then they made for the elevators that would take them down to the lower levels. Soto didn't follow them down. Nor did he need to investigate the dispensary to know that Mason had bought himself some type of speed, there was a wide variety of pills and powders used to keep a person full of energy for extended periods of hedonistic pleasure. Soto was not in a hurry. He had identified his target, and confirmed that LeSean Mason was staying in the resort. Next, he would learn what room his target occupied, and find a way in and out of it. Soto was never rash in his efforts to mete out justice. At times, opportunities presented themselves to him, as they had on Expanse. At other times, he utilized patience and stealth, so that he didn't get swept up in the net of the justice system.

He was on the verge of leaving the concourse and returning to his room for a nap when someone caught his eye. The resort was full of people, even the VIP level. Every ethnicity, and every fashion trend were represented. It was simple to blend in. What one didn't often see was infirmity, but out of the corner of his eye Soto saw a man moving stiffly, as if every step was painful. Soto didn't recognize him at first. The man stepped off the elevator, which Soto knew had come down from the expensive rooms and suites above. He made straight for the nearest dispensary. Soto lingered, pretending to look at a kiosk that sold exotic eye ware. Just like Mason, the stranger knew his business. And just like LeSean, he dry swallowed a pair of pills the moment he stepped out of the dispensary.

Soto marked the way the man's shoulders sagged a little, as if the weight of some great pain had been lifted off his back. He still moved with a stiffness that made it clear he was in pain. He was going back to the elevators, not to the restaurants or shops that filled the VIP concourse. The man had patchy scruff on his cheeks and chin, crisscrossed with faded scars. Dark pouches of flesh hung below his eyes, and his hair was disheveled. He wore a baggy sweater, but Soto spotted the bulge of bandages across his chest.

But it was the eyes that gave the man's identity away. Specifically, one eye that was dark. The white of that eye had been stained red with blood, and Soto remembered inflicting the blow, driving his thumb straight up into the eye of the man who had turned his own blade against him. The stranger looked completely different without his mask and dark hat. He moved differently too, but it was clear that the frail individual was none other than Morgan Black. He was sometimes called the Wraith, an avenging spirit, but he was just a man after all. And Soto had checked the news networks. There were no reports of the death of any law officers on Expanse. Travis Hurts must have struck a blow, and Morgan Black had run to Luxor to recover. Sanada Soto reached up and touched his wounded shoulder. It still ached, but Soto had tended to it properly, and his blades were so sharp that the cut was like the incision of a surgeon's scalpel and was healing quickly.

Black got onto the elevator. Soto watched him in the reflection of a gold-covered planter with palm fronds growing out of it. If

Morgan Black noticed him, he made no indication. Fate had brought Soto to the resort. It was normally against his sense of caution to take out two targets in one confined space, but he couldn't turn away from the opportunity to take down the most notorious paid assassin in the galaxy. Even if LeSean Mason had to wait, Soto would strike at Black and finish what he started on the colony world called Expanse.

3

The *Purgatory* dropped out of hyperspace in the Schwizer system and immediately moved into orbit around Tavos. It was a small, vibrant planet, with very little animal life, but a thriving agricultural industry. Known for its vast wineries and nature preserves, there were only a handful of small cities, and very little technology was in use. It was a green planet, with limited imports and some of the most exclusive wine labels in the galaxy.

"This is it?" Ava asked. "It's beautiful."

"Sure is," Travis said as they looked out the *Purgatory's* wide front viewscreen. It wasn't a projection or vid display, but a transparent steel front to the ship. It was like looking though a glass window at the small planet. In the distance an orange sun glowed through a haze of dust that hadn't coalesced into a solid planetary body.

"You really think she's down there?"

"I went through the records and it's the only place that makes sense," Travis said. "If she's not there, we'll find some clues as to where she might be."

"Victoria Hennings-Mabry," Ava said. "She sounds rich."

"She is. And not just from the corruption scheme on Las Brazzas. Her family has been wealthy for a long time."

"Why get involved in crime if she didn't have to?"

Travis shrugged his shoulders. "Who can say? Excitement, respect, rebellion against her family, there's no telling what motivates these people."

"And you think she's here?"

"Harrison Poe kept records of everything," Travis said. "Like everyone else in their scheme, Victoria had several shell companies."

"What are shell companies?"

"They're incorporated businesses that exist only on paper," Travis said. "They aren't real, no employees, no work or products, just the legal framework and bank accounts. It's used as a way to hide money. An investigator might find one, but the money from whatever criminal enterprise the person is engaged in just flows right through these shell corporations. It's a way to hide what they're really doing with the funds."

"And Victoria had some?"

"Eight," Travis said. "If we didn't have Poe's records, we might have found two or three, but not all of them. The corporations are listed on different planets, and each planet has its own legal hoops to jump through. Some would cooperate, others wouldn't. Most are willing to help but insist their own people handle the investigation into their banks and industries. And as you can imagine it's a pretty low priority. The GCIB has jurisdiction to prosecute crimes that cross systems, but it's a hard job getting the locals on board."

"But you could follow the money trail?"

"Some of it," Travis said. "Banking records are protected, but property records aren't. I did searches on each of the eight worlds where she had a shell corporation. The only one that owned any physical property was a winery on Tavos called Château l'Abri."

"Sounds exotic," she said. "What does their wine taste like?"

"I don't know," Travis said. "They don't bottle their own

vintage. I think they sell their grapes to other wineries instead. But I know what the name of the place means. Château l'Abri means *Castle Hideaway*."

"That's pretty on the nose," she said.

"Yep, and all the upgrades to the property are on record. It really is a castle, not a huge one, but a fortress made of stone, with a thirty-foot wall, guard towers, and a massive gate made of iron wood."

"The perfect place to hide out," Ava said.

"It could just be a simple getaway for a paranoid person," Travis said. "Or maybe it's Victoria's emergency plan. We'll land in Tratoria, which is about fifty miles away from her fortress. I'd like to get a feel from the locals about the place."

"What if they tell her we're asking questions?"

"Then things might get dicey," Travis said.

"I don't like it. Someone like that can hire the best security firms to protect them."

"True enough. Which is why we won't go straight to the Château. We'll pose as newlyweds on a country tour."

"Sounds like fun," Ava said.

They landed in Tratoria. The buildings were all old-looking. They were made of stone and timber, the streets were paved with cobbles, and there were more animals than people. Horses, mules, donkeys, and even oxen were everywhere. Some were being ridden, but most pulled carts and wagons full of wooden crates and big barrels. The town was loud with the sounds of industry, only no machinery was in evidence. Everything was being done in open-air workshops. Travis and Ava, with Kaylee wrapped against her body, went out and explored the town. It wasn't hard to look like tourists when you were visiting a world for the first time. Everything was new, and every workshop was like a show. The people of Tavos practiced all the old arts. From blacksmithing, to barrel making, the residents were masters of their trade. The town was rich with the smells of nature, industry, and of course, food and wine. There were tiny shops and cafes, most with outdoor seating, and open-air buildings where huge windows were open wide. The temperature was comfortable, with a gentle breeze that wafted the smell of freshly baked bread and ripe grapes through the city streets.

They spent hours watching woodworkers and glass blowers. When evening came, they settled in a little tavern where a trio played instruments in the corner, and everyone spoke in hushed voices. Ava couldn't drink alcohol since she was feeding the baby, and Travis didn't want to impair his own judgment. But they ate bread and cheese and fruit while they listened to the conversations around them. Eventually, they got some of the information they wanted. Château l'Abri was well known, and not a favored estate.

"They waste their time," said one server who waited on the off-world trio. "They grow grapes, of course, but poorly. It is all a sham."

"Really?" Travis asked.

"Do not waste your time going there," the server said. "They do not take visitors. And the employees all carry weapons."

"How mysterious," Ava said.

"It is no mystery," a heavyset man at the nearby bar said. He was leaning against the wooden structure, nursing a tall glass of very dark wine. He had a bushy mustache and there were tiny droplets of wine on the tips of the whiskers. "It isn't the first estate to hide a wealthy owner."

"Who owns it?" Travis asked.

The man at the bar shrugged, and the waiter moved on to help another customer, but a woman at a table nearby, clearly there for the music, but also eavesdropping on the conversation, spoke up.

"Offworlder," she said. "A wealthy woman with two last names. Some people come here in hopes of hiding. Rumor has it, her husband was abusive. Perhaps a criminal of some kind, we don't know. But she never comes out of that fortress she built. My Tony, God rest his soul, was a stonemason all his life. He spent more time up there than he did at home."

That night they returned to the *Purgatory*, but the following morning they leased a wagon with two strong horses and set out on their camping adventure. The countryside was rolling hills, the road little more than a track set through forest and along the side of sweeping vineyards. Much of the land was neatly cultivated, but a portion was also left wild. Bees buzzed in the warm air, and white fluffy clouds drifted across a deep blue sky. The journey was idyllic. They stopped at a small farm selling fresh vegetables for lunch before pushing hard through the afternoon.

It took all day to reach a place where the fortress was in sight. They camped on a small hilltop, in a copse of trees. Château l'Abri was across a wide valley that was terraced and lined with grapevines. It was late in the growing season, and the air was heady with the scent of ripe grapes. But Travis saw no one working the vines, or harvesting the grapes. At the top of a tall hill was the fortress. It was a simple structure made of stone, at least what could be seen above the walls. Light spilled out from the compound, but little was actually visible from outside the protective barricade.

"How do we get inside?" Ava asked.

"Great question," Travis said.

"You don't know?"

"Not yet."

"Is this how you make a living?" she teased him. "You just wait around for outlaws to stroll up and surrender?"

"No," he said with a chuckle. "It's not that easy."

"So how does it normally work?"

"You were on P2," Travis said. "Most outlaws don't hide in fortresses."

"She has money."

"A lot of it."

"What's the reward for her?"

"Two fifty," Travis said.

"Wow, that's a lot of money."

"It is. I don't normally chase the big bounties."

"Why not?" Ava asked.

"I've always pursued the people that don't have that much heat," Travis said. "The big rewards draw a lot of attention. And sometimes, even when you capture the outlaw, you have to fight to hang onto them."

"Like Grant Stevenson?"

"Exactly," Travis agreed. "It's not that we can't do it, but the goal is to get criminals off the streets and back behind bars. I usually go after the criminals no one else is looking for."

"For less money."

"It's never been about the money."

"But you took this job?"

"It wasn't broadcast," Travis said. "No one else is looking for Victoria, just us."

"Which brings us back to the question at hand," Ava said, spreading a blanket in the back of the wagon for them to sleep on that night. It wasn't going to be as comfortable as the bunk on the *Purgatory* or a bed in a roadside inn, but there was a sense of adventure to camping out. And she had spent many nights under the stars on P2 before her husband was murdered.

"We watch the place," Travis said. "For a few days at least. Circle around the castle. See what the routine is. Maybe they come and go. There's bound to be a way in, that shouldn't be hard."

"What will be hard?" she asked.

"Getting out again," Travis admitted. "We'll need to get you and Kaylee back on the *Purg*. There are very few satellites in orbit, so we'll probably need to move the ship closer so we can maintain radio contact."

"What's my job?"

"You get us the hell off this world once I've got Victoria in custody."

They watched the castle until it was time for bed. Travis and Ava slept with the baby between them. Travis got up with Kaylee and changed her diaper during the night. He wanted Ava to get as much rest as possible, but also to get a look at the fortress he would have to infiltrate to get close enough to Victoria Hennings-Mabry to carry out the job.

Early the next morning Travis was up with the baby, and the vineyard workers left the fortress. Travis watched as men pushed hand carts from the castle walls. They went to the rows of vines and began to harvest the ripe grapes.

"They're working outside the walls," Ava said with a yawn as she crawled out of the back of the wagon.

"Yeah, with pistols on their gun belts," Travis pointed out.

"You think that's unusual?"

"Very," Travis said. "I don't think those are vinedressers at all. Or seasonal laborers."

"Hired security?"

"That'd be my guess," Travis said.

They spent the day on a long walk around the estate. Most of the time they stayed in the woods, only coming out to get a look at the castle from a different angle. By lunchtime Travis was convinced there was only one way in and one way out. There was a massive gate with towering double doors made of dark wood with black metal supports. Inside one of the doors was a smaller, man-sized door. It opened to let the workers in and out. Travis couldn't be certain, but the workers in the vineyard were taking their carts back to the castle full, and returning to the fields empty. He guessed they were processing the fruit inside, and doing who knew what with it. The harvest was the last thing on his mind. It was time to go back and get their ship.

"Tomorrow we go back to Tratoria," Travis said.

"Already?" Ava said in a playful tone. "We could forget all this fugitive business and you could build us a cabin to live in."

"I think you know I'm not much of a builder," Travis said.

"It's nice here. Everything seems slower, somehow easier, than on a regular planet."

"It is," he said. "Do you like that?"

"I do," she said. "But I'm starting to get antsy."

"How bad would you love a steak right now?"

"Don't tease me," she said. "I'm eating for two, you know."

"We can always come back," Travis said, "for a visit."

"Yes, for a visit," she said. "I love the smell of ripe grapes and fresh baked bread."

Travis waited until dark, then snuck onto the estate property, where he stole a cluster of grapes. They were nearly overripe, and not good for eating. The fruit was dark purple, and fragrant. The juice was flavorful, but not very sweet, and the meat was bitter.

"Not my favorite," Travis said.

"Can't eat that," Ava agreed. "And our bread isn't fresh anymore."

"The honeymoon is over, I suppose," Travis told her. "We'll head back at first light."

"Then the hunt truly begins."

"Yeah," Travis said. "The dangerous part."

4

Augustine Ward got lucky. He had lingered at the fringes of the growing crowd of inmates. A few tried to get close to him, but he held them off with threatening looks. And then Leon Hurts appeared. It was obvious right away that he was a leader among the inmates. Not all flocked to him, but a sizeable group congregated around the man. He was tall, thick chested, with veiny arms and streaks of white in his beard. He wore his hair long and tied back out of his face. While his cohort got in on the act of tormenting the newcomers, Augustine made straight for the man.

"That's far enough," a huge man with a bad eye said.

"I need to speak to Leon Hurts."

"The father don't speak to fresh fish like you," the man said.

Another inmate joined the big man. He was skinny and had a scar across his throat. When he spoke, it was with a gravelly tone.

"The father wants to see him," the newcomer said.

The big man looked confused and angry, but didn't stop the man with the scar from taking Augustine to where Leon had settled on a stack of plastic crates.

"He came asking for you," the man with the scar on his throat said. "Just like you said."

"Indeed," Leon said. "Ain't much to him."

"Reedy," the scarred man agreed.

"Give us a minute, Nester," Leon said. "We'll have communion soon."

"And a show?"

"Sure," Leon said.

Augustine didn't have a clue what they were talking about. But it seemed pretty clear that the inmates were segregated into groups. Any sort of thing might qualify as a reason to congregate together; race, home planet, criminal affiliation, even the crimes for which they had been imprisoned. Leon's group seemed quasi-religious. Augustine knew of religious groups, cults mostly, that ran criminal rings. The Infada came to mind, as did the old Brotherhood of the Sine. But Augustine was not a religious person, and wasn't a member of organized crime. He was a shootist and gambler who relied mostly on his reputation to get favor with the locals wherever he went. From free drinks to winning at cards, his small-time celebrity had been enough for the gunslinger. But he was in a completely different world in the prison camp on Lucerine, and he had no guns. He would have to find protection and support from one of the many groups congregating in the open cavern.

"Got word you'd be coming," Leon said. "You Ward?"

"I am," Augustine said.

"So? What's the message?"

"I'm supposed to tell you that Iona Freeze of the Incendius Organization has a job for you."

"I don't work," he said with a wicked chuckle. "I'm retired."

"She's got a plan to get us off this rock," Augustine insisted.

Leon laughed out loud at that remark. Augustine felt frustrated. The big man was bullheaded, and couldn't see an opportunity when it was right in front of him.

"The guard's going to pick you and me," Augustine said, "next week. Corpse pickup."

"I don't do that sort of work," Leon said. "Bad plan. I believe you've been sent on a fool's errand, Ward."

"I ain't no fool," Ward said. "I met with Freeze herself."

"And she misled you," he said, his tone growing darker, more menacing. "There is no way off Lucerine. Them that try ... die."

"You want to stay down here, be my guest," Ward said. "I'm leaving."

"You think it's so simple?"

"I think the Incendius Organization is making an offer. I don't care what they want, or how they do it. If they can get me out of here I'm gonna do whatever they say."

"A week down here ain't easy," Leon said. "Let me give you some advice. Drop the tough guy act, and beg one of my followers for favor. They might offer you some protection."

"I'm obliged for any help, but I ain't no one's kicking dog."

"You'll be dead if you're not careful," Leon said, shooing Augustine away.

A beefy hand grabbed the shootist by the arm and flung him away like he was a rag doll. Augustine crashed into a mob of people who were shouting and tormenting four of the new inmates. Clothing was torn, as the newcomers were hit and kicked, pushed and pulled. Augustine was slapped. A sense of rage filled him and he shoved the slapper, only to have another man drive his fist so hard into Augustine's side that it knocked the breath from his lungs. Someone else grabbed the neck of his shirt from behind and yanked hard enough to rip the prison jumpsuit. As Augustine Ward was whirled around the tear got larger. Most of the prisoners were punching or slapping, but some were grabbing and pinching his exposed skin. He did his best to protect himself but there were just too many people, and the crowd was in a frenzy.

Eventually he fell to the ground. His jumpsuit was torn from the collar down his back and across his right leg to the cuff.

Someone slashed his back with a sharp rock, blood welled, and things were on the verge of getting truly ugly, when big strong hands grabbed Ward. They yanked him up and Augustine was thrown across a massive shoulder. He lost consciousness for a second or two. When he came back to his senses, the man who had initially blocked his way from getting to Leon Hurts dropped him next to the cavern wall.

"You're mine now," he growled. "Do what you're told or I send you down to the creepers."

Augustine had no idea what the man was talking about but he didn't move. The night turned into a hellish scene. While the other inmates ate and drank there were fights. Those that lost were humiliated or killed. It was the most frightening hour of Augustine Ward's life. When the larger crowd finally lost interest in fighting or tormenting the new arrivals, the crowd around Augustine grew quiet. It was then that Leon Ward got to his feet and began to speak.

"We're the chosen," he said.

"Chosen! Chosen!" his followers chanted softly.

Not everyone in the cavern was listening or joining in. There were groups all around the cavern, hundreds of men, some clinging to one another, others watching for violence to erupt. Leon spoke to his following.

"We're a family. The only family that matters anymore."

"Family! Family!"

"We are no longer individuals," Leon continued. "We are one. We are the source of life here in the caverns, and in the grottos. We move through the tunnels and dig the mines. And everything we do, we do as one."

"As one! As one!"

"And we are the blessed, the favored," Leon said, his voice haunting. "It may not seem so, but we have let go of every trapping the world rushes to gain. We have rid ourselves of all selfish desires and made ourselves whole again."

"Tell us of the beginning," someone in Leon's family called out.

"It is a dark tale," Leon said.

"Tell it! Tell it!" the group chanted in unison.

"I will tell it," Leon said. "And you will remember. For we were there. We, the chosen watchers, saw it all, just as it was meant to be. In the beginning there was darkness all around, and cold and pressure. We knew only pain then, in that beginning, but there was a spark. It drew us to the truth, to the way, and we followed. That spark grew into a flame that burned out the darkness, and it burned out each and every one of us. It grew, and we became the inferno. The universe couldn't contain us. The dark, the pressure, it all exploded in an instant and we spread through the cold vacuum. We built worlds and stars, comets and quasars, formed galaxies from the fringe to the core."

"From the fringe to the core," the people chanted.

Augustine felt strange. He was wounded, and hurting, scared and hungry, but the tone and rhythm of Leon's voice entranced him. He had heard creation stories before, but nothing like what Leon spoke of. Scientists once held the view that all matter in the universe had been condensed for a time before a sudden explosion sent it hurling out in all directions. But of course, not even they could explain where the matter came from, what made it condense, or explode. It was just another story as far as Augustine was concerned, a failed attempt to make sense of the questions every person asked.

Normally, Augustine was not that deep. He had always lived to please himself. He did what he wanted, took what he couldn't afford, belittled, fought, and killed anyone who tried to stand in his way. He didn't spend time thinking about what he couldn't have, or what he couldn't know. It left gaps in his soul, but he was a master at ignoring the daunting questions, and avoiding uncomfortable topics of discussion. And he couldn't understand why Leon's recitation of what was clearly a metaphysical explanation of human origins felt so entrancing. But he could see things in his mind that he had never even thought of before. He saw himself without a body, and without form, just a consciousness in the dark, trying to understand something that was beyond his grasp.

"And then came the separation," Leon said. "The great deceiver lied to us. He told us we could be happy if we just moved apart. He tempted us with the concept of individuality, and sold us a pack of lies. Naively we followed along, hoping the expansion of our community would result in the expansion of our minds. Little did we know that with separation came isolation, that with enlightenment came disillusionment. Everything we had known was lost in an instant as the deceiver spread us out across the vast expanse of space, pitting us against one another."

It seemed a sad tale to Augustine, who was himself at that moment feeling lost, isolated, frightened, and alone. He couldn't understand that he was hearing exactly what he wanted to hear, or that he was being lured in by a master con artist.

"But the truth could not be denied," Leon said. "Even here, at the lowest point of all human conditions, we, the chosen..."

"The chosen!" the group chanted.

"We found one another," Leon said, his voice rising with energy. "We came together and formed a greater, stronger unity than ever before."

"Yes!" someone cried.

"That's right," another person in the group shouted.

"We have shaken off our chains and come together in a unity that none of us imagined possible. Out of this unforgiving rock we have carved a new life that will lead us back to the place we belong. This is not our end."

"No," the musclebound man beside Augustine cried out.

"Not even," someone else bellowed.

"Never!" a high pitched, feverish voice shouted.

"This is our new beginning," Leon pressed on. "This is the freedom we crave. This is the life we were meant for. Not digging in the ground, but joining together in a bond so strong no force in this universe can bend it or break it!"

The group erupted in raucous shouts of joy. They jumped to their feet, grabbing one another, dancing, leaping in the air, spinning around. And some bowed at Leon's feet.

The celebration went on for nearly an hour. Augustine saw that something was passed between the members of Leon's family. He knew a drug when he saw one. It wasn't a pill, but some kind of powder. They licked their fingers, dipped them into the powder, and rubbed it on their gums. At one point someone even rubbed some into the gash on Augustine's back. He felt euphoric for a while, and then slept deeply despite laying on an uneven cavern floor.

The next day when he awoke, he was alone in total darkness. For a long time he thought he was dead. He couldn't see anything, or hear anything, but he could feel the floor, and smell human excrement. He had no idea that it was his own urine dried in the ripped-up jumpsuit he had been given. Eventually, the big man returned with a light. It was so harsh to Ward's eyes that he had to close them and tears spilled out.

"Down!" someone snapped.

A hand pushed Augustine down on the floor. They were in a little nook, a small side cave, and four sweating men came in. They had food, none of which they shared with Augustine. The huge man who had carried him out of the melee the day before was there. The others called him Bro Cyphus. They gave Augustine water, and someone put more of the powder into his back wound that wasn't yet scabbed completely over.

He saw vivid colors that night, and the voices of the other men became like the growls and barks of wild animals. Yet he felt so good, and he wanted to join in with the others, only he was too weak. Hunger gnawed at him. Augustine was naturally thin, and had very little reserve to carry him without nourishment.

He eventually passed out, and the next day Bro Cyphus

returned with an ore sack. Inside was a safety suit. It was a thin, plastic suit with a zipper. Gray industrial tape covered small punctures in the suit, until there was more tape, it seemed, than the plastic suit material.

"Put this on," Bro Cyphus had ordered him.

"I can't," Augustine said.

The big man pulled a rock hammer from the sack. It looked small in his massive hand, but still terrifying.

"Put it on or die," the big man threatened.

Augustine wasn't comfortable moving. His body was covered with bruises, some from the beating and some from sleeping on the cavern floor. But he moved. His muscles quivered and threatened to cramp, but he pulled on the safety suit. Augustine realized that Bro Cyphus had one too. He handed Augustine the rock hammer and ore sack, then pushed him down a winding set of stairs, past other nooks and hovels that were clearly homes for the inmates.

At one point they stopped and waited until two other prisoners came up. The newcomers had on head coverings with clear plastic to see through, and a pitiful little filter to breathe through. The newcomers took their head coverings off, and handed them to Bro Cyphus and Augustine. It was dirty, damp, and smelled horrible inside, like the depths of an unflushed public toilet. But that was just the beginning of the horrors that Augustine discovered.

Bro Cyphus led him down a deep mineshaft. At the bottom was a tunnel. Everywhere he looked people were pecking away at the walls and floor. Eventually they reached an empty spot at the end of a narrow tunnel.

"Dig!" the big man ordered.

For hours Augustine chipped at the hard stone. Whenever there was any color to the rock Bro Cyphus moved in and took it. Eventually he filled his sack. Then he ordered Augustine to keep digging.

"Fill it," he snarled. "You come out with less, you're dead."

Augustine worked for hours more, filling his own sack with

pebbles and chunks of colored stone. He had no idea what it was, or what it was for. But, on the verge of exhaustion, his sack only half filled, he decided death was better than digging. He left the tunnel, wandered for a while with no sense of direction or purpose. He wanted to pull the stinking head covering off, but he could see the dust and knew the danger. He didn't want to die down in the dark tunnel.

Eventually he saw others with full sacks leaving the tunnels. He followed them. The stairs nearly finished him. He was wheezing with fatigue by the time he reached the level where more prisoners waited. He pulled off his head covering and handed it over to the next person, who put it on without complaint. Then it was up more stairs. He was seeing sparks at the edge of his vision and his thighs were cramping by the time he reached the big, main cavern. There he saw people clustered in groups. Bro Cyphus saw him, got up and dragged him to a water fountain. Augustine leaned against the wall and let the water spray into his mouth. He sucked it down eagerly until Bro Cyphus pulled him away.

"Not too much!" the big man barked.

He led Augustine to the ore machine. It scanned Augustine's neck tattoo while he poured in his haul. The dusty display showed one point eight ounces of ore. Augustine knew it was wrong, the machine had cheated him, but it also produced a loaf of lightly seasoned protein and fat. It looked like three protein bars mashed into a single loaf. Fortunately, it wasn't as dense or hard to chew. Bro Cyphus took the loaf from the machine with his dirty hand and gave it Augustine.

"Eat it," he snapped.

The food was terrible, and wonderful at the same time. It tasted like powdered gravy and salt. Augustine didn't care. He ate it, and slurped more water. His strength began to return. An hour later he followed Bro Cyphus to the hovel where they slept. Time was lost to him. He was still deeply slumbering when the big man woke him, and the nightmare started all over again.

Evolving Threat

And that was his new life. Every day he produced a full sack of ore for Bro Cyphus, who in turn gave half of his haul to Father Leon. Bro Cyphus wasn't the only middleman extorting other prisoners. It was a common practice. The strongest of the prisoners thrived by forcing the weaker to provide for them. The strong ate like kings, while the rest of the inmates worked like slaves to produce enough ore to survive on. And many didn't.

5

"There, that looks promising," Travis said.

Ava brought the ship down in a clearing less than a standard mile to Château l'Abri. There were trees on all sides, which would hide the vessel from easy view. The locals didn't care much for spaceships, or any kind of high technology. They certainly wouldn't want it on their land, but there was a lot of common land and preserves on Tavos. Enough to find a spot where they wouldn't be noticed easily.

"You better check the comlinks," Ava said. "It won't do you any good to get inside that place and not be able to call for help."

"I will," Travis said.

It was late at night, and he didn't waste any time gathering a few tools of his trade. His Range rifle went onto the sling that was normally hidden under his duster. But that garment was ruined and left on Scye with Eduardo Hernandez. The tailor hadn't finished new garments yet. Travis had one last shirt with the laser absorbing fibers, and a bulky coat that made him look like a mountain man. He put it on over the rifle, holstered his Kicker in a reverse draw holster that strapped to his left thigh, and put his

Slinger in the quickdraw holster low on his right hip. To his weapons he added a tiny comlink device that fit deep into this ear canal, and a small range finder with night vision capabilities went into one pocket.

"This plan seems a little crazy," Ava told him after she shut the ship's flight systems down and made sure life support systems were in the green.

"It is," he said.

"What if they don't let you in?"

"Then we'll have to give them a reason to take her out of there," Travis said.

"I'm not sure if I should be more nervous about your back-up plan, or the fact that you came up with something like that so quickly."

"It doesn't have to be a bad thing," Travis said. "You catch more flies with honey than with vinegar."

"Which is what they're probably making with those awful grapes," Ava said.

"Funny how something can look so good and smell so delicious, but be just dreadful when you taste it."

"There are a lot of things like that in life."

"You're right about that," he said. "Okay, stay here, keep your weapons handy, and the comlink turned on."

"You know I will," she said. "Don't get killed."

"Never have," he said with a grin.

"Don't get cocky," she called to him as he left their living quarters and slipped out the airlock.

The air was cool on his face as he moved through the trees. He was going slowly, watching for any hint of discovery. The last thing he wanted to do was blunder into someone who might shoot him. His chest still ached from the burns that Morgan Black had given him. The assassin's Ripper had burned through his shirt, and some of the most expensive body armor a person could buy. It left him with second degree burns, but he was still breathing, and not many people could say that after being shot with a powerful laser pistol. His own Slinger, even at full power, hadn't stopped Morgan Black for long. Which just went to show the difference between the small, quick draw weapon, and the heavier Ripper, which was beefy enough to burn through layers of armor.

The walk felt good, despite his nerves, and the need for stealth. It felt good to be outside, on a clean, vibrant world. It might have been better if Victoria Hennings-Mabry was in a tavern with a couple of guards, the way that Grant Stevenson had been. Victoria was more cautious. She had prepared for the inevitable day by building a fortress to protect herself in. And the only question that lingered was, could Travis get inside? He preferred a straightforward approach, but that wasn't always an option. And he guessed that he looked enough like a day laborer to at least convince whoever was guarding the compound.

He came up on the back side of the castle, and spent a full hour circling to the front side. He stopped periodically and searched the walls for any signs of surveillance. If Victoria was employing cameras to keep watch over her estate, they were very well hidden.

Travis settled into a grove of trees for the last hour of darkness, and once more searched the estate with his viewfinder, while testing his comlink.

"Can you hear me, partner?"

"Loud and clear," Ava said. "Where are you?"

"On the far side of the estate," Travis said. "How's Kaylee?"

"Changed, fed, and sound asleep again. I wish I was half as calm as she was."

"Don't worry," Travis said. "I've been doing this a long time."

"But Victoria has hired guards to stop people like you from arresting her," Ava said. "They might even kill you, Travis. Don't take it for granted that you're going to get the bad guy every time."

"I won't," Travis said with a smile. "You never underestimate your target. That's the golden rule in this game."

"It's not a game," she said.

"Why are you so worried?" Travis said. "You weren't like this on P2, or on Las Brazzas."

"And I had to save you from being killed in both places."

"True," Travis said with a chuckle. "Point taken."

"No, it's not that," she admitted. "I think it's Kaylee. When it was just me it didn't feel as scary. Now ... well, it seems really important to me that I protect her, and make sure that the people who love her aren't doing anything stupid."

"We can call off the entire operation," Travis said. "Except we're pretty deep in the hole with Eduardo."

"I don't want you to call it off," she said. "I just want you to be careful."

"I will be," he told her. "Promise."

The sun began to lighten the sky and Travis saw the first of the harvesters come out of the compound with their hand carts. They were simple wooden contraptions, a wooden box with a wheel in front, two supports in back, and two handles. On some worlds they were called wheelbarrows although Travis could tell that the wooden components weren't very efficient. Metal bearings or even a rubber tire would make the small cart much easier to move, especially with a load of ripe fruit, but Travis respected the stance that the people of Tavos had taken. He didn't feel the same way about technology, or the best way to protect natural resources, but he didn't look down his nose at the people on Tavos for standing up for what they believed in.

He waited until the sun was a little higher, and made sure no one would see him coming out of the woods. Once he was on the road, he made quick progress to the massive gates and stepped into the compound. There was no armed guard at the door, and Travis found himself in a wide courtyard. There was space around the tall, protective walls, and the castle itself. He guessed forty feet, maybe fifty, in the area he could see. All around him were people working with traditional presses, preparing for the harvesting. Barrels were being rolled out across the cobblestone courtyard.

Mules were being harnessed to wine presses. It was a very active area as the harvesting operation geared up for the day.

There was a platform built into the inside of the wall, about four feet from the top. It was narrow, and had a short wooden railing to the inside. Travis didn't see any armed guards walking the wall, but he knew that was what the platform was built for. The castle itself was plain on the ground level. Grey stone, narrow windows, nothing ornamental in the stonework. The doors were narrow, but made of thick wood. More than one was open, although it seemed like the equipment and goods were coming from behind the castle.

Travis was no expert on grapes or what they were used for. But it wasn't a leap to imagine the people on Tavos using every part of the grapes, not just the juices. Wine, vinegar, jellies and jams, even pies could be made from a single harvest. And those were just the uses that Travis could think of. The busy commerce around the castle certainly seemed to confirm that harvesting the grapes was big business.

"Don't know you," a heavyset man in a stained apron said. "You here to harvest?"

"I'm looking to work, yes sir," Travis said. "I can do whatever needs doing."

"What's your name?"

"Ned," he replied, ignoring the chuckle from Ava that he heard via the comlink in his ear.

"We're paying one twenty a day," the man said. "Lunch is provided. You can stay on the ground, but not in the castle. But we work here, Ned. No lollygagging, no shirking your tasks."

"Yes sir," Travis said. "I'm here to work."

"Good enough. Head around back and get a hand cart. We need as many people in the vineyard bringing in the harvest as possible."

He hurried around the side of the castle, dodging the busy people and the occasional animal. There were rows of storage sheds built onto the wall. Many of the big doors were open and Travis saw barrels stacked everywhere. In the back was a low barn where the animals, mostly mules, were kept, along with stacked bales of hay. Another building was clearly storage. A woman was writing names on a chalkboard that was hung on the inside of the storage barn door. She took his name, Ned Travers, wrote it in a column labeled *Harvesters,* and gave him a set of pruning shears and one of the wooden carts. He made his way back out of the castle, going around the opposite way from the route he took to the back. There were more storage sheds. He could tell they were well built. Most were open with crates and barrels stacked inside. There was also an awning over a wide platform. Travis saw dozens of what appeared to be sleeping mats. Which made sense, considering the work went on from dawn to dusk.

Travis made his way to the vineyards, was assigned a row, and began harvesting the grapes. They were thick and dark purple. The clusters were so ripe that he had to be careful not to bruise the skins, or dislodge the grapes along the edges. The pruning shears were sharp and made the harvesting easy. In less than an hour his cart was full, and he had only gone halfway down his row of vines.

The sun rose, the day grew warm, and Travis Hurts worked hard. Not that tracking down fugitives and capturing them was easy, but it was a different kind of work. Travis enjoyed the simplicity of the task at hand, and seeing his cart fill up with the ripe grapes. The smell of the rich fruit, the soil, the plants, the fresh air, all combined into an invigorating mixture. He had feared that, never having harvested grapes before, he might be exposed as a fraud. But there was really nothing to the work. In a normal vineyard where the grapes were grown to produce different vintages the harvest work was different. Certain varieties of fruit ripened at different paces, and the type of wine required grapes at different stages of ripeness. Travis had no eye for any of that, but didn't need it. At Château l'Abri the fruit was on the verge of ruin. Every grape needed to be brought in, which made harvesting simple. Whatever fruit Travis saw, he clipped off and set gently in his cart. When the cart was full, he pushed it back up to the castle, where the grapes were dumped into a vat. From there they went into a press. The juice was collected in barrels, which were labeled with chalk and hauled to the storage sheds. The meat and skins were collected as well. There were artisans plying their trade to make the overripe fruit into various products that could be sold.

At one point, a man on a huge wagon, pulled by six of the largest draft horses Travis had ever seen, arrived at the castle. His wagon was loaded up with barrels of grape juice, which he then hauled to another winery. Only a small portion of the harvest collected at the castle was used to make wine on location. It was all a big production, most of which Travis had very little interest in.

Lunch was served in the courtyard. Travis collected a bowl of spicy, vegetarian hash. He couldn't tell exactly what he was eating, and didn't particularly care for it. But after working hard in the vineyard all morning, he was hungry. He joined a couple of the other harvesters, and after introducing himself, listened to their conversation. It didn't take long for talk to turn to the owner.

"It's a shame," said Heston, the oldest of the men in the little group of harvesters that Travis was eating his lunch with. "She doesn't know a thing about her business here."

"Rich woman," Jase said. He was young with round cheeks and thick, bushy hair. "It's all a write-off to her."

"Don't think they should sell good land to off-worlders," Guy interjected. "Property in town is fine. But not the farmland."

"It's a huge disappointment," Heston said. "This could be one of the most productive wineries in the valley."

"At least they pay good," Jase said.

"Yeah, can't complain about that," Raul said. "And they harvest so late in the season, I can bring in my harvest before coming out here."

"Sure," Heston said. "It works for us, I get that. But it's still a shame."

"What do you know about her?" Travis asked. "Does she ever come out of the castle?"

"I never seen her," Guy said.

"Oh, she comes out sometimes, but not too often," Heston said. "That's what I'm saying, she just doesn't care. I think she'd let the fruit go to waste if it didn't make her look bad."

"You mean she would leave thousands of credits to wither on the vine?" Jase asked. "That's insane."

"She's already settling for a fraction of what this vineyard could produce in financial return," Heston pointed out.

"She doesn't need the money," Raul said. "Good for her."

There was much more to learn. It wasn't until the end of the day that Travis' luck took a turn for the better. Dinner was served to the workers who chose to stay the night, which was most of them. Some lived in the castle, but most were seasonal help. A meal of pasta, bread, and of course wine was served to the workers. It didn't take long for some of the help to get drunk.

Travis was chatting up a young woman named Katrina who worked at the castle year-round when the trouble started. Travis hoped that she might get him into the castle, although he wasn't having much luck. She was practical, and he was seasonal help, which meant he would leave when the work was done, and Katrina didn't want to get too close to someone who wouldn't be around long. Then a couple of the men, Raul and a stableman named Drex, got into a fight. Raul was tall and lanky. He landed a solid punch that knocked Drex backward. The smaller man drew a knife. It was a short, thick bladed weapon, more of a tool really, but enough to cause serious harm. Travis wasn't looking to get involved. Most of the people around were just watching, but the introduction of the knife changed the situation. Drex charged Raul. They crashed together, stumbling toward where Katrina was leaning against the wall of the castle.

Instinct kicked in, and Travis grabbed Drex. With one swift move Travis flipped the smaller man over his hip in a well-rehearsed judo throw. Drex fell to the cobble stone with a thump, but managed to hold onto his knife. Raul had a small cut on his arm, and flew into a rage, intent on getting his hands on Drex. Travis lashed out with a powerful side kick that drove the heel of his boot into Raul's stomach and sent him stumbling backward.

Drex tried to stab Travis, lunging up at him with the knife. Travis swayed back out of reach of the weapon, but simultaneously grabbed Drex's wrist and wrenched it hard. The smaller man shouted in pain as the knife fell to the ground. He started to twist Drex's arm the other way, to fold it behind his back. But he caught himself and released Drex, who moaned, cradling his arm against his chest. When Travis turned the fight had gone out of Raul, who was holding his gut and straining to catch his breath. He shook his head as if to say he didn't want any more.

Travis stepped away from the fight, not sure what was going to happen. But the crowd actually applauded. Katrina was looking at him in a completely different way. Travis preferred to fly under the radar. He didn't like being the center of attention, and joined Katrina in leaning against the castle. Drex's friends went to help him. Travis heard the man say he was all right. He got to his feet flexing his hand, then picked up his knife. It went back into a sheath on his belt, and Drex gave Travis a dirty look before going off with his companions.

"That was impressive," Katrina said. "I thought they were going to crash right into me."

"I wouldn't let that happen," Travis said.

"Maybe I underestimated you," she said. "I thought you were just another day laborer."

"Oh, I've got some depth," he replied.

A few people nodded appreciatively at Travis. They didn't mind a fair fight, but no one wanted to see Raul get seriously hurt or killed. Likewise, they didn't want to see Drex get into serious trouble just because he was angry. Things had ended without any injuries or the need to call in the authorities, and that was exactly how they wanted it. And not just the workers. It wasn't long until a man in a dark gray uniform appeared, with a laser pistol in a high holster right on his belt. He was the only person Travis had seen with any sort of modern technology in his possession.

"You need to come with me," he said.

"How's that?" Travis asked.

Travis was sitting on the edge of the sleeping platform and waiting for Katrina, who was fetching him a blanket. He was prepared to spend the night with the other laborers and trying to decide if he was going to break into the castle, or just keep working until a better opportunity presented itself.

"Your presence is requested," the man said. "Now come along."

"Am I in trouble?" Travis asked, pretending to be afraid of losing his job.

"No, just the opposite."

The man led Travis into the castle. The ground level, just like the space outside the castle, was utilitarian. They passed a large kitchen and several storage rooms. One of the rooms was open and had shelves filled with cleaning supplies and a pegboard wall with tools hanging on it. Past the storage rooms they came to a narrow set of stone stairs. The man in uniform led the way. Travis followed him up. The stairs came to an anteroom with several tables. There were plates, silverware, glasses, and wine carafes set out in neat formation, ready to be used at a moment's notice. There were also several bread boxes and a refrigeration unit with a clear front. Travis saw bottled drinks inside, along with cheese and what he thought might have been tins of caviar.

They went through the anteroom and into a dining room. There was a long table, the surface cut from a single slab of wood taken from the heart of an enormous tree. Around it were high-backed, uphol-stered chairs. They passed through the dining room and into a larger room with big windows. Travis hadn't seen windows of any type on the upper floors of the castle like those he saw now. He wasn't sure if the walls were some type of display panels, or highly camouflaged one-way glass that looked like the stone walls of the castle from the outside. He decided it was more likely the latter, since several of the windows were angled open to allow in the cool night breeze.

The room had a bar against one wall, and high-end sofas around a holographic entertainment system. On the wall opposite the bar was a large fireplace, with two very comfortable looking chairs set close to the empty hearth. In one of the chairs sat Victoria Hennings-Mabry. She was reading a book. Not on her data slate, but an old fashioned leatherbound book with actual paper pages. On a little table beside her was a goblet of dark wine, and a long, slender cigar smoldering on the edge of a golden ash tray. She didn't bother looking up as he was ushered into the room.

There were other people there. Several more men in uniform stood looking out the windows. Occasionally, they glanced down at the voices floating up from the courtyard below. On one of the ornate sofas was a pair of women in what appeared to be evening gowns. They looked at him with appraising eyes, and Travis nearly missed the tiny laser pistols that were strapped to their legs. They were just visible in the slit along the bottom of the dress.

Travis counted six guards, and those were just the ones he could see in the room. Odds were that Victoria had more, maybe a lot more, hidden around the castle in other rooms. He guessed there were probably more hidden windows, and at least enough guards to keep watch around the fortress at all times. Getting her out of the compound wouldn't be easy.

"Come and sit by me," Victoria said, without looking up from her book.

"Yes, ma'am," Travis said. The guard didn't follow him over, but stood with his legs slightly apart, his hands clasped behind his back, near the bar.

Travis sat down. The chair was soft, but he didn't lean back or relax. Instead, he sat on the edge of the seat, his hands on his knees.

"You can relax, Mr. Travers. Can I call you Ned?"

"Yes ma'am," Travis said.

"Good," she replied. "I heard about your intervention in the scuffle down there."

She waved her hand as if she was too good to concern herself with the people who worked for her. They were just *those people* who lived and worked literally beneath her.

"Just a misunderstanding," Travis said.

"Yes, a misunderstanding with a deadly weapon," she said. "My people tell me that Drex has a temper. If he had stabbed the other worker it could have been unpleasant."

Travis knew exactly what she meant. It could have led to the authorities coming out to her fortress and looking a little closer at her false identity. She did not want to keep running. Victoria had obviously spent a small fortune on the castle, and she was hoping to stay there as long as she wanted to.

"Yes, ma'am," he replied.

"You're new," she said, looking up from her book for the first time. "Tell me about yourself, Ned."

He had a well-rehearsed backstory. From a little farm near Tratoria, he made a living as a laborer most of the year, but worked in several of the wineries when there were jobs to be had.

"How did you hear about us?" Victoria wanted to know.

Travis shrugged. "Everyone knows about the Château l'Abri."

"We have a reputation," she agreed. "Unfortunately, it's not as good as I would like it to be. I tried to hire a decent manager, but they're more interested in who they work for than in money. The big labels have already snatched up all the best vinedressers and managers. What's a person to do?"

"I don't know," Travis said.

"I would bring in talent from off world, but that's somehow seen as worse than having no one at all. Old man Berington has us in more grapes than we know what to do with, but the quality is poor. The best we can do is sell the juice to wineries off world that produce subpar wine and depend on our harvest to be able to say their juice comes from Tavos."

"At least you're turning a profit," Travis said.

"Profits are less concerning to me than unwanted attention," Victoria said. "All I really want is to be left alone. My people say you proved yourself this evening. I need someone who can keep the peace until the harvest is complete. I'm hoping that you might be that person."

"I'm not sure I understand," Travis said.

"I want to make you property manager," Victoria said. "Your main responsibility will be to keep everyone happy until the harvest is over. After that, you split your time between the estate and your home. My people will see to the interior. Your job will be maintaining the property outside the walls."

"Oh," Travis said. He didn't have to feign his surprise. His plan had been to get close to Victoria and take her into his custody. He hadn't expected to earn himself a promotion. "I'm sure there are others with more experience than me," Travis said.

"I don't need experience," she said. "I want someone the people working down there respect. My people say you handled yourself like a professional. They think maybe you've had training."

"I don't like to talk about it," he said.

"Off world?"

Travis nodded. "I took a job as security on Putnam station when I was eighteen. Spent six years in that tin can, before moving to Tavos."

"There's something wonderful about the clear skies and clean air," Victoria said.

"Yes indeed," Travis told her.

"All the more reason you should work for me. People here don't readily accept outsiders."

"If I'm being honest," Travis told her, "I'm not sure working for you would move me up or down in their estimation."

"Then they can go to hell," she said savagely. "You can live here full time. Are you married?"

"No, ma'am."

"You live alone?"

"Yes, ma'am."

"Then there's no reason to leave," she said. "I'll pay you two hundred thousand credits a year. That's more than you'll make doing just about anything else. You'll work with Estelle Bonet; she oversees the castle and staff. Old man Berington is the vinedresser, but I want you in charge of everything else. Keep the riffraff away, and ensure that the property is maintained. Can you do that, Ned? I think you can."

"Well ... yeah," Travis said. "I can do it. I won't let you down, ma'am."

"I'm sure you won't," she said, turning her attention back to the book she held. "Donald will show you your quarters, and let Estelle know you'll be joining the team."

Thanks," Travis said. "I can't tell you how much this opportunity means to me."

"I'm sure," she replied, lifting her wine glass in dismissal.

It was an unexpected turn of events, and just the sort of opportunity he was hoping for. They were one step closer to taking Victoria into custody. He couldn't ask for more than that. All he had to do was keep up the charade long enough to put a plan together and see it through. He couldn't believe his good luck.

6

Sanada Soto had an expensive suite in the Khafa Pyramid, but he was back in the *Rising Sun* to utilize his supercomputer. It hadn't taken long to hack into the resort's computer system. The casino and financial systems were inside an almost unbreakable firewall, but the guest information and security systems were left vulnerable.

Sanada used the video footage from the elevator and hallway cameras to trace back his two targets. LeSean Mason was staying in an executive room, not a full suite, under the name Lee Mack. Morgan Black was in the Presidential suite, and had around the clock care medical care. It was an exclusive amenity for high rollers. The resort had a concierge doctor, and a group of RNs that offered nearly every service a person could think of. The only thing they couldn't do was prescribe medications, but Morgan was self-medicating. His bill was enormous, which told Soto that Morgan was a man of means.

He had also gotten access to the *Dymetr*. He couldn't get inside Morgan's ship, but he knew where it was and had put a hold on the vessel. The resort could lock down private ships to keep people from fleeing while they still owed the resort money. Morgan had prepaid for the Presidential suite for three weeks, and the round the clock nursing care. His bill had been two and half million credits, and that was before food, beverages, and drugs. Soto shook his head at the thought of such waste. He was a man of means himself, who rarely took cost into account in his decision making. But he couldn't deny that some people were foolish with their money, wasting millions of credits for no reason at all. Soto's suite was forty thousand credits per night. But the Presidential suite was a cool one hundred grand a night.

How people spent their money was of little concern to Soto. He didn't target people because they were rich, or because they were careless spenders. His calling was to eliminate evil from the galaxy, to find those who broke the law and got away with it. And Morgan Black was the epitome of a broken system, and a people who all too often celebrated the success of criminals like Morgan Black. There were books written about him, not just true crime accounts, but fictional stories about The Man In Black. Soto planned to bring that to a swift and conclusive end.

But first, he was going to bring justice to LeSean Mason. It would be an easy enough task. The criminal was sleeping off a twenty-four-hour party binge. In fact, Soto was certain that given a year's time, LeSean Mason would probably overdose on drugs, or get himself killed. He spent nearly twenty-three hours clubbing. The Luxor was a twenty-four hour a day party, and LeSean had embraced that lifestyle, using uppers to keep himself awake and give him energy. But the clubs on the lower levels were crowded places. Soto had already made a plan to deliver justice to the man.

He could get into Mason's room, but that would force Soto to flee the resort. Normally, Soto preferred for his victims to know who had delivered the killing stroke, and why. LeSean Mason needed to pay for his crimes, and that included knowing why he was dying. But his execution had become secondary to the need to make Morgan Black pay for the darkness he cast into the universe.

And Soto had no intention of underestimating the famed assassin. Black was a survivor. He wouldn't weep and beg for his life like so many of Soto's victims did. Until his very last breath Morgan Black would be deadly.

Patience was the key to getting to Black. Soto would wait and watch, from his ship, from the concourse, from restaurants and lounges. He would study Morgan Black until he was familiar with the assassin's every move. And during that time Soto's own injury would heal. Still, it wouldn't hurt to have a plan in place to ensure that he wasn't fighting Black. It was better if Soto could strike first, ideally a mortal blow, but one that allowed the assassin to remain conscious for a few minutes. Justice demanded that Soto make it clear why Black was dying.

In the meantime, Soto made plans to get close to LeSean Morgan. The criminal slept nearly eighteen hours. Food was delivered to his room, and soon two escorts arrived as well. Soto watched from the *Rising Sun* which was tied into the resort's surveillance system. It wasn't long before Mason appeared at the door to his room. He was wearing a dark blue jacket, over a tee-shirt and baggy slacks. His hair was slicked back, his cheeks and chin covered with dark stubble, but his eyes appeared sunken, and his face was gaunt. The two women with him were in tight fitting dresses that were short and stretchy, allowing for freedom of movement in the dance clubs. One had curly hair and wore a sequined dress. The other was wearing a wig of straight, pink hair cut in a bob, and a dark red dress. They each took one of LeSean Mason's arms and walked with him to the nearest bank of elevators.

Soto preferred peace and quiet. He wasn't looking forward to the throbbing music that would assault his ears, or the press of bodies in the resort clubs, but they allowed a form of camouflage that the executor could use to his advantage. Sanada dressed in a lightweight, designer jogging suit. The pants were a perfect match for the jacket, which he kept zipped up. It was not his preferred style, but it was what the majority of men in the clubs on the bottom floor of the pyramid wore. Soto left his Kodachi short sword, and took only the knife he had wounded Travis Hurts with. It was made of the same steel as his Kodachi, but was thin, almost delicate. The blade was straight, double-edged, and ended in a point. At its widest point the knife was the width of Soto's pinky, and five inches from the guard to the tip. It fit easily into the waistband of his jogging pants.

After tying his hair up into a topknot, he put on a designer ball cap with a flat bill. His Asian heritage played in his favor. Even at half a century of age, his hair was still dark and full, his skin still smooth. In the disguise he could pass for someone in their late thirties, which in Soto's estimation was still too old to be wearing such clothing, or frequenting night clubs. But the resort was full of older men trying to relive their youth. He left his ship, and entered the resort's main level. It was warm in the massive dome. There were people everywhere, eating at outdoor specialty restaurants, and laying out on the sandy beach around the lake at the center of the resort. Soto could hear the sounds of voices and the steady swish of waves lapping. Palm trees lined the broad avenues, and in the distance he could see the gold tops of other pyramids, each one housing hundreds of guests. They were massive structures. The resort's promotional materials boasted that each one was seven hundred and fifty feet on each side, the ground floor occupying 13 acres with shops, restaurants, night clubs, and various entertainment venues. Soto went directly to the Khafa pyramid. He could have arrived through the tunnels that led up from the VIP docking port where he kept the *Rising Sun*, but he wanted to enter from the outside, both for security and personal reasons.

Soto normally stayed away from crowds. He wasn't agoraphobic, but he didn't enjoy being in large gatherings either. Security among so many people was impossible. And the barrage of sights and sounds overwhelmed him, disrupting the peace he worked diligently to maintain. Going into the busy lower level of the pyramid was a way of acclimating himself to the crowds and the sensory overload.

Inside the pyramid was the opposite from outside, where it was always daytime. Inside the structure no outside light was visible, creating a sense that it was perpetually nighttime. The many restaurants, bars, theatres, and night clubs all advertised with bright, flashing signs. Tall pillars with faux torches lit the gloomy interior which was filled with kiosks, booths, and stalls selling everything a person might desire, from earplugs, to clothing, to mind-altering substances. It was a mashup of capitalism with hedonism. Soto saw people making out in the shadows, and everyone seemed to have a drink of some kind in hand. He stopped at a bar, purchased a cranberry juice with vodka and soda with a twist of lime, on the rocks. The alcohol consumption in the resort was vast. Some drinks were strong, intended to get a person drunk as quickly as possible, others were weak. Soto sipped his cocktail and could hardly taste the alcohol among the other flavors. But that was a good thing. Soto wanted to blend in, and to do that he needed a cocktail.

He lingered at the cocktail lounge, which was really just a narrow booth serving drinks. It was surrounded by a tiki bar with Egyptian themed decorations. From there, Soto could see the elevators where he knew LeSean would descend from the VIP sections of the pyramid. Nor did he have to wait long. Within a few minutes, LeSean exited an elevator with an escort on each arm, and headed for the nearest club. Soto followed from a distance. The club had loud music, and flashing lights that were caught in a haze of fog that was pumped out by machines to enhance the lighting. The club smelled of sweat, liquor, and the chemicals from the fog machine. Soto found it offensive in every regard, but LeSean Mason went straight to the crowded dance floor. His uppers were kicking in. The designer drugs sped up the messages between his nervous system and brain, giving him an exaggerated sense of energy, focus, self-confidence. But Soto had already noticed the toll they were taking on him. He looked tired and stretched, his body not designed for so much wear and tear. People on stimulants often forgot to eat and drink. That, combined with the increased metabolic state the drugs kept their bodies in, and the lack of sleep, took a high toll on a person's body. Soto knew that if left to his own devices, LeSean Mason would have a breakdown eventually, if his heart didn't simply give out on him.

But Soto didn't want Mason to party himself to death. Nor did it seem fair that he might die suddenly, without warning, and without fear. Death, and the life to follow would be punishment for his crimes in this life, but he should be ushered along in the knowledge that he was dying because he profited from the pain and misfortune of others. Soto lingered by the bar, and turned away three different women who asked if he wanted to dance. They gave him hateful looks when he said no. It seemed that middle aged men weren't the only people in the club trying to pretend they were young again.

After an hour, Mason sent one of the escorts to the bar for drinks. Soto was still sipping his own. It was down to the melted ice, but he didn't care. He started toward the dance floor, bobbing to the beat of the music like so many of the other dancers were doing. He had to move with the flow. It wouldn't do to have people remember him. He was just another face in the crowd, his features hidden by the darkness around him, and the shadows of his ball cap. His body bobbed and weaved through the crowd until he was close to LeSean Mason. That's when the knife came out. He waited until Mason's companion returned with drinks. As expected, LeSean popped another pill. It only took a few seconds for the drug to hit his system, and he threw back his head and howled. His companions laughed and they gyrated faster, rubbing their bodies against his.

Soto's hand shot forward and back quickly. He thrust the knife into LeSean's lower back, puncturing his kidney and lacerating his small intestines. The knife was so sharp, and LeSean Mason's senses so masked by the stimulant he had just taken, that he hardly noticed the deadly wound. Soto pulled a silk square from his pocket, and cleaned Mason's blood from the blade of his knife while still dancing. He started immediately working his way toward the nearest edge of the dance floor. It took nearly a minute before LeSean realized that he was in pain. When he shouted in fear the other people at the club thought it was simply another howl of delight. His escorts didn't notice even though LeSean stopped dancing. At the edge of the dance floor Soto stood back, watching.

LeSean held up a bloody hand. In the flashing light it wasn't clear what he was trying to communicate. One of the escorts slapped his hand, as if he were wanting a high-five instead of showing them he was hurt. LeSean started shoving his way off the dance floor. Inevitably someone shoved back. LeSean went down. Soto made his way out of the club, and lingered at a kiosk with a view of the establishment. It didn't take long for emergency medical personnel to rush to the scene. Soon, they were carrying LeSean out on a hover gurney. His clothes were damp with sweat and blood. Soto saw the crimson stain on his hands. His eyes were open wide. The stimulants in his system were probably masking the pain somewhat, but they were also making him acutely aware that he had been assaulted. What he didn't know yet was that he was dying. That information would come soon. Soto had ensured it. His kidney was ruined, but the real issue was the filth from his small intestines that were leaking into his body cavity. The internal bleeding was serious, especially with his increased heart rate. His stomach was filling with blood. Germs and toxins were leaking from his gut into his bloodstream. If he was to receive medical care immediately at a fully staffed hospital he might survive. But LeSean Mason had pushed his body beyond its limits with the use of drugs. His heart was worn down, his body just didn't have the reserves to survive the shock of being wounded. And Soto knew that guilt would play a role. LeSean Mason knew what he had done, and also what he deserved for his crimes. He would die knowing that he was reaping what he had sown. Soto didn't need to see him breathe his last breath. Instead, he headed for a restroom. There, he disposed of the designer jacket and ball cap. The resort had massive garbage disposal units, the chutes from the restroom went straight down to the incinerators. There wasn't much blood on Soto's hand. His blade had gone in and out quickly, but he washed what blood there was away, then returned to his ship. The murder would be reported, but the response would be tepid at best. Surveillance footage might show a man in a hat dancing near Mason before he was wounded, but they were all too close together to know who had struck the killing blow. It could have been any number of people. Soto would set an alert on the resort security system to warn him if his name came up. But he didn't think it would. When Mason's identity became known, the investigation into his death would lose so much momentum that it would stall. In the meantime, Soto would set his sights on a much bigger fish. It was time to deal with Morgan Black.

7

Travis' room was actually quite comfortable. Larger than most, with a small sitting area with a desk. Estelle Bonet was a sour faced woman who enjoyed being in charge. What she didn't like was the owner hiring someone who was essentially her equal. It was obvious she had enjoyed unchecked power in the castle's lower levels, giving orders to the maids and kitchen staff. Travis wondered what she would do when Victoria Hennings-Mabry was taken off world to face corruption, bribery, extortion, and money laundering charges.

He spent the night comfortably, rose at dawn, and met Drex in the stables.

"You're the new land manager, huh?" Drex said, rubbing his sore arm.

"Hired just last night," Travis said. "That a problem?"

Drex didn't answer, instead he cleared his throat and spit. Travis couldn't help but smile. He wasn't interested in making Drex's life any harder than it already was.

"You oversee the animals?" Travis asked.

"Her majesty," he said with disdain, "keeps six riding horses, and eight mules. I manage the stables."

"And do a great job from what I hear," Travis said. "I'm looking for an assistant. Someone who doesn't mind riding the grounds with me today."

"You know how to ride?" Drex asked.

"Sure," Travis said.

"Well, good for you," Drex said. "We weren't all raised with a silver spoon up our—"

"All right," Travis cut the stableman off. "You don't ride. That's fine."

"I brush 'em, feed 'em, shoe 'em when necessary. There ain't time for joy rides through the country."

"I feel like you're angry with me about something," Travis said. He had tried the carrot, but Drex wasn't interested in being friends. That left the stick, and Travis had no qualms about using it. "If you have a problem, I can let you go today."

"The hell you can," Drex snapped.

"Let's get one thing straight here," Travis said. "I'm your boss. No one is asking you to like it, but if you piss me off I'll send you packing. You and I both know there's not a lot for me to do, and taking over your job won't put me out. I know how to care for animals too. So, are we going to have a problem?"

"No," Drex said through clenched teeth.

"You're still mad about last night. But if you had murdered Raul you'd be in jail, or swinging from a rope."

"That mutt had it coming," Drex growled.

"Maybe so, but you should be thanking me. If you can get over your attitude problem I'll see that he's let go."

That got a response. Drex stood up straight and looked like he'd been slapped in the face. "How's that?"

"It's not hard to find an excuse to cut someone loose. You don't like him, that's good enough for me."

"You'll fire him?" Drex asked.

"Yeah, that's the point," Travis said.

Drex didn't believe Travis, that much was obvious. And in reality, Travis didn't have any intention of firing anyone, not even Drex. What he wanted was to get close to someone with knowledge of the guards, and of Victoria's habits.

"You send that mutt packing; you won't have any trouble from me."

"No more knife fights?"

Drex grinned. "No more," he said. "I get a little testy during the harvest, that's all. Everyone does. It starts out okay. It's almost sort of festive, but then the temps start getting uppity, as if they're better than the rest of us who work here year-round."

"What's it like during the winter?"

"Boring," Drex said. "Especially when her highness isn't here."

"She leaves?"

"She's never been here this long," he said. "Usually just comes a few times a year, never stays more than a few days."

"How long has she been here this time?"

"Ten days," Drex said. "And no word on when she's leaving either."

"What's a woman need all the security for?" Travis asked. "I saw four guards with her last night."

"Four?" Drex snorted as he started saddling one of the horses. "She's got three times that number, friend."

"Twelve?"

He nodded. "All off-worlders, and that's just the men. She keeps six female bodyguards too."

"I saw a couple of them in her quarters."

"Nah, you was on the common level," Drex said. "Ain't no one allowed on the upper floor. That's all her highness's. They say she's got a small fortune up there. And who knows what she needs all that space for?"

"That many off-world guards? How'd she get all of them here?"

"In her fancy spaceship I reckon. She's got a crew for that too, but they stay in Champsborg. You'll see the landing area when you ride around the property. I usually pick her up in the buggy when they come down here."

He pointed at the ornate, covered buggy. It was big enough for four passengers inside the covered portion, which was all leather and polished wood. There was also an elevated bench seat for the driver, and a small platform on the back for cargo.

"Anything else I should know?" Travis said.

Drex led a horse from its stall. It was a big grey gelding with a white star on its forehead. "Try not to fall off and break your neck. At least not until you fire Raul."

He continued to mumble curses at the harvester who had gotten the best of him in the fight. Travis checked the saddle. He had to lengthen the stirrups. Drex watched. It should have been his job, and he might have been insulted that Travis rechecked his work, but it was always a good idea to check an animal's riding gear before using it. And Drex obviously wanted to see just how competent Travis was with a horse. He climbed easily in the saddle and held the reins steady while the horse shimmed to the side. They were still in the stable, and Travis had to duck his head to keep from hitting the support beams.

"I'll be back after I check the grounds," Travis said.

"We'll be here," Drex said.

Travis let the horse walk through the grounds. There were a lot of long looks from the other workers. He had been at the castle just over a day, and already he had been promoted to a high-ranking position. Most of the country estates were working vineyards, the staff filled with professionals at every level. Travis was an unknown, and that only fed the rumor mill after breaking up the fight the night before, and being promoted to land manager.

He left the courtyard and rode down through the section of the vineyard that was being harvested. Raul was out with the other seasonal workers, filling a cart with overripe fruit. Travis ignored him, and kept riding, waiting until he was out of earshot before tapping his comlink.

"Morning Ava, you awake?"

"We've been awake," came Ava's reply. "How did you enjoy getting a full night's uninterrupted sleep?"

Travis smiled, glad she couldn't see him. When he spoke, he tried his best to sound sincere. "I missed you," he said. "Kaylee too."

"We miss you. How is everything going?"

"Better than expected," Travis said, then filled her in on his new position.

"Two hundred thousand a year?" Ava said. "Maybe we should just stay here."

"Can't," Travis said. "I'm starving. They don't eat meat on this planet."

"That's a small price to pay," she said. "I mean, sure your boss is a wanted fugitive, but it's pretty here. Fresh air, lots of space, and the wine is delicious I'm sure."

"Best I ever tasted," Travis said. "But I still don't care much for it."

Travis reached the landing area. It was located in the middle of a wide field. There were grapevines on all four sides, but the heart of the field had been cut out to make space for a landing pad made of concrete. There was nothing old world about it. In the middle of the vineyard was a modern landing pad with ugly paint, and a refueling tank.

"Tell me you've got a plan for getting to Victoria," Ava said.

"I've got one cooking. Another couple of days, and we should be able to get to her."

He marked the landing pad in his mind, and gave her directions. She logged the location in the ship's navigation app. It was nearly noon when he got back to the castle. Travis had seen first-hand what Heston had meant by the wasted opportunity of the property. Three fields that had once been filled with grapevines were left fallow. Weeds had taken over, and the vines had fallen from their trellises. Many even had fruit, but the clusters were sparse, the grapes smaller than in the cultivated vineyards. There were sixteen growing areas in total. Three had been neglected, and the field with the landing pad was kept neat, but the fruit was left unharvested. Six had already been gleaned, but the remaining fruit on the other six fields looked overripe to Travis. He didn't know much about agriculture, but it was obvious that poor planning had wasted much of the year's harvest at Château l'Abri.

When he got back to the stable Drex wasn't around. Travis unsaddled his horse and rubbed it down with a stiff brush. He even scooped it some sweet corn, which it munched on happily. When he came out he was met by Heston, who had a list of ideas for him to consider. Travis took the list and was impressed with the harvester's initiative.

"You show these to anyone else?" Travis asked.

"There was never anyone to show them to," Heston said.

"What about Berington?"

"He's crazy," Heston said. "And hardly ever comes out during the harvest. He's too old and set in his ways."

"Why aren't you a vinedresser?"

"Was," Heston said, "worked at the Grand Trianon. But there was some shady business going on there. We didn't know it, but ..."

"But now you can't get work as a vinedresser," Travis said, getting himself a cup and filling it with water instead of the jugs of wine that were set out for the workers.

"A good name is to be chosen rather than great riches," Heston said, with a little bit of chagrin. "And favor is better than silver or gold."

"I agree," Travis said. "And I'll take these ideas of yours into consideration."

"I could stay on," Heston said. "Help you implement some of them. We could make old man Berington listen to us."

"You deserve it," Travis said. "But I'll be frank with you,

Heston. There's some shady business going on here. You wouldn't want to be associated with a bad vineyard twice in your career."

Heston looked hard at Travis. It was obvious that the older man wasn't sure if Travis was lying or not. Then he nodded. Travis wasn't sure if it was in agreement, or just resignation. He wanted to help. There were a lot of good people working at the castle and helping with the harvest. But Travis wasn't a manager, and he couldn't ignore the fact that Victoria Hennings-Mabry was a wanted fugitive from justice.

With a sigh he skipped his lunch and went looking for a guard. He had the beginnings of a plan in mind, and the quicker he could implement it, the better off the people working at the castle would be.

8

Time had no meaning to Augustine Ward. His life had blurred into one long, hellish nightmare. If he had to guess he was mining sixteen hours a day. Climbing out of the mines to the main cavern just to get a loaf of poorly flavored nutrition was exhausting. He was barely holding on, and probably would have been killed, but those plotting against him were in no hurry. The one thing they all had was time.

Augustine saw the dead bodies. Some had succumbed to life in the mines. They collapsed onto the ground, or tumbled down the steps. They were left where they lay unless they happened to be in someone's way. It was sad, and yet Augustine also felt envious of the dead. They weren't hurting any more. They weren't suffering the way he was. The muscles in his back and shoulders ached from standing on his feet chipping away at the rock walls in search of minerals to fill his sack. But it was his legs that hurt the most. Climbing the stairs left them trembling and weak. In the mornings, or what he considered morning, after sleeping on the rock floor, he was stiff. His quadriceps and hamstrings ached terribly with every move he made, and cramped frequently on the long crawl back up from the mines.

He had just finished giving Bro Cyphus his first haul of the day, when a pair of inmates appeared at his back.

"You're Cyphus' new grunt," one said. "Ain't much to look at."

Augustine would normally have reacted angrily to being insulted. He would have insisted on satisfaction, and nothing but a duel with pistols would suffice. But that seemed like another life-time to Augustine. Everything before arriving at the prison camp was like a dream. He could remember the taste of whiskey and the sizzle as it flowed down his throat. He could remember the feel of a woman's touch, and laughter with friends, but it all seemed like a fantasy to him. Nothing from his former life seemed real any longer.

"He can send a message though," the other newcomer said. "Send it loud and clear."

"Written in blood?" the first one proposed.

"What else?"

"I'm not looking for trouble," Augustine said.

"What you want don't play into it, fish," the first speaker said. He was smaller than his companion, but his voice was cold and cruel.

"You went looking for help from the wrong people," the other man said. "The family ain't nothing but a gaggle of old ladies."

They came at him fast. The smaller one raised his rock hammer with the intention of bashing in Augustine Ward's skull. But despite his fatigue, and even his envy of the dead, Augustine's self-preservation instincts kicked in. And he was still faster than the two men there to do him harm at the end of the tunnel he was digging.

The smaller man's hammer came down but connected with nothing but air. Augustine had already twisted out of the way. And as the other stranger raised his hammer to strike at Augustine, the gunslinger thrust his own tool right into the larger man's face. Their head coverings were just stiff enough to stand up. It was a bit like wearing a bucket on his head, with a dirty, sweat smeared window in front. But it did nothing to protect the wearer from a physical blow. The top of the hammer head smashed in the clear plastic and smacked hard against the big man's face. Augustine saw a flash of blood gush from his nose before he stumbled back into the tunnel.

The smaller man grabbed hold of Augustine's hammer, but Augustine threw himself toward him, bending his arm at the elbow and smashing it into the shorter man's head. The assailant was knocked into the side of the tunnel, which was solid rock. Augustine, in a fit of rage, with all the fear and resentment of being in the prisoner flooding through him, rammed his shoulder into the shorter man over and over again. The assailant was knocked repeatedly into the rock wall, his head crashing against the unmovable stone. His head covering was soon torn, and the man was knocked unconscious.

Augustine put the boots to the smaller man, who fell to the ground. When he heard the other man scrambling back down the tunnel, he snatched up his rock hammer and chased him down. The second figure was on his hands and knees when Augustine reached him. The gunslinger chopped down with his rock hammer. The pointed end pierced the man's head covering and punctured his skull. He fell dead instantly. Turning around, Augustine realized he was alone. The danger had passed. He had no idea who the men were, or why they attacked him. It was just one more horror in the prison camp on Lucerine.

Eventually, after catching his breath and regaining his composure, Augustine stepped over the bodies and went back to work. He got lucky that day with a chunk of mercury that was well over three ounces in weight. When he was finally at the end of this strength, he carried his sack, a little over half full, back toward the stairs. The climb up was difficult. The fight had drained Augustine. He was so thirsty he felt like his tongue was swelling in his mouth. Everything hurt, and despair was like a thousand-pound weight on his back. He had to literally crawl the last hundred feet up, stopping after four or five stairs to just lay there and try to catch his breath.

When he finally reached the main cavern, he got to his feet and walked slowly to the water spigot. He rinsed off his dirty hands, and splashed water on his face in between sessions of gulping the tepid liquid. Bro Cyphus came for him, and Augustine never heard the big man coming. He grabbed the gunslinger by the arm and flung him away from the water spigot. Augustine tripped and went rolling across the floor, barely able to hang onto his bag of ore.

"You killed Kizer and Burton!" Bro Cyphus snarled. "You little maggot!"

"They tried to kill me," Augustine argued.

The big man didn't care for explanations. He swung a meaty fist at Augustine, who honestly would have just fallen over dead if the blow had landed. But the gunslinger was revived by the water. He was still exhausted, his muscles quivering, but his mind was clear. He ducked under the punch, and drove his fist into Bro Cyphus' groin. The big man grunted in pain, but tried to backhand Augustine, who managed to get his rock hammer up to block the slap. But he wasn't prepared for Bro Cyphus' power. The big man slapped the hammer right out of Augustine's hand. It went clattering across the cavern floor.

The two men looked at each other. Augustine was still on his knees, with Bro Cyphus towering over him. The big man raised his hands together and swung them down hard. Augustine rolled backward. The cavern floor was uneven and hard. He felt his bones pinching what little muscle tissue he had left as he rolled over his back and shoulder. The bruising was inevitable, but adrenaline was pumping through Augustine's system. He came up on his feet just as Bro Cyphus was stumbling toward him. Augustine still had a sack full of ore. He swung it hard. The rocks in the sack connected with the big man's face and tore through skin and bone. His scream was loud and echoed in the canyon. He toppled sideways, and lay on the floor clutching his face. Blood flowed from several gashes where the pointy edges of the rocks had torn the skin. His left eyeball was out of the socket, which was pulverized. His cheekbone and several teeth had been smashed. He lay in a growing pool of blood, whimpering.

Augustine turned, looking for more threats. There was only a fraction of the number of people in the cavern compared to when Augustine had first arrived. But Leon Hurts was there. He was surrounded by half a dozen people. They were looking at Augustine with suspicion, but none made a move against him. The gunslinger retrieved his rock hammer and considered finishing off the big man. But it was soon apparent that Bro Cyphus was no longer a threat. He lay passed out in his own blood in the middle of the cavern, one eye dangling in front of the other by the optical nerve, his breathing shallow. Augustine knew a blow to the head could put a man in a coma, or even kill him if the brain swelled. Augustine was in prison for murder, but had only fought to protect himself from Bro Cyphus. It was one of the only truly justifiable killings of his career.

He returned to the water, drank his fill, then turned over his sack of minerals. It was enough for two full nutrient loaves. They were flavored to taste like chicken. Augustine ate them all, and was about to go down to his hovel simply because it seemed safer than falling asleep in the big cavern.

"Hold up there, killer," Leon said, as Augustine started to get up from where he had been gobbling food. "Looks like you did Bro Cyphus in for good."

"What choice did I have?"

"You coulda died," Leon said. "Plenty of people would have."

"Instinct," Augustine said.

"Come sit with me a while," Leon said. "We got business to discuss."

They sat alone, as more and more people arrived in the cavern. Many gave Augustine hateful glances, but more than a few looked at him with respect. Leon questioned Augustine about the meeting with Iona Freeze.

"Don't know her," Leon said. "Never heard of her."

"Maybe someone in the IO feels they owe you," Augustine suggested.

"Doubt that," Leon said. "I suppose they would have just killed me here if that's what they wanted."

"That'd be my thought," Augustine said. "I guess maybe they have a job for you to do."

"Not sure what an old crust like me can do for them," Leon said. "You might not know this but your benefactor over there, the one you conveniently bludgeoned to death, was planning to take over the Family. And he wasn't acting alone."

"You've got enemies?"

"We all do. Some more than others. There's plenty that feel I've been on the throne too long."

"When is the corpse roundup?" Augustine asked.

"Tomorrow. Free food for everyone too. My guess is I'll be dead one way or other before the day is over. The only question is, do I go down swinging, or do I go up there with you?"

"If you're dead either way," Augustine asked, "what do you have to lose?"

Leon looked nervous. "I know what I'm facing down here. Up there?" He shrugged his shoulders.

"Could be freedom," Augustine said.

"You make it sound easy," Leon said.

"Why not?"

"Because, I been down here too long. I won't be able to see what's coming up there. I ain't sure if I'm cut out for it anymore."

"Well, if it makes a difference, I'll be with you," Augustine said. "You won't be alone."

"You saying we could partner up?"

"If it's agreeable with the Incendius people," Augustine said.

"You're the only reason I've got a chance of getting out of this hell-hole. I suppose I owe you for that."

"All right then," Leon said. "We'll be partners. Come hell or high water, we face it together."

Augustine felt a small sense of pride. He was tired, bone tired. But his stomach was full, and for the first time since arriving at the prison camp he wasn't afraid. Best of all, he had hope. And that tiny spark of hope in the darkness of despair was enough to blind him to the fact that Leon Hurts was manipulating him. The crafty old con man was playing games, ensuring that whatever happened, he had someone to push into the line of fire while he made a hasty retreat. It was his way, and being a sociopath, he had no qualms about who he hurt, or what happened to anyone other than himself.

9

By the third day of his new gig as property manager Travis had a pretty good idea where everything stood. There were twelve guards in the castle. They were, from what Travis could tell, trained security professionals, the type one might hire to watch over a business after hours. He would have to deal with them, but he wasn't expecting it to be a problem, since they were all lulled into a sense of complacency by their duties and restrictions. Victoria Hennings-Mabry spent most of her time on the upper level of the castle, which was off limits to the male security force. The only people allowed upstairs were Victoria's four female bodyguards. They were the real issue for Travis.

Unlike the men, the four female bodyguards were highly trained experts. There were always two with Victoria. The other two remained on the second floor with the other guards, and on that rare occasion when Victoria was needed, only one of the two remaining females could go up and request that she come down.

Like everything else on Tavos, there was no electronic communication system in the castle. The only technology was the holographic entertainment system on the second floor. And that, along with the fact that there were no emergency vehicles on the property, played directly into Travis' favor.

On the third night, after a clandestine meeting with Ava to collect a few things earlier in the day on the edge of the Château l'Abri property, Travis was ready to make his move. The harvest was winding down. Grapes were still being collected each day, but each cluster had to be examined before it was processed. The fruit was going bad, and soon the entire operation would be shut down. Travis had debated on waiting for that to happen. It might have been easier to get Victoria out of the castle without being seen when the courtyard wasn't so full of people. But the activity also made it easier for Travis to get the attention of the guards. He couldn't just go upstairs and start shooting. He needed to take them out of commission slowly and very quietly, so as not to alert the bodyguards who were with Victoria. They might not have a way out of the castle, but he didn't want a shootout when he was outnumbered by so much.

The first priority was to get Drex good and drunk. The stableman was spending his nights in the barn with the animals to ensure none of the seasonal workers, who he didn't dare trust, got in and stole anything. Travis had been around long enough to know the stableman's bias against the seasonal workers was unwarranted. They were salt of the earth types, who were happy to be working, even if they did feel that the waste taking place on the property was a crime. They were paid daily, in hard currency, which was standard for seasonal workers on Tavos. But they were paid top wages for their work done late in the season, which was for most a financial boon to their yearly income. No one was looking to steal anything, not when the pay was so good.

Travis spent the evening ensuring that Drex drank enough wine to get completely soused. When Drex finally passed out on the little bunk he had created with some blankets and a few bales of hay, Travis breathed a sigh of relief. He got the big grey horse he had ridden each day saddled, and out of its stall. He tied the animal up just inside the stable doors.

His next priority was to check the gate. There was only one way in or out of the castle. The big double doors of the gate were rarely opened. But Travis could lead his horse out through the man door, which was kept locked at night with a simple metal bar. Under the guise of his new job, Travis had made a show each night of walking the castle courtyard and inspecting the gate. He did so again, and made sure there was nothing other than the metal bar blocking the man door. It could easily be removed, and that was one more item he didn't have to worry about.

The real issue was getting upstairs. He needed an excuse for being on the second floor, preferably one that would set the guards at ease. Travis could go in shooting, but his Slinger made a reasonably loud report for such a little gun. Plus, it only fired six shots on a single power cell. Travis could swap it out, but he didn't like the idea of getting into a gunfight if he could manage it. The workers who lived downstairs might not like the idea of seeing the owner carried out of the castle grounds. They didn't respect her, but they liked getting paid. There might not be a lot of pride in the operation of Château l'Abri, but the money was good. Who knew what would happen to the property once Victoria was arrested? The GCIB would undoubtedly freeze all her assets that were known to them. Which meant they would take possession of the property. They might keep the employees on to manage everything until a trial could be held, but Victoria was part of the corruption case on Las Brazzas and there might not be a trial for years. So, with the fate of every employee at stake, it was best if Travis could get Victoria out of the castle with as few people knowing about it as possible.

At midnight, he made his move. The workers in the courtyard were all asleep. The kitchen staff rose earlier to begin preparing for the long days and extra mouths to feed, but they wouldn't be up for a few more hours. Travis went up the stairs to the second level and was stopped immediately by one of the guards.

"What are you doing up here, Travers," the guard asked.

"It's Estelle," Travis said. "I think maybe she's having a heart attack."

The guard looked more frustrated than concerned, and didn't seem skeptical at all. Estelle was a heavy-set woman, always angry about something. She lorded her position over the rest of the staff, and could be very unpleasant to deal with.

"And ..." the guard asked.

"And I think we need to get her some help. Are any of your people trained in medical emergencies?"

"No," the guard said.

"Don't you think we should alert Ms. Hennings-Mabry?"

"You want to wake her up?" the guard asked.

"I think we should," Travis said. "Come and see what's going on if you think I'm overreacting."

"Alberaz, Levins, you're with me," the guard said.

Two more guards joined the one at the top of the stairs. They followed Travis down. He led them to his room. It was the one real risk in his plan. If they knew where Estelle slept, they would know he was up to no good. He had his Slinger tucked into the pocket of his coat, but fortunately, he didn't need it.

In his room he had staged what looked like a sudden medical emergency. A table was knocked over, and covers were pulled off his bed, covering the shape Travis hoped would look like Estelle Bonet. And, just as he had hoped, all three guards entered his room, but none went close to the pile of blankets.

"She passed out?" the main guard asked.

"Yeah," Travis said, pulling out his Storm KV stun wand. "Just like this."

He pressed the wand into the back of the nearest guard. It crackled, shooting fifty-thousand volts into the man who stiffened and toppled over. The other two guards watched their companion in shock. It was that moment of hesitation that sealed their fate. Travis shocked the second guard, so that only the man named

Levins was left. He went for his gun, but Travis hit his forearm with the wand. He yelped in pain, and then Travis pressed the end of the device with the electrical nodes against his chest and fired it. Like the others, Levins stiffened as the electrical charge shot through his body, contracting his muscles, and overwhelming his brain's electrical activity. He dropped to the floor and Travis quickly got restraints on all three men.

His plan had been to go back upstairs immediately, but he found two of the other workers in the hallway. One was Katrina, who was still very friendly with Travis.

"What's going on?" she asked. "We heard someone yell."

"That was me," Travis said. "Stubbed my toe."

"In your boots?" Torre asked. She was roommates with Katrina and worked in the kitchen.

"I just remembered I left the irrigation valve open," Travis said. "At least I think I did. I'll have to go check it."

"Oh," Katrina said. "That's why you're dressed."

"Yeah," Travis said. "Stupid mistake, but I can't sleep until I know for sure that it's off. I'll just go up and let the guards know what I'm doing."

"They give me the creeps," Torre said.

"They look at us like we're show animals or something," Katrina added.

"Well, who can blame them?" Travis said. "You're both young and attractive."

Travis was, by his guess, two decades older than Katrina and her roommate. And he was not a handsome bachelor, but he was nice and complimentary. Plus, they had seen him in action, not to mention on horseback. When he said they were attractive both of the girls blushed.

"Go on back to bed," Travis said. "I'm sorry I woke you."

They obeyed, and Travis breathed a sigh of relief. The castle had thick walls, even between the rooms, but too much noise would ruin his stealth tactics. He moved to the stairs, but waited until both of the girls had gone back into their room. He looked around, no one else seemed to be up. It was dark, with only a couple of tall tapering beeswax candles lit at either end of the hallway to shed some light into the dark corridors.

He went back upstairs. There were two guards left at the windows. They stood staring out into the darkness. Oil lamps were mounted on stands that stood at intervals along the tall stone walls, casting light down into the courtyard. But beyond the wall, was only darkness. If an intruder didn't come carrying his own light, the guards wouldn't see them. Travis was quiet as he moved up behind the nearest of the men. To his surprise, he heard deep breathing, and just the faintest snore. The guard was asleep at his post. Travis had heard stories of soldiers falling asleep on watch, but he never imagined that a person could actually sleep standing up.

He slipped over to where the other guard stood. He too was breathing in a deep, regular rhythm. Travis zapped him with the stun wand, caught the guard as he fell, then put restraints on him, all with the other guard in the room. The first guard went down just as easily, and then Travis went in search of the room where the guards slept for the night. It was a big room, with six sets of bunks, and its own bathroom. Half of the bunks were filled with slumbering guards. Travis took out a canister of compressed sleep fog. He pulled the pin and rolled the canister into the room. As soon as the chemical agent, which would keep the guards asleep for hours, started to billow, Travis closed the door.

The next room he came to had a guard looking out the wide window, shifting from foot to foot. He was the first person Travis had found awake. Travis strolled into the room, which appeared to be used as an office of sorts. There were boxes on the floor, and on a broad desk. There were shelves against one wall partially filled with old-fashioned books. A small lamp on the desk was the only light in the room. Travis moved quickly behind the guard, who didn't notice him until the last minute.

"Hey, what's up?" the guard asked, thinking that Travis was one of his compatriots.

Instead of responding, he zapped the guard with the stun wand, but the power charge was nearly spent. It only sent the guard to his knees. Travis had hit the man on the back of the head with the wand, which was built for that purpose. He didn't like hurting people when he didn't have to, but the guard was working to protect a wanted felon. If Travis was leading a team of GCIB agents, the guards would be arrested for aiding and abetting.

He put restraints on the man, then went back to the hallway. By his estimation there should be one sentry left, and two of the four female bodyguards should be sleeping somewhere. He made his way quietly through the castle. There were many rooms. Some were completely empty, others looked like storage. He eventually found the two sleeping female bodyguards. Travis had two more canisters of sleep agent. But before he used it on the slumbering security professionals, he wanted to round up the last sentry.

The final guard was posted in a long, narrow room filled with plants. It was a lovely space, but the only way in was through a door in plain sight of the last sentry. Travis replaced the battery in the Storm KV stun wand and took a deep breath, before strolling into the room like he belonged.

"Who the hell are you?" the guard asked the moment that Travis stepped into sight.

"Property manager," Travis said. "Estelle had a heart attack. We're going to have to send for transport. She won't make it to Tratoria by wagon."

Travis had the stun wand in hand, but was holding the device in a reverse grip with his left hand, keeping the wand, which was as long as his forearm from elbow to wrist, hidden behind his arm. He had hoped the explanation would throw the sentry off his guard, but instead the man turned, put his hand on the handle of his pistol and braced himself.

"I don't know you," he said.

"Whoa," Travis said, sounding surprised but purposefully keeping his voice low. "Look, man, I just work for Ms. Mabry. I was told to let you know what's happening. That's it."

"Turn around," the man said, clicking on a small, handheld flashlight.

Travis didn't move. He had lost sight of the sentry in the glare of the light.

"You deaf?" the man snapped. "I said turn around."

He was too loud. Travis knew there was only one way to proceed. He couldn't turn around. The sentry would see his stun wand, and Travis wasn't going to turn his back on his opponent. Instead, he went for his Slinger.

The light bobbed slightly as the sentry went for his gun too, dropping out of Travis' eyes. The sentry had a typical military style pistol, bulky and thick. He wore it on his thigh, and already had his hand on the grip when Travis went for his own weapon. But the sentry wasn't fast enough. He got his bulky pistol out of its holster, but couldn't get it high enough to shoot before Travis gunned him down. The stun blast hit the sentry in the chest and sent him tumbling backward.

Travis didn't go to restrain the man. He knew the odds of having been heard were too great. He slipped into the hallway just outside the room where the two female bodyguards slept. He could hear their whispered voices. Their door was open, and the women were shaking off sleep as Travis pulled the pin on the sleep gas. He rolled the canister into their room, then stood and pulled the door closed.

"Hey!" one of the women shouted.

"Gas," the other said, as the canister started to billow.

"Get to the bathroom," the other said.

They were smart. They would lock themselves in the bathroom until they could find a way to rush through their bedroom and out into the hallway. They probably had towels they could cover their faces with. Travis moved to the end of the hall and waited at the bottom of the stairs that led up to the third floor.

He was in the shadows, his Slinger held ready, as he waited. It wasn't long before the bedroom door was yanked open and the two women with towels held to their faces with one hand, and pistols held ready in the other, lunged out. Travis fired three quick shots. The two women dropped, and when he turned his attention back to the stairs, lights were coming on.

His stealth attack had been successful to a point. Of the sixteen security people, only two remained. Travis feared that Victoria Hennings-Mabry would have a reinforced safe room to hide in. If she got to it and locked herself in, there would be no way to get her out. Travis would have to keep watch for days, maybe weeks until she ran out of food or water. He had no idea how the staff would respond to his failed attempt to take Victoria into custody in the dead of night. He couldn't take the chance that she might slip away from him. He would never have a better chance to bring her in, and he had too much riding on the job to fail.

There was only one thing left to do, one option available to him. And that was to charge straight up the stairs, and hope he could take out Victoria's guards before they got him.

10

"Ava, head this way," Travis said as he ran up the steps.

"Okay, how's it going?" her voice crackled in his earpiece.

"So far, so good," he said. "I've almost got her. See you in a few."

At the top of the stairs, he stopped to get a lay of the land. It was a room much like the main room of the second floor. There was a bar, only instead of hard liquor the surface was littered with wine bottles. More were in a massive, temperature-controlled refrigerator with glass doors and a digital display. There were plates of half-eaten food, and two large charcuterie boards with fruit, cheese, crackers, and slivers of meat. It was clear at a glance that Victoria wasn't a big eater, but she also wasn't a vegetarian like most residents of Tavos.

The ceiling of the third floor was lined with transparent material, either glass or something stronger. He could see the stars overhead. There were windows too, just like the second level, but between them were tall bookcases. Victoria was a collector with thousands of volumes of ancient, printed material. There was no time to study the titles. In a nook, clearly visible from where Travis came up the stairs, was a communication console. One of the two female guards was there, calling for help.

"... immediate evac—" was all he heard her saying into the unit before he shot her.

The stun blast knocked her into the wall. She hit the communication unit hard enough to crack the touch-sensitive display. It went dark, as the guard toppled onto her back. Her nose was bleeding and one eye looked red. She was stunned, not injured from the shot, but the force of the blast had left a mark.

Travis immediately ejected the battery from the Slinger's grip. It popped out easily, and he slid a fresh power cell into the bottom of the handle. It clicked into place, and he slipped the spent battery into his coat pocket.

From the living area Travis moved quickly toward a hallway. The first room he came to had a massage table set up. The second room was filled with exercise equipment. Travis saw no signs of Victoria or the other guard.

"They were calling for help," Travis said. "Check the radar."

"Nothing yet," Ava said. "I'm lifting off now."

"There's one guard left," Travis said. "But they know I'm here."

"I guessed as much," Ava said. "You were bound to be noticed sooner or later."

"Keep watch for company. Victoria is up here somewhere. I just have to find her."

He had passed several guest rooms. They were completely empty, no beds or furniture. Eventually he came to a large room at the corner of the home. It was bigger than any two of the others combined. When he peeked inside he saw a massive bed. It was set on a platform that required steps to get up into it. Only the covers of the near side were thrown back, and light from a nearby bathroom shown into the room.

Travis didn't see any movement, but a laser blast from the other side of the bed burned into the thick paneling next to the door. He pulled back into the hallway.

"I hate traitors!" Victoria screamed. "How could you?"

"I could ask you the same," Travis said. "Drop that pistol and come out with your hands up."

The command was met with more laser blasts. Travis expected as much. He pulled the pin on his last canister of sleep gas and sent it rolling into the room.

"Bastard!" Victoria yelled. "Coward."

"We have to move," her bodyguard said. "Stay right on my hip."

Travis had moved back into the hallway. He knew they wouldn't run straight toward him. Victoria's bathroom was probably larger than his living quarters on the *Purgatory*, and well-stocked. He lay on his stomach and pushed himself around the edge of the door frame. The guard was moving over the bed. They had been hidden behind it, and instead of going around the massive piece of furniture, they had gone up and over. It was the most direct route to the bathroom. Travis fired. His first shot hit the guard just as she was jumping from the bed. The force of the blast knocked her into Victoria, and they fell together. Victoria screamed, then went silent. The sleep gas was across the room, and Travis didn't want to wait for it to settle and fill the space. He took a deep breath and ran in.

Victoria wasn't unconscious, but lay under the body of her guard. She had her own pistol and when Travis approached she shot at him. Fortunately, in her fear and lack of experience, the shot went wide. Travis kicked the weapon out of her hand, bent down, and rolled the guard off Victoria. She did have one arm bent awkwardly behind her. Travis wasn't sure if it was dislocated, or broken, or both. The fact that Victoria was still fighting was impressive. She reached up, her fingers curled into talons, as she tried to claw his face. Travis grabbed her wrist and pulled her toward him. She screamed again, her left arm dangling at her side. She was wearing a dark purple sleeping gown. It had tiny straps over her shoulders and hung to her knees. Travis could see her left arm swelling just above the elbow, and her shoulder on the left side was misshapen too. He felt sorry for her, knowing the pain had to be agonizing. Fortunately, she passed out, and he was able to pull her over one shoulder and carry her out of the room.

"Target acquired," Travis said.

"Damn, you're good," Ava said. "I have to admit, I was worried."

"We're not out of the woods yet," he said. "I've still got to get her out of the compound."

"Will the workers stop you?"

"They might try," he admitted. "How's the radar?"

"Still clear," she said.

He hurried down the stairs. The second floor was clear and quiet. But when he reached the third stairwell, there was light and motion below him.

Travis put his Slinger back in his pocket and rushed down the steps. Estelle Bonet was there in a long, ugly sleeping dress. Her gray hair was a tangled mess, and she held a lantern in one hand.

"What are you doing?" Estelle demanded.

"Someone broke in," Travis said, heading for the nearest exit. "They attacked Ms. Mabry."

"That's Hennings-Mabry to you, Travers," Estelle snapped angrily. "Where are you going?"

"She's hurt," Travis said. "Broken arm, probably dislocated too. I've got to get her to a doctor."

Most of the permanent staff were women. One chef and a maintenance worker were men, but they did nothing to stop Travis. They were all in shock. Travis dashed outside and found the seasonal workers stirring. He ran for the stable. It wasn't easy with a full-grown woman over his shoulder. She was thin, but still weighed over a hundred and twenty pounds. He was sweating by the time he reached the stable.

He yanked the door open. Drex was still snoring on his bed of hay bales. The big gray horse was waiting. Travis stepped onto a stack of feed bags, then threw his leg over the saddle. His back was aching, but he had his arm around Victoria's legs, with her good right wrist his grasp, securing her in place. He let the horse take its lead. He had to duck under the door to get out, and he felt the muscles in his back quivering. They were on the verge of cramping as he straightened in the saddle.

"What's going on?" someone shouted.

"He's taking her," another worker yelled, pointing at Travis.

"The mistress is hurt," he said, urging the horse forward with his knees. "I've got to get her to help."

"What happened?" someone asked.

"She was attacked," one of the permanent staff said.

"Wait, what?" Heston asked, from where he stood on the sleeping platform.

"Ned's going to save her," Katrina declared.

"No," Raul said, coming around the far end of the castle behind Travis. "He's the one taking her."

For a moment no one knew what to do, except to get out of the way of the horse. The big gray's hooves were clopping loudly on the cobblestones.

"Guy," Travis shouted, "Open the man door on the gate."

"Don't do it," Heston called.

"He's kidnapping Ms. Mabry," Raul bellowed.

"I don't know," Guy said.

"She's a wanted felon," Travis said. "Open the gate."

"You do and you're just as guilty as he is," Heston shouted.

"No, he's helping her," Katrina shouted.

"You're a fool," Raul snapped. "Can't you see what's happening?"

"Put her down, Travers," Heston ordered. "You can't do this."

Travis was thinking of pulling his pistol. The fact was he couldn't get down off the horse very easily with Victoria over his shoulder. There was no way to put her on the horse without her falling or being pulled down. And once Travis was on the ground, he was certain the workers would attack him. If he pulled his weapon he might get Guy to move, but the sight of the laser pistol might also convince everyone that he had bad intentions.

"She was involved in the money laundering and corruption on Las Brazzas," Travis shouted. "I'm a licensed Fugitive Recovery Specialist, working for the GCIB. I have to take her in, that's the law."

"Not on Tavos," Raul snapped. "We have our own laws."

"We don't need outsiders telling us what to do!" Estelle screamed.

Travis knew things were about to get ugly. Not having the gate already open was a mistake. There was no other way out of the compound, and he didn't have enough firepower to disperse the crowd. But before he could decide what to do, Ava flew over the castle. She came in low and fast, the repulser lifts roaring.

Her voice was crystal clear in Travis' ear, "Tell them to open the gate or I'll blast the wall down."

He knew the *Purgatory* didn't have guns. She couldn't knock a hole in the wall, or attack the crowd, but they didn't know it.

"That's my ship," Travis shouted. "Open the door, or we'll blow a hole in the wall."

That got Guy moving. He was a seasonal worker and didn't want any trouble. He just happened to be by the door, and he didn't feel any compulsion to stand up for Victoria Hennings-Mabry, or anyone else. He lifted the metal locking bar and swung open the door.

Travis needed to get off the horse but there was no time. He bent down on the big gray's neck and nudged it forward. The horse walked through the man door. Travis felt Victoria's back bump on the door frame. She groaned, and he thought it probably hurt, but there was no time to check on her. As soon as he was outside he turned the horse to the side and gave it a kick. The big gray sped up into a trot, and then a canter, hurrying around the building. Travis could hear people shouting inside the compound. Someone had gone up to check on the guards. Some were surely arguing that Travis should be stopped, but no one followed. He rode to the rear of the castle, then out through the vineyards.

"Travis, there's something on the radar," Ava said over the comlink.

"That figures," Travis said. "Where are you?"

"On the landing pad."

"I'll be there in a few minutes," he said, his back throbbing with pain as the horse sped up into a gallop. "How close is it?"

"Still on the edge of the radar," she said. "forty miles maybe?"

"Are we ready to fly?"

"Sitting on go," she replied.

"All right, I'm almost there. Open the rear hatch."

Travis could see the *Purgatory* ahead of him. He felt both relief and tension build. It was a relief to be out of the castle. He had made it past Victoria's guards, and the seasonal workers. It felt great to be in the wide-open vineyards on horseback, as if nothing could touch him. On the other hand, he was afraid of what was coming. If it was just a transport they had nothing to fear, but he had trouble believing it wasn't something more sinister. A gunship maybe, or even just a security vessel that might have weapons. Whoever was on it didn't want Travis taking Victoria off planet. And if it had the means, it would stop them any way it could.

Travis reached the ship and reined the horse in. Getting off the animal was too difficult with Victoria on his back. He held her wrist and lowered her to the ground. It was more of a controlled drop, and the gray horse stepped to the side, away from Victoria.

"Good boy," Travis said, patting the gelding on the neck. "You did good. Back to the castle now."

Travis stepped out of the saddle and down to the ground. Then he slapped the horse on the rear and watched for a few seconds as the horse turned through the vineyard and cantered back toward the castle. He didn't want to drag Victoria to the ship. It would have been easier on him, but potentially worse for her. He couldn't pull on her dislocated arm, and he feared dislocating the other shoulder if he pulled her good arm. Instead, he sat her up, bent as low as he could, and lifted her onto his shoulder.

"Bastard," she said in a weak voice.

"Glad to be of service," he said as he hurried up the ramp. "Ava, I'm on board. Closing rear hatch."

He hit the button to close the hatch, and immediately the ship started to rise. Travis lowered Victoria carefully to the deck inside one of the holding cells.

"Don't do this," she said. "Take me to a hospital. Please."

Travis ignored her, and closed the door.

"Where's that bogey?" Travis asked.

"Twenty miles out and closing. They've sped up."

"They see us on their radar," Travis said.

"What will they do?"

"I have no idea."

He was headed for the Engineering space when Victoria called out. "I'll pay you. Name your price."

Travis ignored her and went straight through engineering and the living quarters. Ava was in her customary place. There were two pilot seats in the *Purgatory* and two sets of controls. She preferred the seat on the right, and baby Kaylee was strapped into the makeshift safety seat on the left. Travis grabbed the support bar and looked down at the radar.

"Can you bring up the rear vid feed?" Travis asked.

Ava reached out and hit the icon for the rear facing camera. A hidden projector displayed the video on the lower left-hand side of the ship's forward view screen.

"It's good to see you too, Travis," Ava said sarcastically.

"Trust me, you're a sight for sore eyes. That looks like a security ship of some kind."

"Guns?"

"Probably," Travis said. "Are we headed for orbit?"

"Yes, engaging jet engines now."

Travis was nearly pulled off his feet. He had to brace himself as the *Purgatory* jumped forward when the jet engines engaged. For a few seconds they put distance between themselves and the security ship. Travis hoped that it would land at the compound. They had no way of knowing their benefactor was on his ship, but the security vessel increased speed. The radar showed them at sixteen miles directly behind the *Purgatory*.

Ava dialed up the artificial gravity. The system was power heavy when activated in atmosphere where it had to fight against the gravity of an entire planet. Travis looked at the fuel gages. They had over half a tank of fuel, plenty of water and air. The ship's battery banks were over ninety percent. There was no need to stop and refuel. They could break orbit, then jump to hyperspace. As long as the security ship didn't stop them.

A voice crackled over the cockpit's speakers.

"Vessel 212179er, this is Tavos Security. Drop speed and begin a controlled descent. You have human cargo on board without consent. I repeat, drop speed and begin a controlled descent."

"Negative, negative," Travis replied, holding the transmit button on the arm of the pilot seat he was braced behind. "This is the *Purgatory*. We are a licensed Fugitive Recovery vessel with a prisoner on board. Stand down. This is a law enforcement operation. I repeat, we are a licensed fugitive recovery vessel. Do not impede our launch."

"*Purgatory* we do not recognize your ship, or your authority to take anyone from Tavos. Reduce speed and begin a controlled descent or we will be forced to take extreme measures."

A light began to flash. Travis didn't recognize what it was immediately, but Ava did.

"They're trying to lock onto us," she said. "What do we do?"

"Can't give her back," Travis said.

"Will they fire on us?"

"If they do they'd be killing their boss," Travis said. He reached forward and pushed the transmit button again. "Tavos Security, I have Victoria Hennings-Mabry on board the *Purgatory*. Do not fire on this ship. Not if you want to see her alive again."

"*Purgatory* you are threatening a sovereign citizen," the security ship said. "That is a crime on Tavos. Land your damn ship, or we will shoot you down."

"You shoot us, your boss dies."

"We'll take that chance," the pilot of the security ship said.

Travis couldn't be sure, but he felt strongly that the security ship was an atmospheric aircraft only. It had closed to within twelve miles of the *Purgatory*. He wasn't sure what to do. If they landed and gave Victoria back, they would probably kill Travis and Ava just for the trouble. He couldn't risk it. But it made no sense that they might shoot him down with Victoria on board.

"Don't slow down," Travis said.

"What if—"

The ship's defense systems picked up the missile lock and gave a warning alarm. Kaylee started to cry. Travis felt his gut turn to water, but deep inside his instincts told him not to give in.

"Just - keep - going," Travis said.

"They have a missile lock on us, Travis," she said.

"And if they use it, Victoria Hennings-Mabry will die. How close are we to orbit?"

"Sixty seconds," she replied.

"Take Kaylee to the escape pod. I'll fly the ship."

"No," Ava snapped.

"*Purgatory*, this is your last warning. We have a missile lock on your vessel. Reduce your speed and begin your descent or we will open fire. Do not test us. We will shoot you down."

Travis toggled the transmit button again. "I don't think so," he said, looking at Kaylee and wondering how he could possibly risk her life. It felt wrong, he thought he might be sick to his stomach. Sweat was popping out across his forehead, and his legs felt shaky, like they might collapse at any moment. "You won't risk killing your boss," Travis continued. "We both know that if you fire that weapon you'll kill everyone on board this ship, either in the detonation, or when we crash. And trust me, Victoria would rather be alive in custody than dead."

He stood up, staring at the ship on the video display.

"You're risking too much," Ava said. "She isn't worth it."

He knew exactly what she meant, and felt exactly the same way. But before he could defend himself the alarm stopped, and the security ship broke off its pursuit. He exhaled a shaky breath, and when he looked up again, the sky had turned black and was sparkling with starlight.

11

When Augustine woke up the cavern was filling with people. There were bodies being piled up near the gates, at least a dozen, and one of them was Bro Cyphus. Augustine hadn't wanted to kill the big man, but he hadn't wanted to be attacked by him either.

Leon Hurts was across the way. Everyone was eating. The food dispenser was allowing everyone free meals, and there was a festive mood in the air. Augustine got his share of the nutritional loaf, which had a sweet tang to it. Not that it was really sweet, the synthesized protein and fat wafers had been dusted with artificial sweeteners and flavors that left a metallic taste in his mouth. But the other inmates were enjoying the free meal. They had forgotten what real food tasted like, but not Augustine. He ate to fuel his body and kept his rock hammer close.

It wasn't long before an alarm sounded, and then an amplified voice boomed over hidden speakers.

"Inmates, sit on the floor with your legs crossed."

Augustine felt isolated and alone, despite the hundreds of

people around him. He wanted to get out of the cavern and away from all the people, any of whom could be a threat to him. But that wasn't the plan. He knew what he had been told. Plans changed, and he couldn't control it if they did, but the guard had said he and Leon would be selected to help move the bodies. He was trembling all over with hope, and fear that his hopes would be dashed.

Six guards came down the metal stairs. They were in full armor, and armed with laser pistols on harnesses. Two had a hover-sled between them. The guard in front opened the gate. No one moved, as the guards spread out, their weapons held ready to fight back the crowd, but it wasn't necessary. The lead man hit a button that opened the face shield of his helmet. He spoke loudly, his voice echoing off the rock walls of the cavern.

"I hope you're all having a good collection day," he said. "I count seven dead. Not bad. You're all getting along, and that's good. Once we've collected the bodies and are moving back up top, you'll get another treat from the food dispensers."

This got an enthusiastic response. The crowd screamed and cheered. The guard raised his free hand to quiet the crowd, but never let go of his pistol. When the inmates settled, he spoke again.

"I'll need two people to help settle these bodies. New regulation requires inmates to dispose of their own dead. Ward, Augustine and Hurts, Leon, you get the duty. Let's go!"

Augustine stood up and moved through the crowd enthusiastically. It was happening. He could hardly believe it was really happening. They were getting out. He couldn't wait. It took all the self-control he had not to run through the throng of inmates. He was careful not to step on anyone. He didn't want to get attacked when he was so close to being rescued from the hellish prison camp.

Leon got up too, but much slower. He looked suspicious. Not at Augustine, but at the guards. Their faces were completely hidden by dark shields on their helmets, all but the leader of the guards.

Augustine didn't care what Leon thought or believed. He just didn't want the big man to ruin his chance of escape. When he reached the pile of dead bodies he was revolted by the stench, but it was the sight of the two dead men, still in their mining suits, that really made his skin crawl. He had come so close to being in the pile of bodies. And he knew if he stayed in the prison, he would be in the next pile, or the one after that. It was inevitable.

Leon joined Augustine and the guards set the hoversled on the ground. Leon took the feet of the first corpse, and Augustine put his hands under the dead man's shoulders. They carried him to the sled and set him down. Travis had no idea who it was, or how he had died. Three of the corpses had certainly died of exhaustion, and malnutrition. Maybe dehydration had played a role. All Augustine could say for sure was that they weren't heavy enough. Not that he wanted to work harder, but they didn't feel real being so light. Bro Cyphus was another story. The blow to his head by the bag of ore had crushed his skull, and caused his brain to hemorrhage and swell. It hadn't been a swift death, but he had been completely unconscious while his massive body gave up and died. Moving him was difficult, but after some effort they managed it.

One of the guards activated the sled, which floated up into the air. Augustine went first, steering the device with one hand. Leon followed, pushing it. The sled did the work. They went through the gate, then up the metal stairs. Augustine never let go of the railing. His legs burned with the effort of the climb, but Leon didn't seem fazed. The guards kept them moving until they finally reached the top. It had grown hotter the higher they went, but at the surface a hot breeze was blowing. Sand from the surface stung Augustine's skin, the glare from the sun hurt his eyes. He and Leon pushed the hoversled to a ground transport with an open cargo bed in the back. The sled went in, and they were ordered up after it.

They sat on the rails of the cargo bed, Augustine on one side, Leon Hurts on the other. Beside them two guards rode in back, while two more sat in the cab and drove the vehicle. All Augustine could think about was how desolate Lucerine was. There was a landing port, a rugged, sun-scorched guard tower, and in the distance, the incinerator. No one spoke. Perhaps it was the presence of the dead inmates, or just the oppressive heat. The guards had helmets and armor, which likely protected them from the elements. Augustine was in the baggy jumpsuit that was supposed to keep him safe from the toxins in the mines. His head was uncovered, and he could feel the sun burning his skin.

At the incinerator, they put the bodies on a conveyor belt that carried the corpses into a chamber where the sun's rays were focused. Each body dropped from the conveyor belt into the incineration chamber, where they immediately burst into flames. The guards didn't say much, just urged Augustine and Leon to finish the task. Foul, black smoke billowed from the incinerator, filling the air with a horrid stench. As soon as the bodies were dropped into the cremation chamber they loaded back up in the ground transport and went back to the guard tower.

The two guards from the cab went straight into the tower. The other two herded Augustine and Leon back toward the stairs. Fear stabbed at Augustine. He couldn't believe that they were sending him back. Escape had been nothing more than a pipe dream. He was going to die on Lucerine and he was contemplating a leap off the stairs, when one of the guards stopped them.

"That's far enough," he said. "Strip out of those prison clothes."

The two prisoners were marched naked into the guard tower. Augustine recognized the corridor where they had been shaved, showered, and forced to watch the orientation video. One of the guards gave each of them a bar of soap and pointed at the showers.

"Clean yourselves up," he ordered.

"Why?" Leon said.

"Because you smell like animals and everyone will notice," the guard said. "We're only doing this because we're being paid a lot of money. Don't get cute with me, Hurts, or I'll toss you right back down in the mines."

Leon looked angry, and Augustine feared the older man might blow their chances of escape. But he kept his mouth shut, took the soap and went into the shower room. There were no stalls, no privacy. The guards watched through a one-way mirror, as Augustine turned on the water. It was lukewarm but felt wonderful after a week in the same, filthy clothes. Augustine and Leon scrubbed up, then toweled off the excess water.

Leon's hair had grown out, long and stringy. His beard was a long, tangled mess too. The guards had him run a brush through both. His hair went into a ponytail, his beard was clipped short. They both dressed in the guard uniforms, but were not given weapons. By the time they got dressed, an announcement was heard. The shift rotation ship had arrived. Everyone was ordered to the ship that would leave the planet for two weeks, once their replacements had filed off the vessel.

"Keep your mouth shut," the guard told Augustine and Leon. "Take the shuttle up to the ship and someone will meet you there."

"Where are they taking us?" Leon asked.

"Don't know, don't care," the guard said. "Just don't make trouble and you'll be a free man. You both deserve to die down here. This is the only chance you've got. I'd take it."

They did. They wore helmets, as did most of the other guards. The shuttle was big enough for twenty-four passengers. There were twelve counting Augustine and Leon, who sat in the back. The other guards took their helmets off once they were settled in the ship. Taking his off was difficult for Augustine. Fear that they would be recognized and returned to the prison was so powerful that his hands shook.

Leon didn't say anything. He just sat staring straight ahead. The shuttle took its time, the trip to orbit lasted forty-five minutes. Eventually, they docked with the ship that would take them out of the system. Augustine and Leon were the last two men off the shuttle. They found a woman in a uniform waiting outside the shuttle. She was clearly part of the ship's crew. No one seemed to notice or care that the two inmates were on board. Maybe, Augustine thought, they didn't realize it. Or maybe, they just didn't care. For all Augustine knew, they did this kind of thing all the time.

"Where are we going?" Leon asked.

"Putnam Station," the woman said. "Your people are waiting there."

"What people?" Leon asked.

"How the hell should I know?" the woman said. "We'll make the jump to hyperspace within the hour. We'll be at Putnam in four more. After that, you're both on your own."

She showed them to a stateroom with two bunks. On each bunk was a set of standard civilian clothes, nothing fancy or showy, just tan pants, tee-shirts, and jackets. They changed out of their uniforms and waited. Leon slept, his snores rumbling in the confined space. Augustine couldn't have slept anyway; he was too excited. And, if he was honest, too scared. It felt like at any moment law enforcement officials would burst into the room and tell them their escape attempt was over.

But the hours passed, and the only person to come into the room was the female officer. She had changed clothes too, and looked attractive. Although Augustine had to admit it had been a while since he had seen a woman and maybe he was just desperate.

"Let's move," she said. "We're at Putnam."

They didn't have to walk far. The ship wasn't huge, and soon they were inside the docking arm of the space station. A man in a long coat was waiting just outside the airlock.

"I'll take 'em from here," the man said.

"Good riddance," the woman said.

"Don't get cheeky with me," the man said.

Augustine and Leon followed the man in the coat. He led them to an elevator that took them up to the commerce section. The smell of food and drinks hit Augustine like a hammer. He suddenly felt as if he were starving. But the man in the coat led them past the cafes and restaurants. They went past shops and stores with bright signs, and flashing lights. The concourse was filled with people. They were brushing shoulders with strangers who didn't give them a second glance. No one knew they were escaped prisoners. It felt like Augustine was in a dream. How could no one know who they were, or where they belonged? He felt like the prison was a bad smell that clung to them, that everyone should recognize. But no one did. The man in the coat led them to a storeroom. It was plain and mostly empty, unpainted metal walls, utility deck plates, and a heavy-duty table in the corner.

"What's this?" Leon asked.

"This is where we wait," the man in the coat said.

"For what?" Leon asked. "What's this all about? Why'd you want me here?"

"The boss will explain."

"Who's your boss?"

"You'll see," the man said with a smirk.

A moment later the door in the back of the room opened. Four men came in, they were killers. Augustine knew the type. They had long coats too, but he saw their Slingers in low holsters. They were the type of people who didn't shy away from a fight. Behind them came the woman that Augustine had met on Los Mesa, only she wasn't in a business suit any more. She wore tight leather pants, and a leather vest. There were tattoos on her exposed skin. He could see her muscles too, thick and veiny, her thin skin revealing the striations. She had her hair pulled back in a tight ponytail, and her face was quite attractive. But the look in her eyes was deadly.

"Augustine Ward, you did well," she said, but there was no warmth in her voice or in her look. "You've earned your freedom."

One of her men stepped forward and handed Augustine a thick wad of hard currency bills with one hand, and new identification with the other.

"Thank you," Augustine said, taking the money and ID.

"Why am I here?" Leon said.

"For a very specific job that I think you alone are capable of," she said.

"What's that?"

"I want you to kill Travis Hurts."

12

Travis knew things weren't okay, but he didn't want to face it. So instead of staying with Ava in the cockpit, he went to check on his prisoner. They had a clear space from orbit to the jump point. Orbital control had already cleared their departure, which was just further proof that the ship pursuing them hadn't been an official vessel of any kind. And while Travis had been right that they wouldn't shoot the *Purgatory* down with Victoria Hennings-Mabry on board, he knew the stress was getting to Ava. It had to be, Travis knew, because it was getting to him too.

As he had since falling in love with Ava Lynn Baxter, Travis once again questioned why he was continuing to work in law enforcement. It was a dangerous job under the best of circumstances, but a Fugitive Recovery Specialist worked on his own, with no backup, no safety nets. He tracked down the most dangerous criminals and brought them to justice, and for his trouble the most infamous assassin in the galaxy, Morgan Black, was on his trail. He couldn't say why he did it, or why he didn't just hang up his Slinger. Part of him knew he would never be content as a shopkeeper, or a farmer. He didn't have marketable skills other than tracking down people who didn't want to be found.

And Ava didn't want a quiet life either. He had to remind himself that she had chosen to stay with him, and that she loved flying the *Purgatory*. It had been her idea to stay, and she had fought for it, but he knew she had to be doubting that decision. Risking their lives was one thing, but putting baby Kaylee at risk was too much, no matter what the circumstances. He went through their living quarters and then the engineering space, before reaching the cargo bay which was lined with holding cells. Travis had metal bars welded to the deck and to the ship's ceiling to create narrow cages. Each one was big enough for a grown man to lay down at full length, and just wide enough that the prisoners on either side couldn't reach a person who stayed in the middle. There were six holding cells, three on each side of the cargo bay, with room down the middle for Travis to pass through. But he had only one prisoner at the moment. She lay flat on her back, groaning in pain.

Her left arm was broken and probably dislocated. Travis got out the med scanner and went to her cell. She didn't look at him, but he could see tears running down the side of her face.

"If you want I can take a look at that arm," he said.

"Go to hell," she snarled.

"I'm not headed that way at the moment," Travis said. "We're about to make the jump to New Salem. The GCIB has a warrant out for your arrest in connection to the money laundering and corruption charges on Las Brazzas."

"And a reward too," she said. "You know I can pay you more. Tell them you couldn't find me, or better yet, tell them I'm dead. I'll pay you five million credits."

"That would be against the law," Travis said. "I've got morphine for the pain."

"You know what'll happen if you take me in," she said. "You might as well shoot me dead right now."

"Prison is better than death," Travis said.

"I'll never make it to prison. You know whose money we cleaned on Las Brazzas? It wasn't small time dealers. It was the big boys," she said. "Organized crime. It won't matter what I do, the Galactic Coalition can't protect me. No one can. How many people did you lose taking out my security team?"

"None," Travis admitted.

"Where's the rest of your crew?"

"It's just Ava and me," Travis said.

"One man? You took out all my guards by yourself?"

"Most of 'em were sleeping," Travis admitted.

"I'm a fool," Victoria cried.

Travis unlocked the cell. Normally, with the types of criminals he pursued, he would never put himself at risk by going into the cell with them. But Victoria Hennings-Mabry wasn't a dangerous woman. Anyone who was desperate enough could be dangerous, Travis was well aware of that fact, but he knew she was in so much pain just moving was excruciating for her.

"Your people got too lax in their judgment of things," Travis said, activating the medical scanner. "The castle was too secure. They thought it was overkill, and got lazy. It happens."

"Not at the rate I was paying them," Victoria said, as Travis waved the scanning wand over her shoulder and arm. "What's it say?"

"Dislocated. I'll have to secure it."

"No, you can't touch it," she insisted.

Travis opened a little compartment on the back of the scanner. He had anticipated the need to give her something for the pain. The scanner recommended the dosage. He had a hypodermic needle, and a small vial of morphine.

"You won't be awake," Travis said. "I don't have to secure it, but the EMTs that take you into custody will and I can't guarantee that you'll be unconscious."

"Fine," she said. "But don't you think I've suffered enough? I'm a disgrace, cut off from my family. I'll spend the rest of my life in hiding, always looking over my shoulder. There's no reason to turn me in. The GCIB doesn't need my testimony. They've got Poe and he's talking. Please let me go."

"Sorry, ma'am," Travis said, injecting the morphine into her good shoulder. "I can't do that."

"You can," she said, her voice soft. "If you wanted to."

Her eyes fluttered, her features softened, and she fell asleep. Travis made sure she was still breathing, then got to work securing her arm. She moaned in pain several times, but he knew she wouldn't remember it. He pinned her arm across her chest and wrapped it with enough gauze to hold it steady when she was moved. Then he got a blanket for her, and locked the cell door.

When he got back to the living quarters Ava was in her chair feeding Kaylee. She looked at him and he felt guilty. He had made the right choices, but he still felt as if he had done something wrong.

"How?" she asked.

"How what?" he said, putting the medical scanner away.

"How did you know they wouldn't shoot us down?"

"It didn't make sense," Travis said. "If they had gotten in range while we were still relatively low to the ground then maybe, but taking us out after that was too much of a risk."

"And you're a calculator of risk, aren't you?"

"It comes with the territory."

"And how much risk are you willing to take?"

"I prefer no risk," Travis said.

"But you'll risk everything," she said. "And one day you'll lose."

He nodded. "That's always the way I've figured it."

"Do you still?"

"I honestly don't know," Travis said. "A lot has changed."

She looked down at the baby. Nothing else in the universe seemed to matter but the baby when Travis was looking at her. She was so innocent, helpless, and sweet. She could raise her voice and be heard too, and she didn't mind letting you know when something was wrong. But every fiber of his being wanted her to be safe. And he knew she wasn't as long as she was with him.

"We'll have some money when we deliver Victoria to the GCIB. Enough to pay off Eduardo Hernandez, and put back your savings," Travis said. "With around twenty-five thousand credits after we refit the *Purgatory*. I say we take that money and rest up for a while. Give ourselves time to really think through all the possibilities."

"What possibilities?" Ava asked.

"Everything," Travis said. "Career changes, opportunities, our wants and desires."

"You don't want us here?"

"I want you both here," Travis said. "With me, from now on. Nothing else would make me happier, Ava. But ..."

"But your job," she said.

"We can't risk it," he replied. "We can't risk Kaylee. I see that now."

"But you don't want to do anything else," she said, getting up and handing the baby to Travis.

He put her on his shoulder and patted her back until she burped. He could smell her sweet infant aroma, and some of her mother too. She squirmed a little and settled into his shoulder, falling fast asleep.

"I don't," Travis said. "But it ain't about what I want anymore."

"I don't want to give up flying," Ava said.

"There might be bounties that aren't so dangerous," he said. "Bail jumpers, paroles, that sort of thing. Or maybe we go in a different direction. It wouldn't take much to cut out the holding cells and turn the ship into a cargo freighter again."

"You would go crazy making routine deliveries," she said.

"I'm just saying we aren't stuck. We have options. There are things we could do to make a living that wouldn't require sticking our neck out."

"And you would seriously consider them?"

"Yes," Travis said. "And if you want, I could get a job as a marshal on Expanse. We could build out the house, raise some horses."

"And die of boredom?"

"At a ripe old age ... that doesn't sound bad."

"Yes it does."

"Not when I consider this sweet child."

"She's not your responsibility," Ava said.

"Don't say that," he replied, his temper flaring. "She may not be my flesh and blood, but she's the one I choose. And I'd die to protect her."

"I know you would," Ava said calmly. "I didn't mean to get you riled."

"We could get married," he said. "I would never try to take your husband's place, Ava, but I could provide for you and Kaylee. I can do a lot of things if I put my mind to it."

She stepped close. "I know, and I love you for offering."

"But ..."

"No but, let's deliver the woman to the GCIB and settle our debts. We don't have to make any decisions right now."

"Okay," he said.

She leaned over, putting a hand on Kaylee's back and kissed his cheek.

"She's sleeping," Ava said. "We should too."

"All right," Travis said, realizing just how tired he was for the first time since capturing Victoria.

They put the baby down and laid down on the bed together. Ava put her head on Travis' chest. It felt good to relax and close his eyes. But it didn't take long before bad dreams wrecked his sleep. He wanted to believe that Morgan Black wasn't alive, that he wasn't out there somewhere plotting his revenge, but he knew it wasn't true. And he never got anywhere in life by pretending. He needed to finish their business once and for all.

13

While Travis was thinking about him, Morgan Black was making his way from the Presidential Suite in the Luxor Resorts prestigious Khafa pyramid to the recreational drug dispensary in the VIP concourse. He was recovering, but the burns were still painful. The nurses did all they could for him, but they couldn't prescribe medications, and it was against resort policy for employees to purchase drugs. It was the one thing that couldn't be delivered to his suite.

Gourmet meals, entertainment, private medical care were all just a voice memo away. He could tap the interactive menu at his bedside, or activate the voice commands from anywhere in the suite. Then, he just had to say what he wanted. But drugs still had taboos, and intergalactic laws regulated where and how they could be sold. For instance, the resort could sell any recreational drug, but only at advertised dispensaries that were clearly identified and secured.

Morgan was spending upwards of twenty hours a day in bed, with his nursing staff applying medicinal lotions to his chest, neck, and side, every four hours. He washed in cool baths, and occasionally got up to walk around the suite. Some meals were best eaten at a table with utensils, but most of his time was spent in bed. The walk to the elevators, and then to the dispensary in the concourse, was good exercise. Unfortunately, the concourse was also crowded, and it was painful to be jostled. He would have chosen to go late at night, when the crowds thinned, but there was no day and night in the resort. Everyone did what they wanted, when they wanted. Outside was always daytime. It was always sunny and warm, with a slight breeze manufactured by massive air circulators that were expertly hidden around the space station. And inside the pyramids it was always night, with nonstop parties, shopping, and entertainment.

That left Morgan to fend off the crowds as he made his way to the dispensary. The pill shop, as the resort employees called it, was a simple little storefront. Inside, the customer area was a U shape, with glass counters displaying a wide variety of drugs. By far the most popular were the party drugs, Dreamers, Nirvana, Confetti. There was a wide variety of smokable herbs, and just as many drug-laced vape cartridges. There was speed, downers, organic and synthetic hallucinogens. But Morgan had come for the painkillers. They were available, but were not on display. They came in packages of ten, with a limit of one per customer, per day. The ten little pills cost a thousand credits, and lasted Morgan two and half days. His burns had not been deep enough to scar the muscle, or affect his internal organs. But the pain was excruciating. Everything he did made the burned area across his chest and side hurt. He couldn't move without the skin stretching. His nurses applied ointments, but the blisters still formed. The only relief was from the painkillers, which numbed his brain as much as it did the pain. Which was certainly why he didn't notice the Asian man who kept showing up when he made his run to the dispensary.

But things were improving. The redness was starting to recede, and while several of the blisters had burst, they didn't appear to be refilling. Morgan knew that second degree burns took anywhere from three to six weeks to heal, and it might be even longer before his skin had replaced all the burned area. Still, it was all superficial, and with the painkillers in his system, he could function pretty well.

"Back again, Mr. Hitch," the clerk in the dispensary said. "Want your usual?"

"Yes, please," Morgan said as he leaned against the counter. "How's business?"

"Brisk as usual," the clerk said. "I hope you get to feeling better soon. There's a lot of hot babes in the resort right now."

He set a package on the counter. It was the size of Morgan's hand. A piece of cardboard with ten pills in little push through slots was covered with heavy duty plastic that had to be cut off with scissors. The package was covered with warnings about the addictive nature of the drug, and the way it impairs the user. The painkillers were synthetic, and banned on most worlds. The places that sold it did so in restricted numbers to stop dealers from buying in bulk to sell on other worlds.

"Female companionship is the least of my worries," Morgan said, pulling a thick wad of hard credit notes from the pocket of his baggy linen pants.

He wasn't at the resort to spend time on the beach, but he dressed the part. He wore canvas shoes with no socks, baggy, light-weight pants, and an oversized button-up shirt untucked. He rolled the sleeves of the shirt to just below his elbows, but kept the buttons fastened all the way to his neck to hide the laser burns.

Drugs were the only thing on the resort that a person couldn't buy with a signature. Everything else could be charged to the digital credit accounts, but the drugs had to be sold for hard currency. They also had to be taxed. The pills were a thousand credits, and tax on recreational drugs was twenty-eight percent. He fanned out thirteen hundred credit notes and handed them over.

"Want your change?"

"You keep it," Morgan said.

"Thanks Mr. Hitch. I hope you're feeling better soon."

"You and me both," Morgan said as he left the dispensary. The trip back up to his room was uneventful. His nurse that day was a cosmetically enhanced woman with thick blond hair. She met him at the door of his suite and he handed her the pills.

"Breakfast just arrived," the nurse said.

"Wonderful," Morgan said. "You'll join me?"

"Sure," the nurse said.

Morgan didn't need company. He was a solitary individual, but he was paying for help and he preferred to keep an eye on the people around him. The Presidential Suite had excellent views. From a small table in the oversized bedroom portion of his suite he could see down into the resort. Thousands of people lounged on the beaches around the crystal-clear waters in the center of the resort. He could see the other pyramids and temples, the fantastic statuary, and the exotic palm trees. But it was almost like watching a vid. No sounds from the ground far below reached him. The people all seemed tiny, their features indistinguishable. Still, it was a great view, and Morgan settled on a chair at the table. His meal was under a silver dome.

The nurse joined him with a tray that had her own food, as well as juice and coffee. It was breakfast, and they each had a stack of pancakes with real bacon, sausage, and fruit. Morgan poured syrup onto his pancakes and cut himself a bite while the nurse opened the package of pain pills. She popped one from the package and set it beside his glass of orange juice.

"Thank you, my dear," Morgan said.

He took the pill, ate his bacon, and went back to bed. A few more days and he would leave the resort. It was nearly time to resume his mission. If Travis Hurts wasn't dead soon, the Incendius Organization would send people to kill Morgan Black, and that would muddle his plans. Not that he was afraid of being killed, but he did fear getting stopped before his business with Travis Hurts was complete. He needed the bounty hunter to die knowing that it was Morgan Black that did it. After that, he didn't care what happened to him. He could die knowing he had won, but of course, once Travis Hurts was dead there would be no reason for the gangsters to want Morgan dead. Perhaps he would retire, move to a tropical planet and live the good life. It was a pleasant fantasy, but Morgan knew that he would inevitably turn to drugs out of boredom. He wouldn't live happily ever after. Without the hunt, without the kill, he would be purposeless. A man without meaning. And that wouldn't do at all. He fell asleep with thoughts of revenge dancing in his chemically altered mind.

14

The *Purgatory* came out of hyperspace in the Francisco system near the New Salem space station. It was becoming a familiar sight. Travis activated the communications system, thinking he would let the authorities know he was bringing in Victoria Hennings-Mabry, but was alerted of a message waiting for him before he could do anything else. Travis pressed the icon and a woman's face appeared on the front viewscreen.

Ava was in the pilot's seat, although they were on a straight trajectory toward the station and there wasn't much flying to do. She wore Kaylee in a wrap. Travis had reclaimed his seat in the cockpit. The message played in front of him.

"Fugitive Recovery Specialist Travis Hurts, my name is Sabrina Astor. I'm the Special Prosecutor on the Las Brazzas RICO case. I need to meet with you when you are back in system. This is a priority for my office and it is imperative that you contact me ASAP. I look forward to hearing from you."

The message ended. Ava looked at Travis with her eyebrows raised.

"What?" he asked.

"That did not sound like a friendly invitation."

"She's a lawyer," he replied. "They don't do friendly."

"But what does she need to see you for?"

"I testify in a lot of cases," Travis said. "It's probably about setting up a deposition, or she might have questions about what happened on Las Brazzas."

"You would know better than me," Ava said. "But watch your back. I don't think that was a run of the mill type request."

"Duly noted," Travis said.

He texted a reply to the Special Prosecutor's office, then another to Chief Investigator Logan Brand. The autopilot maneuvered them into a docking slip, and when Travis opened the airlock he found a team of four officers waiting to take Victoria Hennings-Mabry into custody. Three were trained EMTs. They had a hover-gurney. The fourth was Logan. He looked exhausted, and like he hadn't changed clothes in three days.

"It's probably best that you come on board and take her," Travis said.

"She causing problems?" Logan asked.

"No, but she's in a lot of pain."

"How'd she get injured?" Logan asked.

"When I stunned her bodyguard they fell off an elevated sleeping platform," Travis said. "She tried to catch herself."

"That kind of impact fracture is pretty unique," one of the EMTs said. "If it's a spiral break, that usually only happens when a person tries to catch themselves when they fall backward. Dislocation isn't unusual either."

"At least there's no traumatic brain injury," Logan said. "We need her testimony."

Travis led the group to Victoria's cell and unlocked it. She was only semi-conscious. Travis showed the EMTs exactly what he had dosed her with, and how much. They got her on the gurney and strapped her down.

"I'm dead," she whimpered, not opening her eyes. "I'm dead."

"She in that much pain?" Logan asked.

"I think she's referring to what she believes will happen to her," Travis said. "According to her, the people they were working with won't want her testifying."

"Fear is a powerful tactic," Logan said as the EMTs maneuvered the gurney back out of the airlock.

Ava came through the engineering section and into the cargo hold.

"Good to see you, Ava," Logan said, his tone sounding anything but happy. "I need a word with the both of you."

"Is something wrong?" Ava asked.

"The RICO case is big," Logan said. "It's historic, really. And that means there are a lot of people who want to be involved."

"And probably a lot of people who don't," Travis joked.

"I'm talking about people with political ambitions," Logan said, undeterred by Travis' attempt at humor. "There are a lot of cooks in the kitchen right now, and a lot of pressure for us to cast a wide net."

"Okay," Ava said. "Travis got a call from the Special Prosecutor."

"I heard," Logan said.

"What does she want?" Travis asked.

"I have no idea, but she's a politician. All she cares about is herself, and she doesn't mind burning bridges, or stepping on the little guy."

"And I'm the little guy," Travis said.

"'Fraid so," Logan said. "Tread lightly, keep your head on a swivel, and be careful what you say to her. Have you heard about LeSean Mason?"

"I don't even recognize the name," Travis said.

"Harrison Poe named him as one of the people heavily involved in the corruption on Las Brazzas. He was hiding out on the Luxor Resort, but got himself stabbed."

"Really?" Travis asked.

"Really. He was pretty strung out on speed of some kind. No one in the club knew what was wrong with him. By the time the medics got to him, he was too far gone."

"He died?"

"Yup. His heart gave out due to blood loss from a deep knife wound. Small blade, extremely sharp according to the initial findings by the medical examiner. We just got that info shortly before you arrived."

"Any chance you have a lead on who did it?"

"The bogeyman," Logan said. "It's not Morgan Black's MO, he doesn't normally kill with blades."

"He was stabbed in a night club on a resort space station and they couldn't identify who did it?"

"They have footage of nearly sixty people dancing close enough to Mason to have done the deed. Resort security was running names, talking to people, but they don't have a clue. Whoever took him out is a pro."

"Didn't you have a FR specialist tracking him down?" Ava asked.

"We did," Logan said. "She never even got to the resort. Had no idea where he was."

"What about the others?"

"No word yet," Logan said. "You're the first one back with your fugitive."

"That's good, right?" Ava proposed.

"Yeah, having Victoria Hennings-Mabry will help us lock in some of the claims that Harrison Poe is making. Especially if she cooperates and becomes a witness for the prosecution, but I'd watch your back, Travis. I have no idea what Sabrina Astor is up to, but she's capable of anything."

"Will do," Travis said. "Thanks for the heads up."

"Anytime," Logan said.

Travis and Ava secured the ship, then set off through the space station. Travis went to the GCIB executive offices, while Ava went shopping for Kaylee. The baby was growing fast, and going through diapers even faster. They made plans to meet in a couple of hours at a small food market near the docking arm where the *Purgatory* was berthed.

The GCIB took up an entire level of the space station. New Salem wasn't their only set of offices, nor was their main headquarters, but it was where the Racketeer Influenced Criminal Organization or RICO case was being put together. The Galactic Coalition Investigation Bureau consisted of law enforcement personnel and special prosecutors. Usually, the prosecutors were lawyers with a lot of trial experience, but there was the occasional political appointee. Travis wasn't surprised that Sabrina Astor had been put in charge. He didn't know her, but had heard her name before. And when he reached the GCIB level, it was clear very fast that everyone was working to please the new Special Prosecutor.

Travis checked in then sat waiting for over an hour. He wasn't necessarily surprised. They didn't have an appointment on the books, and he couldn't expect the Special Prosecutor to drop what she was doing to meet with him, even though it seemed she expected that from him. Finally, he was called into an office. It was big, with a massive view screen on the curved wall. Sabrina Astor was a tall woman, with short hair and a perpetual frown. Travis was reminded of an angry librarian.

"Specialist Hurts, thank you for coming in," she said, waving him to a seat in front of her desk.

"No problem," he said, sitting down.

Astor didn't sit. She paced as she asked questions.

"I need you to tell me what happened with Grant Stevenson," she said.

"Oh, okay," Travis said. "I was on Expanse."

"Planet T996 in the GZB 84 system?"

"That's right," Travis said. "I've got a homestead there. Ava and I were taking some time there. Working on a little place."

"Ava?"

"Ava Lynn Baxter," Travis said.

"Continue."

"Okay, well, I went to see Wilford Valentino, the Territorial Administrator about communications out on my property. While I was with him, he informed me that Grant Stevenson was on the planet and staying in Prosperity. He was concerned."

"About what?"

"About the need to bring Stevenson in. About the bodyguards that were with him and the possibility of the locals getting hurt if there was gunplay."

"So, you volunteered to bring him in."

"I volunteered to try," Travis said. "This is all in my report."

"I want to hear it from you," she snapped.

Travis thought maybe things weren't as cut and dry as he thought. He straightened in his chair and continued his statement.

"I went into the hotel where Stevenson and three guards were staying. I assessed the situation, and decided I could probably detain him without things getting rowdy. So, I did."

"You confronted Stevenson?"

"After dealing with his guards, yes."

"Two were captured, one was killed."

"By one of the other bodyguards," Travis said. "Shot in the back."

"And you have proof of this?"

"The bartenders were there, along with six civilians. I don't know if the hotel has video evidence, but it most likely does."

"So, you took Grant Stevenson into your custody?"

"I did, but not for long."

"What does that mean?"

"It means that even though I had him, he wasn't secured. And before I left the hotel with him, I was confronted by a bounty hunter named Jonah Barnes."

"A bounty hunter. Do you know who he was working for?"

"No," Travis said.

"But he was there for Stevenson?"

"Yes," Travis said.

"He told you this?"

"Offered to pay me if I would turn him over."

"And did you?"

"No ma'am."

"And you have proof of this?"

"I have two of his mercenaries that I brought into custody," Travis said. "And the townsfolk who saw me fighting them."

"But during the fighting you lost Stevenson?"

"That's correct."

"How?"

"Well, I couldn't risk him getting killed. So, I left him in an alley while I dealt with the mercenaries."

"And he fled?"

"Warned him not to, but he didn't listen."

"And this is where the story gets foggy. In your report you recaptured him after Jonah Barnes was killed."

"That's right."

"Who killed Jonah Barnes?"

"I have no idea."

"How is that possible? Was it Stevenson?"

"All I know is that I and several of the locals went looking for Stevenson. We found him in the landing field beside Barnes body."

"How was Barnes killed?"

"Looked to me like his throat was cut."

"And it didn't occur to you that maybe Stevenson did it?"

"Jonah Barnes wasn't an outlaw, but he worked with outlaws, and he died like an outlaw. I was just happy to have Stevenson back."

"What did you do with him?"

"I locked him up on my ship."

"That's the *Purgatory*?"

"Correct."

"And then what?" the Special Prosecutor asked. "He just disappeared?"

"No, I then locked up the other outlaws, Stevenson's body-guards, and Jonah Barnes' mercenaries that were still alive."

"And Stevenson was secure on your ship."

"Yes," Travis said.

"So, when did you lose him, Mr. Hurts?"

Travis explained that Ava had been taken by Morgan Black. And that Travis went after him.

"Somewhere along the way, someone got onboard my ship and took Stevenson."

"I'll be frank with you," Sabrina Astor said. "That's a difficult story to believe."

"It's the truth, whether you believe it or not."

"Who is the mystery man?" she pressed.

"I don't know. But I heard about Harrison Poe losing his hands. Maybe whoever did that, kidnapped Grant Stevenson."

"You're saying that you think there's a serial killer targeting criminals?"

"No, I'm just wondering if the two incidents are related."

"What makes think they might be?"

"Jonah Barnes' throat getting cut for one thing," Travis said. "The report about LeSean Mason would be another."

"What do you know about Mason?"

"Just what Chief Investigator Logan Brand told me," Travis said.

"Which was?"

"That he was stabbed while on the Luxor resort, and that he died."

She didn't look happy. Travis wasn't even sure she had heard the news. When she spoke next, it was through clenched teeth.

"I won't have my suspects dying before they face the conse-quences for what they did," she said. "Tell me why Victoria

Hennings-Mabry is in the medical bay instead of a four by eight cell?"

"She fell coming off a platform bed when I shot her bodyguard. They got tangled up, and she fell back on one arm. Broke it, and dislocated the shoulder too."

"Is it normal for you to torture your captives before bringing them in?" Astor asked.

"I did nothing but help Victoria once she was in my custody."

"Or maybe it was you that broke her arm. Maybe you like putting the boots to your prisoners before you bring them in. Maybe things got out of hand with Grant Stevenson and you had to jettison the body to hide the evidence."

"That's the craziest thing I've ever heard."

"Is it?" the Special Prosecutor pressed on. "Tell me what happened to Frank Lee Voss. He was turned over to police custody with a shattered nose and multiple lacerations to his face and neck."

"That happened on Pergamum Prime," Travis said. "Morgan Black released him on my ship, and he attacked Ava Lynn Baxter."

"So you punished him?"

"No," Travis said. "She fended him off with a decksweeper to the face. He was lucky it was loaded with non-lethal pellets."

"And you didn't torture him while in your custody?"

"Absolutely not," Travis said.

"I find that hard to believe. As a certified law enforcement officer, you have a duty to protect and safeguard the prisoners in your custody."

"I make every effort," Travis said.

"Or maybe you let Grant Stevenson go. I think it's possible that either he bought his freedom from you, or that you killed him."

"No, ma'am."

"What proof do you have? I've spoken with Territorial Administrator Valentino. He claims that you left Prosperity on planet

T996 with Grant Stevenson in your custody, but that when you returned he was missing."

"I'm sure that's not all he said," Travis replied.

"This is your last chance to tell me the truth, Mr. Hurts. What did you do with Grant Stevenson."

"Nothing," Travis said. "When I went to face Morgan Black, he was in my ship. When I got back, he was gone. But like I said, Ava was having the baby and I was wounded. Honestly, I didn't know Stevenson was gone until the next day after having treatment."

"If that's your story, then I have no choice but to hold you responsible."

"Responsible for what?" Travis asked.

"I'm charging you with dereliction of duty," Special Prosecutor Astor said. "And imposing the maximum fine in relation to the fugitive you allowed to escape your custody."

"You can't be serious," Travis said.

"I am. Pursuant to the Fugitive Recovery code part four, point sixteen, if a fugitive is confirmed to be in your custody, and you fail to deliver that fugitive to official law enforcement facilities, you can be held responsible for the full reward offered, plus thirty-three percent."

"That clause stipulates that I have no proof of what happened to the prisoner," Travis said.

"Which you have repeatedly refused to give me."

"Because I don't have it," Travis said. "I don't know what happened to him. But there were other people on Expanse trying to take Grant Stevenson off world."

"And your first responsibility was to your prisoner," Astor snapped. "Not to chase after someone else."

She sat down at her desk and started swiping at the motion controls.

"Grant Stevenson's reward was seven hundred and fifty thousand credits," Travis said.

"Yes, with the penalties, that comes to right around a million."

"You can't charge me that much," Travis said.

"I can," she said without looking up. "As special prosecutor, it is well within my approved powers. Furthermore, I have the right to say in what time you need to produce said funds. I think thirty days is more than enough to come up with the money you owe."

"You've lost your mind," Travis said.

"Actually, I'm in the middle of the biggest criminal case in the galaxy. No one is going to sell our fugitives to the highest bidder."

"That's not what I did," Travis complained.

"Then either pay the fine, or your Fugitive Recovery certification will be revoked," she snapped. "I don't care which."

"I'll appeal," Travis said.

"You'll lose. The authority granted in the FR statues are clear, even if they are rarely enforced. No one is going to stand in the way of this office getting the convictions we are aiming for, Mr. Hurts."

"Who the hell do you think you're talking to," Travis shouted. "I'm the one who brought Pete Fox into custody, and turned him over to the GCIB."

"That doesn't give you a pass to break the law," she said.

"I didn't break any laws," Travis said.

"The Fugitive Recovery code is clear on this point, Mr. Hurts. Without proof that you are not responsible for what happened to Grant Stevenson, I can and will hold you to account. This meeting is over. You have thirty days to pay off the remaining seven hundred and fifty thousand credits."

"I thought you said a million," Travis said.

"I put a lien on your reward funds this morning," she said. "The money due you from the capture of Victoria Hennings-Mabry was applied to your fines."

"You can't do that!" Travis snapped. "I need that money."

"It's already done, Mr. Hurts. If you would like to appeal, you are free to pursue that course of action, but as I've already said, my actions are well within my purview."

"You're stealing from me."

"You have responsibilities as a member of law enforcement," she said. "You shirked that duty, and the fine is a reasonable penalty, set into law by GC legislators."

Travis was so angry he wanted to put his hands on the Special Prosecutor, but before he could do anything he would regret, the office door opened and a pair of burly guards stepped in.

"You wanted to see us, Ms. Astor."

"Yes," the Special Prosecutor said. "Please escort Mr. Hurts from GCIB offices."

Travis was furious, but didn't resist. He walked in front of the guards and went straight to the elevator. He was shaking with rage as the doors closed. And when they opened a moment later he was struck by fear. They had used the last of their funds to refuel the *Purgatory*. He had nothing left, and still owed Eduardo Hernandez over a hundred thousand credits. Travis knew that it was possible to earn a lot of money in a short time if he got the right fugitives, but a million credits was a difficult hill to climb. And he only had thirty days to get the money. Worse still, he couldn't just get five hundred thousand credits and retire. Any funds brought in from fugitive recovery rewards were already spoken for. He would be lucky if he could conjure up enough money to keep the *Purgatory* flying.

He stepped off the elevator feeling like he was going to be sick. He needed to tell Ava, but the thought of it was so overwhelming he feared he might pass out. She had volunteered all the savings he had given her. And he no longer had any way of paying her back. His life was over, his career finished, and there was nothing he could do about it.

15

"What are you saying?" Ava asked.

They were in a little cafe. She had just fed Kaylee, and the baby was sleeping peacefully. But Ava was anything but peaceful. She felt as if the ground had dropped out from underneath her.

"I'm saying we're finished," Travis said.

"What happens if you don't pay the money?" Ava asked.

"I'll lose my Fugitive Recovery license," he said. "And, they'll probably sue me."

"So you have to pay it? Seven hundred and fifty thousand credits? That's outrageous."

"I know," Travis said. "I'm sorry."

"It's not your fault," she said, but she sounded like she was angry with him. "This is how the system works. People who do the right thing never get ahead, while people who do wrong get off scot-free."

Travis wanted to argue with her, but he had become the proof of her argument.

"I guess we really are going to talk about what comes next," she said.

"We're in a tight fix," he said. "All our money is tied up with Eduardo."

"And we still owe him," she said.

"I know," Travis said.

"How much money could you make hauling goods in the *Purgatory*?"

"Maybe a hundred and fifty thousand credits after expenses," he said. "It'll take a year, but it's possible."

"Surely, you could make more than that," she urged him.

"Not unless I was hauling contraband. And I'm not going down that road."

"I would never ask you to," she said.

"You can walk away right now," Travis said. "This millstone is tied to my neck. Not yours."

"And do what?" she asked. "I can't work while Kaylee is breast-feeding. And I don't want to leave her."

"So, maybe we could sell the ship," Travis said. "I bought her for seven hundred thousand. If I could get that much out of it, we would come pretty close to paying the rest off."

"And have no way to earn anymore," she said.

"I'm only good at one thing," Travis said. "And working law enforcement doesn't pay that well."

"We took in over seven-fifty from Pergamum Prime," she said. "Why not do that again?"

"I got lucky, there," Travis admitted. "I was aiming for about four hundred grand."

"I never thought I'd say this, but maybe we should go back to P2?"

"No, the planet is burned for me. People know who I am there. I could never get close enough to the fugitives without someone tipping them off.

"There has to be something we can do," Ava said. "We could hire a lawyer."

"We have no money, and the government has me over a barrel. They'll win in court."

"So, paying them back is our only option," Ava said, trying to hold back the tears that were welling in her eyes, but failing.

Travis saw the tears, and they tore his heart to pieces. He had set out to protect Ava, but she had ended up saving him. He wanted to set up somewhere safe, where she could have a good start with the baby. Instead, she had chosen to stay with him, and he had lost all his money and hers to boot. It was the absolute worst feeling he had ever experienced.

"There you are," Logan called out as he came hurrying out of the crowds of shoppers to where they sat at the little cafe.

"What's he want now?" Ava said.

"I don't know," Travis said.

Neither of them felt like seeing Logan just then. They knew the fine wasn't his fault, in fact, Logan had warned them that Special Prosecutor Sabrina Astor was trouble. Still, he was a GCIB agent, and in that moment that made him the enemy.

"Here to gloat?" Ava snapped as Logan approached them.

"What? No, of course not."

"This isn't the best time, Logan," Travis said.

"Yeah, I heard about the fine. It's total BS, but there's nothing I can do about it. The Special Prosecutors have nearly unlimited powers, and Astor has been handed the keys to the kingdom with this case."

"I wish I'd never heard of Las Brazzas," Travis said.

"Me either," Ava agreed.

"I have news that you may not want to hear, but you need to," Logan said. "It just came through a few minutes ago."

"What did?" Travis asked.

"There was a jail break on Lucerine," he said.

Travis felt a cold wind blow through him. It made his skin contract into goose bumps, and hands began to tingle. There were thousands of prisoners on Lucerine, but Logan wouldn't have come hunting them down if the escapees weren't related to Travis or his work. And in this particular case, Travis knew that he was related, literally.

"So, is there a big reward or something?" Ava asked.

"No, no reward yet," Logan said. "Only two prisoners made it out."

"So?" Ava asked.

"Let me guess," Travis said. "One of them was Leon."

"Yeah, the other was Augustine Ward."

"Ward? Didn't we just get him on Pergamum Prime?"

Travis nodded, but he wasn't thinking about the gunslinger.

"Who's the other man?" Ava asked.

"Leon Hurts," Logan said softly.

Ava looked at Travis. She hadn't thought it was possible for him to look worse than he had when he told her about the fines. She was angry about the money, and frustrated too, but she didn't blame Travis. And she had wanted to support him somehow. She would have done anything to keep him from looking so low. But the news from Logan Brand was even worse.

"He's my father, Ava," Travis said.

"Your father ... didn't you ..."

Travis nodded. "I did. When I was seventeen. Took him in to the authorities and told them he was a wanted man. He was falling down drunk at the time and had no idea what was happening to him. Since then, he's had over two decades to think about it."

"You don't think he'll come after you," she said.

"Doesn't have to," Travis said. "I'm going after him."

"Any idea where he'll go?" Logan asked.

"He always talked about going to Dur Rohstoff if the heat got too high."

"Dur Rohstoff is a dead planet," Ava said.

"No law," Logan said. "A lot of outlaws and desperados end up there."

"And some pretty big fencing operations too," Travis said. "A lot of illegal goods flow through Dur Rohstoff."

"Odds are high he'll kill not to go back to prison," Logan said. "Keep that in mind."

"He'll want to kill me either way," Travis said. "He wasn't the forgive and forget type."

"So why go there?" Ava said. "Let's sell the *Purgatory*. You can take a job on Expanse. We'll build a house there and make a life. If the GC wants to come after us for the money, they'll have to get in line."

"Or," Travis said. "I go to Dur Rohstoff, capture my father and some other fugitives, and get us out from under this debt."

"The Bureau keeps a list of wanted fugitives believed to be on Dur Rohstoff," Logan said. "I can forward it to you, but the odds aren't great you'll get off that world alive."

"If I get killed," Travis said, "Ava can sell the ship. She can go anywhere she wants and start over."

"No, that's not going to happen," Ava said.

"Why not," Travis said. "If I get lucky, we might get clear of this mess after all."

"You said you got lucky on P2."

"I can get lucky again."

"We need to think about it," Ava said.

"There's nothing to think about," Travis said. "What we need to do is get moving. Logan, can you send me everything you've got on that prison break."

"Already have," he said. "Looks like the Incendius Organization is involved."

"Good," Travis said. "They'll have an operation on DR. It's a good place to start looking."

"The Incendius Organization?" Ava asked. "As in organized crime?"

"Yeah," Logan said. "One of the major players. They haven't come up in the Las Brazzas RICO investigation yet, but it's probably only a matter of time."

"Someone wants me dead," Travis said. "They hired Morgan Black. Now they've broken my father out of prison. My guess is the IO doesn't want me to testify against Lawrence Pescatory."

"Who's that?" Ava asked.

"A gangster," Travis said. "He was wanted in connection to a murder. I picked up him a few months back. The prosecutor in that case wants me to testify. It's a pretty standard gig. Comes with the territory."

"Pescatory isn't taking a plea?" Logan asked.

"I have no idea," Travis said. "But that makes sense to me. Do we know the IO broke Leon out of prison?"

"Some of the guards were involved. They didn't know who was paying them, but our people traced the money to a shell company set up by Iona Freeze. She's a shot caller with the IO," Logan explained. "An underboss. Our organized crime people say they expect her to take over the entire operation. She's a nasty piece of work."

"Is she wanted?" Ava asked.

"No, not that I'm aware of," Logan said. "You take her down and that could really ignite a firestorm."

"Thanks for the info," Travis said.

"Sure. There will be Marshals on the case. I should let them know you're going after your old man on Dur Rohstoff."

"Go ahead," Travis said. "Then they'll send people and word will get out, and every criminal on the planet will know I'm there."

"Okay, okay," Logan said. "I get it."

"Just give me a week," Travis said. "If you haven't heard from me by then, tell the Marshals."

"Good enough," Logan said.

They shook hands. Ava was holding the baby, and didn't have to shake hands with Logan. It was a convenient excuse. She didn't dislike Logan, but she was starting to dislike who he worked for, and how the GCIB operated.

Logan got to his feet and said his goodbyes. Travis watched him go and then turned back to Ava. If it were up to him, he would leave her on New Salem. But she had no money and he had none to give her. Plus, if he got killed on Dur Rohstoff, which was a very good possibility, she would need to have the ship. It was the only thing of value he had left and he wanted to be sure that she got it.

"We should go too," he said.

"You really think this is the right course of action?" Ava asked.

"I don't believe in fate, Ava," Travis said. "But I do believe there is a God, and sometimes he orchestrates our steps. My father busting out of prison at the exact same time I'm fined by the GC is too big of a coincidence in my opinion. I'm supposed to go to Dur Rohstoff. Maybe I'll die there, or maybe I'll turn our fortunes around."

"I don't believe in fate either," she said. "Going there is your choice. Do you even care what I think about it?"

"Of course I do," he said.

"Good. Maybe I'll tell you once we're underway."

"You'll come with me?"

"Yes, you stupid man. Who else is going to come to your rescue when this crazy plan falls to pieces?"

16

Iona Freeze was waiting. She had already leaked word to the authorities that Leon Hurts and Augustine Ward were on the loose. And she had a ship waiting to take them wherever Leon wanted to go. The plan was a long shot, and not as clean as ordering a hit. But there weren't many button men who would take a job against a well-known bounty hunter. Most had warrants out for their arrest, which meant they were limited in where they could go, and how they could pull off the hit. But the real limiting factor was that none of them wanted to be captured and sent to a penal colony. Better to die fighting, than to get stunned by a lawman's non-lethal blaster and get locked up in chains for the rest of one's life.

When Leon walked into the room a few minutes later, Iona wasn't sure whether to be angry or impressed. The old man had on a long coat, which wasn't unusual. The strange part was that it was dark purple. She couldn't understand what part of blending in the old felon didn't understand. He was not what she had expected. He was charming, but also profane, fearless, yet at the same time uncertain. Along with the purple coat he had a flat-topped black hat. It was quite the combination. Despite his age, he was a big man with broad shoulders and barrel chest. Yet he spoke with a smooth voice that made him seem younger.

"What do you think?" he asked, taking a spin in his new duds.

Augustine Ward was behind him. He had on new clothes, all in shades of brown. He could blend easily into a crowd, especially since she had paid to have the damage to his left hand repaired. The gunslinger had a bionic finger and thumb, both covered with synthetic flesh. Unless a person got a long look at that hand, or shook his hand, they would never know it wasn't natural.

"He looks like he just lost a job at the circus, you ask me," Augustine said.

"No one is asking you," Leon said. "I want the opinion of a lady."

"Ain't many would call me that," Iona said.

"Well, I'm one," Leon said. He was being charming, and he was damn good at it.

"You look fine," she said, deciding not to chastise him for his fashion sense at the last minute. "Now let's get off this station before the Transit Authority spots you."

"They aren't looking for me," Leon said. "They're looking for an old man, who's desperate and trying hard not to be seen."

Iona wasn't sure his logic was sound, but he knew how to stay cool under pressure, and she had gotten both Leon and Augustine new identification. It would pass basic scrutiny, but if it was run through a GC database it would probably be discovered as fake. And no amount of colorful clothes, or good paperwork would change Leon's retinal image, or DNA. If a cop ran those, they were dead in the water.

"I'll still feel better once we're moving," Iona said. "Where do you want to go?"

"I been thinking on that," Leon said. "There's only one place I can think of that my boy might remember."

"Your boy?" Augustine Ward said. "He's a lawman now. Ain't no boy."

Leon ignored the gunman. "Just one place where we can be without hiding: Dur Rohstoff."

Iona Freeze shivered. If there was one place in the entire galaxy she never wanted to go, it was Dur Rohstoff. And it wasn't because of the unstable tectonics, or the roving bands of natives that made her afraid, it was the Scabbers. She was not a traditional beauty. In fact, many people thought of her as too masculine with her muscular build, and almost no body fat. She didn't even have the normal augmentations that most women got to make their figure fit the hourglass shape that so many people thought of as ideal. But she didn't like the possibility of catching a debilitating skin disease with no cure. She would blow her own brains out before she became a hag with open sores all over her body.

"Fine," she said. "We have a territory there. What about you, Ward?"

"He's with me," Leon said.

Iona knew Ward didn't like the idea of going to DR, but he didn't contradict the older man. He just nodded, and that was good enough for Iona. She needed to get back to Dice on the *Incendius*, and ensure no one was trying to replace her in the criminal organization. It was a very competitive environment, and the stakes were life and death.

"Fine," Iona said. "Let's go."

She led the way out of the nondescript meeting room, and through the crowded corridors of the Putnam Station. Fortunately, most of the Transit Authority officers were on the upper levels where the spaceliners docked, and where thousands of duty-free shops were located. They were going down. The *Tuscany* was a legitimate cargo ship. It had docked with a load of sellable goods that were moved from the ship to the vast warehouses in the lower levels of the station. She didn't keep up with the *Tuscany's* cargo manifest, but she knew it hid a small interstellar ship, the *Lo Spet-*

tro, that would take Leon Hurts to Dur Rohstoff without any records for the authorities to follow. She wanted Travis Hurts to find his father, but not the teams of Marshals who were tasked with hunting down escaped convicts.

They took a cargo elevator down to sub level D, and went immediately to the docking arm. Once they reached the *Tuscany* everyone relaxed noticeably.

"We're going to need weapons," Leon said. "Dur Rohstoff is not the kind of place one goes without significant firepower."

"We have what you need," Iona said.

She used the ship's private communication system to alert the crew that she was on board and ready to leave. They immediately began the process of getting permission to disengage from the space station, and make their way to a suitable jump point that would take the ship back toward the galactic core. It would stop of course somewhere between systems to let the *Lo Spettro* out of the giant freighter so that it could take its passengers to the dead world of Dur Rohstoff.

The two escaped convicts followed Iona through the interior of the big freighter. They would be staying on the *Lo Spettro* for the duration of the flight. It was stocked with food, supplies, and a variety of weapons. She took them on board. The only crew were a pilot, co-pilot, and a woman that served as engineer and steward. She met Leon and Augustine in the ship's galley and showed them to the armory.

"This is more like it," Augustine said.

"Everything a boy could want," Leon agreed.

There was a wide variety of rifles, sub-rifles, and pistols, along with plenty of power cells for the various weapons, and even holsters. Augustine Ward found himself a quick draw holster and a nickel-plated Slinger. He put the holster on a gun belt and got it situated low on his right thigh, tying the lower part around his leg to hold it secure. He chose a beefier gun for his left hand, a Ripper made of blue steel. It used a bigger power cell and could fire twelve kill shots on a single charge, while his Slinger could only fire two lethal blasts before he needed to replace the battery.

Leon was not a shootist. He selected an old-style laser pistol with an eight-inch barrel, and a power cell capable of nineteen shots at full power. It fit in a snug, faux leather holster which Leon wore butt out on his left hip, the better to draw and swing with. The heavy firearm would be as effective as a club, and Leon had spent more than two decades on Lucerine where rock hammers were the only weapons. He also picked up a pair of small pistols, what some people called Sixers because they could fire six kill shots on a single power cell. They were sleek and light, but small enough to use as hidden weapons. One went into an ankle holster inside Leon's right boot, and the other was kept in a hidden pocket inside his purple coat.

"I have a contact for you on Dur Rohstoff," Iona instructed the pair once they had their weapons chosen. "Her name is Mallorie McSwain. She's in charge of the import/export operation. Once you land, she'll make sure you've got what you need, including hard currency. I don't care what you do there, as long as you kill Travis Hurts."

"I have a question on that point," Leon said. "Why do you want the boy dead?"

"He's not a boy," Augustine said.

"He's become a problem for the organization," she replied. "Is that going to be a problem?"

"Oh, no, I'll gladly kill him," Leon said. "We've got unsettled business."

"Good. That has to happen. If you fail, the organization will not be pleased. You're sure he'll come?"

"I'm sure he'll be looking for me," Leon said. "He's the reason I was locked up to begin with."

"Your own kid turned you in?" Augustine asked.

"Got me so falling down drunk I didn't know what he was

doing," Leon said. "I woke up in jail. The guards told me what he did."

"That's low," Augustine remarked.

"You have no idea," Leon replied. "He had to tell the coppers where to look for the warrant against me. I wasn't even wanted on that planet, but once he alerted them they were happy to send me packing."

"I believe Augustine has history with Hurts too," Iona said.

"He caught me on P2. I was wounded. Morgan Black shot me in the hand, and your son carried me off. He's got a ship with jail cells in the back. He locked me up with a bunch of other fugitives and took us back to where we had warrants. I see him, he's gonna die."

"I hear he's a real fast draw," Iona said.

"Not faster'n me," Augustine said. "I guarantee you that."

"I don't think he'll be at the top of his game when he sees me," Leon said. "He was always scared of me."

Iona wanted to point out that he wasn't too scared to haul Leon to jail, but she kept that thought to herself. She wanted both men anxious to kill Travis, and it wouldn't help to step on their pride along the way.

"Make sure that it happens," Iona said. "You kill Hurts and we're even."

"What if he don't show?" Augustine asked. "You can't blame us if he don't show up."

"He'll show," Leon said. "He'll come for me once he knows I'm loose."

"If he doesn't go after Leon, I'll send a ship for you both," she said. "You can pursue him across the galaxy if need be."

"He'll come," Leon said.

"And we'll finish him," Augustine swore.

"Then I'll make sure you have transport wherever you want to go in the galaxy after that," Iona said. She looked at Augustine and added, "If you fail, or if you run ..."

"I ain't gonna run," Augustine said.

"Then our deal is off, and you will be killed on sight by anyone in the Incendius Organization."

"I like clear instructions," Leon said. "I can live with that."

"Good luck," Iona said.

She left the two escaped convicts and went to her own ship. It would launch at the same time as the *Lo Spettro*, and take her back to the *Incendius*. Morgan Black was still out there somewhere, licking his wounds. There were rumors he was wounded by Travis Hurts on some fringe world. She wished the infamous assassin was dead, and maybe he had died of his wounds. Either way, she had a better plan in place. And once it was complete, she could refocus her efforts on removing Dice Jester from his seat at the head of the table, and filling it herself.

17

"I can't believe you sometimes," Ava said.

They were back on the *Purgatory*. The baby was sleeping, and Travis was with Ava in the cockpit as the autopilot flew them away from New Salem.

"You don't have to help me on this one," Travis said.

"I understand you want to catch your father."

"Don't want to," he said. "Have to."

"That's just it, Travis. You don't have to."

"You don't know him," Travis said. "He'll want me to come."

"Which is a good reason not to go. Let someone else do it."

"They'll get killed. I can't live with that."

"How am I supposed to live if you die? How is Kaylee going to get by without you?"

"As it stands, you're better off with me dead. I'll sign the ship over to you."

"No," Ava said.

"That way you can sell it. I hope you'll send payment to Eduardo, but that's up to you."

"Travis, you can't die."

"Not planning to, just planning for it. Seems like a good idea."

"Please, just talk to me about this."

"What's to talk about?" Travis said. "I know him. I know where he'll run."

"To a planet with no law enforcement. You'll be completely on your own."

"Yep," Travis said.

"That's insane."

"No different than P2."

"It is different, don't you see that? You aren't the same person. You're not alone, Travis, not anymore. Let's go back to Expanse, or even someplace else. Any place at all, I don't care."

"Can't," Travis said. "People will die if I don't find him. He's my responsibility."

"What about us? Aren't Kaylee and I your responsibility too?"

"Yes, and this is the only way I can think of to get us out of this mess," Travis said. "I have to stop my father, but I can do more than that on Dur Rohstoff. I can fill the ship with wanted criminals, pay off my debts, and ensure we have a fresh start. You don't want to wake up one morning and find that the Galactic Coalition is suing us."

"We can deal with that. As long as we're together we can deal with anything."

"And as long as I'm alive we'll be together," Travis said. "Long as you want to be with me."

"That's the point," she said. "You might die on Dur Rohstoff."

Travis understood her fear. And he understood that going to one of the deadliest planets in the galaxy was a high risk. But he couldn't live under the debt the GCIB had put him under. And he didn't want to simply move on, hoping the debt didn't follow him. He had lived his life facing his problems head on, not running from them.

"Death is all around us," Travis said. "I could drop dead from a brain aneurysm or get hit by a hovercar. More people die from accidents than from crime."

"You think that stat holds true on Dur Rohstoff?"

"I think it might," Travis said.

"You are a stubborn man."

"I'm not forcing you to do anything," Travis said. "This is my issue, my fight."

"We're in this together," Ava said. "Stop acting like I'm a China doll. I don't want to run and hide every time you face danger, Travis."

"Then what do you want?"

"I want to have a say in what *we* do. I'm not going anywhere without you, but I don't want you to make decisions without me. I need to have a say in what we're doing."

"Like a partner?"

"Like a family," Ava said. "I don't want to be a partner, I want to be a wife, and mother. I want you to be my husband, Travis. I want you to be Kaylee's father."

"I'm not her father," he said.

"But you could be. She'll never know my late husband. She'll never see how quirky he was, or how excited he would get over a new idea. But she'll also never see how wrapped he got in those ideas. She'll never feel the sting of knowing he would rather work on a new invention than spend time with her. Or the ache of knowing he doesn't think she's smart enough to understand what he's doing. I miss him, Travis. But what I have with you is so much more than I ever had with him. You make me feel like I can do anything. You make me feel loved and cherished and empowered all at the same time. I feel trusted, and accepted, and seen for the first time in my life. I want Kaylee to have that too. Not just from me, but from you, Travis. I want you to be her father. I want you to be with us."

"I want to be with you too," Travis said softly. "I just can't live with this debt hanging over me."

"We can fight it," Ava said. "No one in their right mind can blame you for losing Grant Stevenson."

Travis knew that wasn't true because he blamed himself. On Expanse, knowing that Morgan Black had Ava, all Travis cared about was saving her. And while he hadn't said that Soto could take Grant, he had said it would be possible. Soto had held up his end of the bargain. He had distracted Morgan Black long enough for Travis to save Ava. And if that cost him the reward for Grant Stevenson, he was happy to pay it. And if the GCIB wanted to blame him for losing Stevenson, he would gladly face that penalty too. Because Ava was safe, and Kaylee too. That was all that mattered to Travis.

"I don't have any way to make a living in the meantime," Travis said. "We talked about going somewhere and getting a big haul. Maybe Dur Rohstoff is that place."

"Okay," Ava said. "I'm open to that. But I want to see that list from Logan before we make a final decision. I want to be sure we've thought of everything."

"All I can think about is my father."

"Tell me about him."

"He's a monster," Travis said. "He killed my mother ... beat her to death when I was little. I never knew her."

"Oh, Travis," Ava said gently.

He plowed ahead, wiping the tears that sprang from his eyes. "They locked him up for that. Ten year stretch somewhere. I was bouncing around the system, trying to survive. I didn't think life could get worse, but I was wrong."

"He came back? Surely they didn't just let him have you."

"No, he wasn't supposed to, but he kidnapped me, and fled to Rote Nine. You ever been there?"

"No, I've never even heard of it."

"There's not much to hear about. It's mostly a salvage world. Very rough. He had a gang there, ran the usual rackets, extortion, gambling, drugs. He used to let his people beat me up. I had to learn to defend myself, and learn to fight back. Right after I turned seventeen he got falling down drunk. I was his way home when he did that sort of thing. Only I didn't take him home that time. I took him to the security station, told them he had a warrant on Traegen Major for kidnapping, abuse, breaking his parole. I didn't even realize he was also wanted for murder there. They kept him, I took his money and bought a one-way ticket off Rote Nine and never looked back."

"Travis, that's a tragic story," she said.

"It made me who I am."

"I think you are who you are, despite that, not because of it."

"Either way, it's why I do what I do," Travis said. "Finding fugitives is all I've ever been good at. I scrimped and saved for nearly twenty years just to get the down payment for the *Purgatory*. But with this ship I can earn good money catching people that slip through the cracks in the system. I can make a difference in the galaxy."

"Yes, you can do that. You've already done it."

"That's why I want to go to Dur Rohstoff. It's not just because of my father. Although, if he's there, I will stop him."

"Okay, I get it," Ava said. "But let's be smart. Let's work together. Let me help you."

"You already have," Travis said.

"And I can do more," she insisted.

"Then let's go and fill the *Purg* up with wanted fugitives. We'll pay off the debt and then some."

"All right," Ava said. "If that's what you want to do, I'm with you."

"But if things get dangerous, you have to leave," Travis insisted. "You have to take Kaylee and get off world."

"What about you?"

"If it comes to it, you have to be willing to leave me behind."

"I would never do that, Travis."

"Yes you would," he said. "Because you are smart, and you are capable, Ava. If it gets dangerous, you let me worry about me, and you make sure that Kaylee is safe."

"Until you make contact with us," she said.

"Yeah, until then," Travis said. "You can go to Expanse. Borrow money until you can sell the *Purgatory* and keep our little one safe."

"Is that really how you feel?" she asked. "I want you to. I want you to feel like Kaylee's yours, but it's a big thing, Travis. Don't say it just for me. Only say it, if you really feel it."

"I don't want to overstep bounds, and I never thought about having children. But that little angel took up space in my heart since day one. I'll be proud to raise her as my own, if that's what you want."

"It is ... more than anything, Travis. That's what I want."

"Then it's settled," Travis said. "We'll make it official once we're back from Dur Rohstoff."

"All right," Ava said.

They embraced. There was still a lot of emotion in both of them. Hopes, fears, relief, all mingling together. It was bittersweet, and lovely at the same time. They might have stood there in each other's arms for a long time if Kaylee hadn't woken up crying.

"I'll see to her," Ava said.

"I'll check to see if Logan sent that file."

"Okay, and set a course for Dur Rohstoff. I want to know how long it will take to get there."

Travis got the nav computer working on their course, and checked the communication system for the message from Logan. It was there, a list of over twenty wanted felons believed to be hiding out on Dur Rohstoff. Several had rewards of over a hundred thousand credits. Travis would track down as many as it took. He would have preferred to have his new coat, but he would have to rely on the one shirt he had from Eduardo with the laser absorbing fibers and on his speed with his Slinger. All he could hope for was that it would be enough, and that his father really was on the dead world. Travis would never feel safe no matter where he was, or what kind of protection he had, until Leon Hurts was back in prison, or six feet underground.

18

S oto had been watching his target for days. The security
team on Luxor had done a standard search of every person
in the club the night that LeSean Mason was murdered. It
had been a simple task to delete his name from the list long before
the security agents had the chance to question him. Since then, his
name had not come up in their reports or their investigation. Soto
even intercepted messages from the GCIB with the promise that
help was coming, but it had yet to materialize.

That left him focused on Morgan Black. The assassin had the
Presidential Suite reserved for only one more day, and according to
Soto's surveillance, he only came out of his rooms for drugs. Soto
had decided it was time to make his move. The nurses were on a
regular rotation, eight-hour shifts, caring for Morgan Black. They
obviously had no idea who he was. Soto didn't waste time
wondering what type of therapy they provided. But he did get to
know their movements, and was in place near the elevator when
Sofie Turner approached just minutes before her shift was set to
begin. Soto activated the surveillance loop on his computer via a

remote. It overrode the resort's live footage, and when he stepped from the shadows to follow Sofie Turner into the elevator no one saw it. Nor would there be a record of it when he made his way to the Presidential Suite. He punched the number for his own floor, and stepped aside as Sofie inserted her employee card that gave her access to the top level of the resort pyramid.

The doors closed and the elevator started up. Soto turned to face Sofie.

"I am sorry," he said.

"Excus—"

Soto abhorred firearms. They were, in his mind, a coward's weapon. He preferred for his opponent to be face to face, and within striking distance, when he fought them. But he used a spring activated dart gun to render Sofie Turner unconscious. She never saw the small device. The dart hit her left arm, which was bare beneath the very short sleeve of her nursing uniform. The dart was laced with a fast-acting drug that would render her unconscious for several hours. It went to work the moment it broke the skin, and Sofie looked at him with horror before passing out. Soto caught the nurse and held her over his shoulder when the door to his floor opened.

He had been prepared to act quickly if another guest was waiting, but there wasn't one. He tapped the button to close the elevator doors and it continued up to the Presidential Suite. Soto used Sofie's employment card to get into the suite, and quickly let Sofie's body slide off him and onto the floor. The nurse finishing her shift was ready to go. She appeared just as Soto got a new dart into his little spring powered gun.

"Who are you?" she asked before the dart hit her stomach. Soto let her collapse onto the tile floor, and moved quickly into the suite.

He had hoped to find Morgan Black in bed. Soto didn't want to underestimate the assassin. Catching him unaware would be the best result, but when he moved through the empty sitting room, he heard the shower start. The bedroom door was open, and probably the bathroom as well. Soto stopped outside the bedroom door, listening. The only sound was the shower. He stepped into the bedroom and saw steam coming from the bedroom. The bed was empty. A tray of food was left half eaten on the small table. The entertainment console was off. But the bathroom door was open, the lights on, the shower running.

Something wasn't right, Soto thought to himself. He looked around for any signs of weapons. There were dirty clothes, mostly vacation type garb. There were large containers of burn salve next to the bed. A medicinal smell was strong in the bedroom. Soto started for the bathroom, and didn't hear the closet door behind him slide open.

Morgan Black was wearing grey slacks, black socks, but no shoes. His shirt was made of fine silk, and buttoned up the front, only Morgan left it unbuttoned. His body was thin and marked by scars. Some were from his childhood; others were mementos of his long career. The largest was the burn scar from the laser blast that Travis had shot him with. It left jagged lines of thickened skin, like lightning bolts streaking across the night sky. Between the crooked, white lines, the skin was bright red. It was all covered with a thin glaze of burn salve.

Morgan never went anywhere without a weapon. His usual pistols weren't allowed on Luxor, and he carried a tiny Sixer instead. It was made of carbon fiber, which would only hold up to five or six shots from the laser pistol. After that, the weapon would break down. It was a throwaway but useful piece, custom made at great expense, for the express purpose of being able to pass through normal security checkpoints.

As Soto reached the bathroom door, Morgan followed as far as the bedroom door. He recognized the assailant. It was the same man he had fought on Expanse. The one who had nearly cost Morgan an eye. That eye was healing, but still had blurred vision.

Morgan stepped through his bedroom door, leaving only his gun hand and half his head exposed. It was his bad eye, but Morgan didn't need to aim. His Asian counterpart was only a few feet away, along the same wall Travis was hiding behind.

If he had gotten the shot off without making a sound, the threat would have been over. Instead, a button on his open shirt bumped into the door frame. It made a slight ~*tick!*~ sound. Morgan fired a second later, but it was just enough time for Soto to hear the sound and spin away. He didn't have to think about what he heard or what it might portend. His body was trained to react to sound or smell, just as surely as to sight. He ducked and spun backward, drawing his Kodachi short sword. Unlike Morgan Black, Soto had ways to defeat traditional security check points. He carried his weapons inside his luggage in a special compartment lined with copper alloy that defeated metal detection systems and x-rays. The blade came out with a deadly hiss, and as Morgan pivoted to fire again Soto dove to the side. He rolled over a shoulder, came up on his feet and slashed his Kodachi at the assassin's gun hand.

Morgan fired a second shot, missed, and started to withdraw. He felt that he was too close. It saved his hand, but not the laser pistol. The hardened steel chopped into the carbon fiber, missing Morgan's fingers by a fraction of an inch. The laser focusing apparatus was ruined, as was the barrel. Morgan flung the pistol at Soto and dashed backward, looking for something else to fight with.

Soto ducked under the pistol Morgan threw at him, then straightened and followed his target from the bedroom.

"What the hell are you doing here?" Morgan snarled.

"Happenstance brought me to this resort."

Both men were moving through the suite's sitting room, carefully circling around the furniture.

"LeSean Mason," Morgan said. "It was you."

"His was a darkness that needed to be extinguished from the galaxy."

"Is that what you do? You avenge wrong doers?"

"I am a force for balance," Soto said.

"You're a damn, killer," Morgan snapped. "No different than me."

"You are an assassin. You kill for money."

"Money, honor, the universe, whatever ... it's all the same thing."

"I am not surprised that you see it that way," Soto said.

"Oh, you're looking down on me? That's rich. What happened to Grant Stevenson? You chop him up into little pieces with your sword? What are you supposed to be, anyway? There haven't been Samurai in over a thousand years."

"Samurai is not a thing to be, it is a frame of mind."

"Confucius say, the future looks dim for you," Morgan said in a sing-song voice.

"Confucius was Chinese. My ancestors are Japanese."

"You go far enough back and we're all from the same place," Morgan said. "So, you're a holy crusader?"

"I am what I am," Soto said.

"You're a dead man now," Morgan said.

He snatched a pillow off the sofa and flung it at Soto, who cut it half with his sword in one clean stroke. But Morgan used that one second of time when Soto's attention was diverted. He snatched up an imitation of an antique chair. It was made of wood fibers and some sort of binding agent. The chair wasn't heavy, but it was bulky enough that as he swung it, Soto had to back up. He could have tried to block the chair with his sword, but he recognized that the chair had more mass. His Kodachi might cut through it, but it would continue on and crash into him. Instead of fighting against it, he stepped back out of the path of the bulky piece of furniture.

Soto stepped back then lunged forward with his sword. Morgan saw the attack coming. He dropped the chair, and twisted to avoid the sword. It caught in his shirt and sliced through. At the same time, Morgan grabbed hold of Soto's arm. He yanked the intruder off balance. Soto hit the back of an overstuffed sitting chair and flipped over it.

Morgan tried to follow up with a punch that Soto managed to avoid. He jerked his sword arm free, turned the blade around and slashed at Morgan. This time it was the infamous assassin who saw the attack coming and dodged back out of the way. The sword missed him, and he picked up a vase full of fresh flowers with water at the bottom. He hurled it at Soto.

The assailant reached out with his free hand and batted the vase to the side, but not without a grunt of pain from the wound in his shoulder. It was no longer bleeding, no longer a threat, but it hadn't healed completely. The force exerted by this left hand was painful to Soto. Morgan grinned.

"Hurts don't it," he said.

Soto didn't reply as he sprang to his feet. Morgan fled to the wall, ripped a painting down and tried to bash in Soto's skull. Soto brought his sword up and caught the frame on the Kodachi's guard. At the same time his foot shot forward and hit Morgan's knee. The leg flexed backward, sending a shockwave of pain through Morgan's body. He stumbled backward toward the door to the suite. There was a table in the entryway. He used it to steady his balance. Soto was stalking forward. There was another vase on the table, a narrow cylinder of mirrored glass. Morgan grabbed it and swung the base at Soto. His sword shattered the lower portion. The mirrored glass fell to the floor in a tinkling symphony, but left Morgan with the upper part of the vase, which had held together. The shattered end was full of sharp shards. Morgan shoved it toward Soto's stomach. The silent assassin leaned forward, but flexed his back out of the way. It almost worked, but the vase shards caught on Soto's shirt. He wasn't wearing his normal clothing for a kill. His Hodo, and Kayahan undershirt were missing. Instead, he wore typical business clothes. The glass shards shredded his clothes and a few jagged tips even reached his skin, leaving shallow cuts.

But Soto rammed down with the hilt of his sword. It hit

Morgan on the wrist. He dropped the vase and drew back holding his bruised arm. His back was to the door.

"You have nowhere left to run," Soto pointed out. "You will die for the innocent lives you took."

"The lives I took were no more innocent than those you killed," Morgan said. "At least I don't have to delude myself with some religious mumbo jumbo to justify my life."

"There is no justification for you," Soto said. "You are a blight on the galaxy that must be removed."

He thrust forward with his sword. The tip caught on the door as Morgan flung himself sideways. Soto jerked the weapon free, and at the same time Morgan grabbed the knob and twisted it open. But he couldn't just run through it. Not without Soto slicing him up. Instead, Morgan kicked at Soto. His foot rammed upward into Soto's groin, but on impact his injured knee sent a stab of pain up into Morgan's thigh. The kick wasn't as powerful as Morgan had intended, but it did make Soto grunt in pain and take a step back.

Morgan spun around and leaped through the doorway. He felt the tip of the sword slash down his back. It wasn't a deep cut, but he felt it. The pain spurred him forward. The emergency stairs were to the side, through a narrow utility doorway. Morgan limped for it, and burst through. Then, just as Soto was following him, he threw all his weight into the backside of the metal door. It bashed into Soto and sent him staggering backward.

Morgan flung himself forward again, with both hands on the narrow rails on either side of the stairway. He caught his weight on his good leg and lunged forward again. The door opened with a crash behind him, just as Morgan reached the first landing. He whipped around and dove down the next flight of steps. Soto's feet were ringing on the metal steps behind him. Morgan rushed headlong away from his assailant. He had to go down ten full flights. Soto followed, but didn't go too fast. He was careful not to lose his footing.

Morgan was sweating, his shirt in bloody tatters as he threw himself against the utility door that opened onto the VIP Concourse. He hurried to the bank of elevators nearby. A couple in beach clothing had just stepped inside. The woman screamed when she saw Morgan. He grabbed her companion and flung him out of the elevator.

"Hey! What gives man?"

Morgan ignored him and hit the close door button on the elevator. The woman in her damp swimsuit, smelling of suntan lotion, jumped out past Morgan as the doors began to close. Morgan hit the button for the docking level. When the doors closed and the elevator started down, he sagged against the wall. Somehow he had survived. He cursed himself for being so careless. The assassin had followed him to the Luxor resort somehow. If Morgan could just get to his ship he could escape, or better still, get to his weapons and finish the sword-toting buffoon.

When the elevator chimed and the doors opened, Morgan expected to find Soto waiting to finish him off. But there was no one there. Just an empty hallway, and signs pointing to the guest docking arm. The lower levels of the resort weren't as opulent as the upper level. The lighting was low, fewer light fixtures than the levels where guests spent their time, and they were further apart. That meant shadows, and Morgan was normally a denizen of shadows, but in his weakened state, the shadows were no longer his allies. He knew the silent assassin could be lurking anywhere. The one thing that was absolutely certain in Morgan's mind was that the sword-wielding assailant had not given up. It had been a long time since Morgan had felt the chill of mortal danger. Even on Expanse, so near to death, everything had happened fast. But as he limped out of the elevator and down the service corridor, he felt death breathing down his neck.

His burns were healing, but they were still tender. And the painkillers, while effective at blocking the pain, had also blocked his digestive system. His muscles felt weak, and he was bloated and slow. Morgan couldn't help but appreciate that his assailant had come after him in a time of weakness. It was smart on the other man's part, but Morgan wasn't the type to give up. He could feel his knee swelling. It hurt to put his full weight on that leg, but he had struck a blow too. The silent assassin was bleeding. Maybe the wound wasn't deep or debilitating in any physical way, but he knew that it would impact his opponent's mental state.

Soto was lingering in the dark near the main guest docking bay. Morgan had surprised him. There was no doubt to the man's resourcefulness. He was a dangerous foe, a worthy opponent, Soto thought. Perhaps he was the yin to Soto's yang, his dark counter-part. They were both killers, but for very different reasons. Still, despite this ruined clothing, and the cuts he had endured from the broke vase, Soto was solidly focused on taking Morgan Black down. He had one last chance before they would be seen fighting on the docking arm's security cameras. Soto hadn't anticipated the battle raging so long, or so far from the Presidential Suite. He hadn't both-ered to hack the security camera feeds in the docking arm. It was a failure of foresight. But Soto wouldn't let that stop him from striking one last blow at his opponent.

Morgan turned the corner. The docking arm was only fifty paces away, through a set of double doors. But his survival instincts were telling him there was danger all around. And his knee was throbbing with pain. When he came to a maintenance closet that someone had left open, he looked inside and pulled out a mop handle. It was made of some type of plastic, but it was strong enough for Morgan to lean on. He unscrewed the handle from the mop head, and continued toward the entrance to the docking arm.

When Soto swung out of the shadows, slashing at Morgan with his sword, the mop handle saved his life. Morgan brought the plastic pole up purely on instinct. It didn't stop the well-honed steel, but it deflected Soto's strike. The sword cut through the mop handle near the end that screwed to the mop head, and changed the trajectory of Soto's attack. It also gave Morgan just enough time to duck.

Before the severed end of the handle could hit the floor, Morgan flipped the lower section upward. It hit Soto's elbow. The blow wasn't that powerful, but the mop handle impacted Soto's funny bone. It was one of those freak occurrences that happened in a fight that no one could predict, and that made every fight's outcome a mystery. Soto's hand went numb, the sword falling to the deck. Both men saw the look of surprise on their opponent's face. Morgan tried to hit Soto with the mop handle again, but the silent assassin ducked under the blow and tried to sweep Morgan's legs out from under him. Morgan, sensing the attack, hobbled back out of range. He tried to follow up with an overhead chop using the mop handle, but it hit the wall, and then the ceiling. By the time it came down toward Soto, he was ready for it. Grabbing the mop handle Soto jerked hard. Morgan was thrown off balance. He bent forward, trying to keep his weight off his injured knee. Soto's kick smashed Morgan's nose. Blood flew out as Morgan arched backward, and Soto moved in for the kill. He didn't need a weapon to end a life. He spun around and chopped vertically with his hand stiff. It was a strike he had perfected over time, breaking boards and even cement blocks as he trained his body to be the weapon he needed it to be.

But Morgan saw the strike coming. He couldn't avoid it, so he leaned into it instead, raising his shoulder and lowering his jaw. The chop should have hit Morgan just below the corner of his jaw and snapped his neck. Instead, it clipped his shoulder and hit Morgan in the side of the head. For a split-second Morgan lost contact with his senses. He didn't feel his feet fly up into the air, or his body flip nearly sideways before falling to the deck. But the crash brought him back to himself. He was almost helpless. No weapons, not even the mop handle, to protect himself with. Prone on the floor, his reflexes were dampened by the painkillers, his injured leg unable to support his full weight. In that moment Morgan realized he was going to die. And had Soto rushed to finish him, he would have. But instead, Soto hesitated. Morgan looked up; his vision blurred from the chop to his head.

"You have killed so many," Soto said. "How does it feel to be facing your own demise, Morgan Black?"

Morgan didn't respond. His mind was still reeling, searching for a way out of the mess he found himself in.

"Extinguishing your darkness from the galaxy will be a great victory," Soto said. "But I wonder if anyone will realize who you really are? Surely, this quivering, drug addled, fop isn't a great man."

Morgan had to spit a mouthful of blood from his broken nose out of his mouth to draw in a shaky breath.

Soto continued mocking him. "In the end, he was helpless to save himself."

"Go to hell," Morgan snarled.

Soto reached down and grabbed the front of Morgan's open shirt. He could see the pain on Soto's face as he pulled Morgan closer with his left arm. At that moment Morgan remembered that Soto had been cut in their fight on Expanse. He lunged forward, his fingers grabbing Soto's shoulder and digging in. Soto was smaller than Morgan, a thin man, his body honed for battle just like his weapons. Morgan felt the hard muscles, but continued squeezing. He saw the pain register on Soto's face. The smaller man screamed in pain, but he also lashed out with his right hand. Soto's open palm hit Morgan with enough force to snap his head back. He dropped to the floor, and Soto staggered backward, away from Morgan.

Later, when Morgan Black remembered the fight, he would recall the voices. Someone was coming toward them. They hadn't turned the corner yet, but they were coming. Soto heard them too. He snatched up his sword as blood from the reopened wound in his shoulder soaked into his shirt and jacket.

"Hey!" a stranger shouted. It was a tall man in a maintenance uniform. "What happened?"

Soto glanced up. The man was just a resort worker. But he had stumbled into a fight that he shouldn't have seen. Behind the man came a woman. She had on a chef's jacket that was stained from what was probably a long, frantic shift in one of the resort kitchens. And with her was another man, much smaller than the first. He wore a janitor's coveralls.

"We need help," Soto said in a shaky voice.

The tall man hurried up to Soto, but his eyes were on Morgan, who lay on the floor, spitting blood from his mouth and nose.

"He's hurt," Soto said.

"Hey, mister, don't worry," the tall man said as he dropped to one knee beside Morgan.

He never saw Soto's Kodachi before it stabbed through the side of his neck and severed his brain stem. The tall man died instantly, collapsing on top of Morgan Black. Soto's sword came free easily, as the woman screamed. She and the janitor were still ten paces away. Soto charged them. The janitor, to his credit, stepped between Soto and the woman. His hands were raised to fend off the blow he knew as coming. But Soto was swinging his Kodachi with full strength. It severed the janitor's hands and the tip slashed his throat. At Soto spun around the man, a fountain of blood erupted from the janitor's wounds. The woman screamed again, feinting before Soto could strike. She dropped to the deck one way, the janitor fell to his knees, then toppled over the opposite way. Soto killed the woman who could identify him, with a quick stab of his sword. Then he turned back, intending to finish Morgan Black. But the infamous assassin wasn't there.

Morgan had seen the tall man die. The maintenance man's body fell onto his, and Morgan didn't move until Soto dashed away to kill the others. Then he flung the maintenance man aside, climbed to his feet, and pushed open the door to the docking bay. Morgan didn't know about the security cameras that were hacked, and those that weren't. All he knew was that his ship, the *Dymetr* was in docking slip fourteen. He ran, ignoring the pain and weakness in his knee. It was all compartmentalized in his mind.

Breathing was hard, his knee was on the verge of giving out. But escape was in sight if he could reach his ship. And to his surprise the doors behind him didn't slam open. The assassin with the sword didn't chase him down. Instead, just as he reached his ship, Morgan looked back the way he had come. The passage was empty, as far as he could tell. His vision was still blurry, probably the result of a concussion, he surmised. Morgan passed through the airlock on his ship and ordered the computer to lock it down.

Soto watched from the shadows on the far side of the docking bay doors. They had large windows in the upper portions, giving Soto a clear line of sight to Morgan running for his life. He would have chased him down, but that would have revealed his actions to the cameras. Instead, Soto reached up and undid his top knot. His long, dark hair fell to either side of his face. He returned his bloody sword to its hidden scabbard inside his jacket, then slowly opened the door. He walked calmly down the hallway, knowing that security officials would watch and rewatch the footage dozens of times. He moved with confidence. Maybe they would see a spot of blood on his clothing. Soto didn't know where the cameras were located in the docking arm. He just knew he couldn't avoid them all, and didn't have the time to erase them. He reached his ship, the *Rising Sun*, and went inside. Like Morgan Black, he ordered it to begin leaving the resort. The ship's operating system did everything, from communicating with the flight control computers, to running the preflight checklist.

There were less than sixty seconds between the *Dymetr* and the *Rising Sun* launching from the resort space station. Morgan made a full throttle dash away from the resort. Soto moved more slowly, tracking his prey. He didn't want it to seem obvious that he was chasing the *Dymetr*. He took his ship in a different direction entirely, but kept his systems focused on Morgan's ship. It was black and hard to see visually, but Soto's radar had a lock on the smaller ship. His own space yacht was moving at a leisurely pace, all the while tracking the *Dymetr's* trajectory and calculating the possible destinations. At the last minute it turned hard, then disappeared into hyperspace.

Soto knew it was possible that Morgan would jump to empty space, and then change to a different direction. It was what Soto would do. But it had left on a direct course to Putnam Station, which was only a forty-minute flight from Luxor. Soto set course for the popular space station and made the jump.

19

The rich food from Putnam station hadn't sat well with Leon. He had stayed in his cabin for the flight out to DR. Dur Rohstoff wasn't on the fringe of the system like Pergamum Prime. It had once been a thriving world, rich with natural resources. But those resources had been so thoroughly stripped from the planet that it was left with an unstable surface. Earthquakes were common. Not that such natural phenomena couldn't be dealt with, but the planet had been abandoned long ago. Only the poorest of the poor had been left behind. It was a forgotten planet, a system off the regular trade routes, that no one seemed to care about any longer. Which made it a perfect place for criminals to flock to.

Only they weren't the only people on DR. The natives were fiercely territorial, and hated everyone but their own kind. It was an understandable bias, given the fact that they had been abandoned on a dying world. Most scientists believed it was only a matter of time before the planet fractured to the point that it broke apart. And the natives understood that the newcomers to their world were there to continue the legacy of exploitation. So they killed anyone they came across as they roved over the poisoned, unstable landscape.

Mining had been a major industry on DR. The toxic runoff from the mining trickled down into the water system. Entire native species had gone extinct. And one of the lingering dangers of the tainted water was a sickness that covered a person in open sores. It wasn't contagious, but the locals believed it was. Anyone found to have contracted the disease was either killed, or exiled. The exiles banded together for safety and went slowly marching across the planet in search of food and water.

It was a planet in constant conflict. The natives were deadly, but didn't have the resources that the criminal organizations brought to the forgotten planet. That didn't stop them from raiding the towns and settlements that were set up by the career criminals who used DR as a base of operations. Some were big and others were small. The Incendius Organization had their fencing operations based on Dur Rohstoff. It was the perfect place to hide stolen goods, which could be warehoused easily, and then resold on other planets later for a profit. It was also a good place to lay low after a hit, or if a warrant was issued for someone's arrest. Normally, a person could just flee to another planet, but occasionally they needed to get completely off grid. DR was the perfect place to hide out, long or short term.

The *Lo Spettro* set down inside a compound of prefab buildings and open storage. There were a lot of metal storage containers, the kind often used on freight ships for moving goods. Nothing on DR was stable, so buildings were often compromised in the frequent earthquakes, and fences or walls crumbled. The most durable of structures were the old-style storage containers. Made of hardened steel, and just the right size to be extremely strong, the storage containers were the safest of structures. Entire cities and compounds had been made from them. The Incendius Organization territory was filled with hundreds of them. Some were turned into domiciles, others were used at bars, cafes, brothels, drug dens, and entertainment venues. Not that traveling acts visited the dead world, but because so much stolen property passed through the operation's compound, there was no shortage of the latest tech.

When the *Lo Spettro* landed it was met by a woman in a long dress, with a quick draw pistol on a gun belt she wore high around her waist. She wore a short jacket and wide-brimmed hat.

"You Hurts?" the woman asked, as Leon and Augustine Ward left the small spacecraft.

"Who's asking?" Leon replied.

"I'm McSwain," the woman said. "This is my facility."

Leon looked around. The compound looked more like a trade show than a hideout of wanted criminals. He saw smart-looking wheeled vehicles parked in neat rows, bundles of boxed goods wrapped in plastic and sitting on pallets just waiting to be loaded up and hauled away. The shipping containers were metal rectangles. Made of dull-looking metal, many had been marked with graffiti. They were everywhere. Leon could see the layout of the compound. The ground was mostly paved, although it was cracked and crumbling into a kind of gravel. There were people everywhere too, some looked busy attending to tasks, others just strolling about.

"I'm Hurts," Leon said. "He's Ward."

"I got word you two were coming," McSwain said. "How's it feel to be a free man?"

"Damn good," Augustine said.

"I'll let you know once my debt is paid," Leon said.

He looked up at the sky. The blue sky was hidden behind a pale, yellowish pall of smog. The air was breathable, but had a metallic tang to it, and smelled industrial to Leon. Still, it was all an improvement over Lucerine.

"The bounty hunter comes out here, he'll be looking for you boys on the strip," McSwain said. She turned and started walking away from the *Lo Spettro* had landed.

"What's the strip?" Augustine asked.

"That's where the fun happens," McSwain said. "We keep our goods in the center of the compound. We're on the flight line now."

She pointed to the various ships parked in a long line.

"North and West are domiciles," she said. "With automated security systems. We've got auto cannons that will hold off an army of Scabbers and any three tribes of natives. None of them are really big enough to worry about, and they don't get along, so there's little danger they might band together, but if they did they wouldn't get in that way."

"The strip is to the south?" Leon asked.

"You've got a good sense of direction," McSwain said. "That's our connection with people who aren't Incendius."

"The locals," Ward said.

"We do some trading with the other organizations on world," McSwain explained. "And a pretty brisk business with people who have no affiliations. I've got a good crew here. We all know each other."

"Someone you don't know comes snooping around?" Ward asked.

"We don't go heeled for nothing," McSwain said. "But mostly, it's just the natives you have to worry about. They like to raid."

"What do they look like?" Leon asked. "I wouldn't want to get caught off guard."

"You wouldn't," McSwain said. "They don't wear much in the way of clothing, and they paint their bodies. You see someone like that, shoot first and ask questions later."

"They armed?" Ward asked.

"Some are. Mostly older projectile weapons, but some have laser rifles. They take whatever they can get their hands on. Clothing, weapons, vehicles, tech of any kind. They don't know what to do with most of it, but they take it all."

She showed them a pair of cargo containers that had windows cut into them. The big metal doors had been replaced with what looked like sliding glass. Inside they were decorated and furnished.

"Home sweet home," McSwain said. "Iona said to set you up with the best. Normally, we charge ten thousand a month for these, but you're on a mission for the boss. She said to give you some money too."

Leon was staring at the box domicile. It had clearly had a lot of work done to turn the metal container into a nice-looking home. It was nicer than anything he had ever lived in. Even before being sent to Lucerine, he never lived in anything but old slums and junk shacks.

"You won't hear me complaining," Ward said, as he took a roll of coins from McSwain.

"That's enough to keep you well fed and in good company for about a month," she said. "I won't tell you how to do your job, but I would take it easy on the booze and drugs until the bounty hunter is taken care of."

"And after that?" Ward asked.

"Depends on what you want to do," McSwain said. "You can stay on world, go to work for me, or we'll arrange for you to get off DR."

"What about the earthquakes?" Leon asked.

"Tremors mostly," McSwain said. "You'll feel 'em two or three times a day. Just a low vibration. The bigger ones are pretty rare. We aren't near any of the main fault lines. There are places where the tremors are dangerous. I'd stay away from the mountains and the coast. And don't go looking at the sink holes. They can be pretty unstable."

"Hot damn, it feels good to be back," Augustine said. "Money in my pocket, a gun on my hip, all I need is some female companionship and I'll be right as rain."

"Speaking of rain, it's not exactly toxic. But try to find cover if a storm blows in."

"What about the law?" Leon asked.

"Ain't no law on Dur Rohstoff," McSwain said. "But I've got a security team to make sure our goods don't get poached. Back shooters, and instigators are either exiled or killed. Don't go making trouble just for trouble's sake."

"We weren't planning to," Ward said. "Just looking to have a little fun."

"You've got vehicles, money, access to the strip and beyond," McSwain said. "Do whatever you want, just don't kill my people, and don't get yourselves killed. Least not until the bounty hunter's six feet under."

"He comes around, we'll be ready for him," Ward said.

"He'll come," Leon said.

"You sure about that?" McSwain said.

"We've got unfinished business," the older man said. "He'll come for me, or I'll go after him."

"I'll leave you to it, then," McSwain said. "Just know that's all the credit you'll get from me. And if you crash these cruisers, I'll have something to say about that."

She was referring to the sleek-looking land vehicles. They had four wheels and big shocks. They looked as if they could go anywhere. Leon hadn't driven a vehicle in over twenty years. Just sleeping on a bed was taking some getting used to. He had one shot of whiskey on Putnam Prime that went right to his head, and made him sick afterward. And he hadn't been with a woman in so long he wasn't sure how it would go. For years he had dreamed of escaping Lucerine, although he never really thought it would happen. In his mind he was still the hard charging, fast living tough guy he'd always been. But since leaving Lucerine he was struggling to adapt. He needed to take things slow, but he couldn't show weakness. All he wanted to do was to take a nap, but when Augustine suggested they check out the nightlife, Leon didn't protest.

The strip was only a few hundred yards from their new domiciles. They walked. The afternoon was fading into a long, dull twilight but the strip was already busy with locals. Some were part of the Incendius Organization, others were people who lived outside the compound. There were plenty of nomads, short timers, and people just laying low. They made money selling stolen goods, or doing gun work. The big compounds had their own security against the native tribes, but the unaffiliated had to pull together when the roving bands came raiding. Some were flush from big heists, while others ran for their lives to DR in hopes of getting away from law enforcement. They all wanted what the Incendius Organization was selling on the strip. Real food, booze, drugs, the latest tech. It was a carnival of the flesh. Leon found himself in a bar that was really just another cargo container, but it had small tables and less noise than some of the others. It was called the Oasis.

"This place is dead," Augustine said. "Let's go somewhere else."

"You already been to see a sporting girl."

"Man's got needs," Ward replied. "I'm surprised you didn't want to find one for yourself."

"Never paid for that," Leon said. "Ain't about to start now."

"Whatever," Ward replied. "Let's find a place with some card games, or entertainment."

"This place is good enough for me," Leon said.

"Fine, suit yourself," Ward said. "You need me, I'll be where it's the loudest and brightest."

Leon watched him go. There hadn't been a tremor on DR yet, but there was plenty inside Leon's mind. He was a master con man and could pretend that everything was fine, but in reality he was coming apart at the seams. There was too much space, too many people, and no one looking for him. It all felt wrong. After twenty years on Lucerine he felt like he had stepped out of his life. On Putnam he had put on a good act, and the fear of getting caught was so strong that it hid most of his insecurities. On DR, there was no law, no fear of getting taken back to prison. He couldn't understand what exactly he was afraid of. But he was terrified. Nothing was like he thought it would be, and he just hoped he could hold himself together until Travis showed up.

The heat of his hatred for his own son's betrayal had filled him and fueled him for a long time in prison. But Leon was desperate to see a familiar face. Not that he thought he would recognize his son. Leon had forgotten what Travis looked like. But he wanted to see him, to face him, to make him feel the pain that Leon had felt. All he had ever done was look after Travis. He had rescued him from the foster care system, and made a man out of him. But Travis had betrayed Leon. It was a deep wound, and one that Leon had to focus on to get him through the night. He was drinking beer, sipping at the intoxicating beverage and just hoping it wouldn't go straight to his head. But he could feel things getting wobbly. An hour after Ward left him, Leon finished his single drink and decided he had done enough.

He was halfway back to his ship container domicile when two shadowy figures approached. Leon heard their boots scuffing behind him, but didn't turn around. They talked in low voices, but he could hear them.

"You sure that's him?" one said.

"Pos-I-tive," the other said, drawing out the syllables. "Seen 'em come in this afternoon. Has to be him."

The pair fell silent as they closed in on Leon. Of all things he was uncertain of, the one thing that remained with him all his life was violence. He wasn't sure if he wanted the pair of shadowy figures to kill him or not. It might have been easier to just take a shot in the back and let all his fears go away into the void. But instead, he stopped walking and turned around. The pair were just a few paces out of reach. They both had pistols in their hands, and crowded close to one another.

"Who are you two fools looking for?" Leon asked.

"Heard us about a prison break," the shorter of the two said. "They's bound to be a re-ward," he said, pronouncing reward as if it were two separate words.

"One's an older fella," the taller stranger said. "Been in the pen 'bout as long as I been drawing air."

"That a fact?" Leon said.

"It's more of a rumor than a fact," the short man said.

"But we're keen for opportunities," the taller man said. "Don't much get past us."

"I find that hard to believe," Leon said.

"You're kinda mouthy for fella with two shootists already pointing their pistols at you," the tall one said. "Best if you just answer the questions we ask."

"You one of them jailbirds?" the shorter man asked.

Leon didn't speak, he just nodded his head.

"Told you," the shorter man said. "Go ahead and put your hands up. Don't get wise with us, or we'll air out your insides."

"No," Leon said.

"You losing your hearing old timer?" the taller man said. "He said get 'em up."

"I heard him," Leon said. "The answer's still no. Tell you boys what. I've got a roll of hard currency in my pocket. Why don't I save you the trouble of wrangling me off world, and dealing with the law to get a reward. It might be that if you bring me in, they might try to arrest you too."

"Hadn't thought about that," the shorter one said.

"We ain't wanted for nothing," the taller man said.

"That we know of," his companion insisted.

"Here," Leon said. "Let me give you this money."

He reached in his coat, pulled out the roll of coins. He held it in his hand and waited for the fools to come and get it.

"We can take it," the tall man said. "Save us some trouble."

"That's what I'm talkin' about," the shorter man said, suddenly bubbling with excitement.

The taller man stepped close to Leon and reached for the money, but before he could take it the older man drew his pistol and bashed the man in the face with the heavy barrel. He dropped to the ground, groaning in pain. The shorter man stared at his companion in shock. He would have come to his senses in a second,

164

maybe two, but that was more than enough time for Leon to step toward him and slap the gun from his hand.

The shorter man jumped back, clearly frightened. He turned to run but Leon kicked his leg sideways. It flew into his other leg and the man went sprawling onto the gravel. Leon walked over and stomped down with the heel of his boot on the back of the man's neck. The man screamed as his face pounded into the gravel. Leon looked back at the other man. He wasn't moving, or making noise any longer. For the first time since leaving Lucerine something felt right to Leon. Dishing out pain was always something he did well. He was strong, with a wicked sense of cruelty.

He bent down over the bloody faced man. "I guess you just weren't man enough to get the job done."

With a powerful, chopping motion, he brought the butt of his pistol down onto the side of the man's head, knocking him out cold. He got slowly to his feet and looked around. Normally, he would search the bodies of his victims, taking whatever he wanted. But he had money, and doubted the desperado had anything to add. He picked up their pistols. They were old, and looked about as likely to blow up as to actually shoot. And that was if the batteries weren't already dead. He tossed them both away into the darkness like garbage, and left the bodies behind him. Things were starting to feel less chaotic and big to him. So much had changed, but some things hadn't. He could still fight. Maybe he just needed some time. Maybe things would work out to his advantage after all. He strolled back to his domicile with a spring in his step and murder in his heart.

20

"Where are we going?" Ava asked.

They were skimming over the landscape just a hundred feet off the ground.

"I already told you."

"But why not just call in, get coordinates?" Ava asked.

"Because, the comms are most likely being monitored," Travis said. "And I don't want anyone knowing we're here."

It took nearly two hours to find Hogan's cabin. It was a small structure, just a prefab building next to an old style well. There was a corral next to the cabin with half a dozen horses grazing on the grass inside. Ava landed the *Purgatory* about fifty feet from the cabin, then held Kaylee and watched as Travis went outside. He was wearing his cowboy hat, and a poncho that was thrown back over his right shoulder. His Ranger rifle was slung over his back, the barrel pointing upward. She thought he looked roguish in his outfit, but also a little dangerous. He wasn't trying to hide his weapons, which was a little different for Travis.

Outside, Travis moved slowly to the well. Some of the horses were watching him, but others had no interest. About the time he reached the round stack of rocks around the old well, the door to the cabin opened.

"What are you doing here?"

"Came to see an old friend," Travis said.

"It's been a while."

"Has," Travis said.

The man stepped out of the cabin. He was old, his face a mass of wrinkles and wiry gray whiskers. He wore an old-style military pistol in a holster with a flap. His back was a little hunched, and he hobbled more than walked.

"Most folks don't come around less'n they need something."

"We all do," Travis said. "I brought someone with me."

"Prisoner?"

"No," Travis said. "She's ... well ... I'm not sure what we're calling it. More than a friend, but nothing official. Not yet anyway."

"Well, what the hell are you waiting for?" the old man said. "Don't keep an old man in suspense."

Travis turned and waved. Ava came down out of the rear hatch and walked toward Travis.

"What's she toting there?" the old man said.

"A baby," Travis said. "Little girl ... Kaylee."

"Yours?"

Travis hesitated a moment, then nodded. "Yeah," he said. "Kaylee is my daughter."

"Never thought I'd see the day," the old man said.

When Ava reached him, Travis introduced her. "Ava, this is Mick Hogan."

"Hello," Ava said.

"Pleasure to meet you," Hogan said. "Let's go inside. This sun will addle your brains you stand around in it too long."

They followed the old man into the cabin. It was a single room with a narrow bed in one corner, a cook stove next to a refrigerator unit on the opposite wall. Between them was a sofa and a couple of well-worn recliners.

"You'll have to forgive my humble abode," the old man said. "There hadn't been much call for updating in a long time."

"We're not here to judge," Travis said.

"Why are you here?"

"You haven't heard?"

"I hear a lot of things," the old man said. "But less than I used to. Ain't as much call to go to town as there used to be."

"How do you two know each other?" Ava asked.

"I'm the one taught him the business," Hogan said. "Joined with the Rosenthal Detective Group when he was just a baby."

"Hogan was my mentor," Travis said. "I worked with him for three years."

"Till they forced me out," the old man said.

"We tracked down missing people," Travis added. "Usually, wives that ran off with their lovers, or children who ran away from home."

"He used to come visit me regular," Hogan said. "I taught him to ride and to shoot. Then he got it in his head to buy a ship. I guess it worked out."

"Pretty much," Travis said.

"How many prisoners that rig hold?"

"Six comfortably," Travis told him.

"Well," the old man said. "This calls for a drink. Whisky, or iced tea? I got both."

"Tea," Ava said. "I can't drink alcohol while I'm nursing the baby."

"Don't see why not," Hogan said. "In my day, it wasn't unusual to rub a baby's gums with whisky when they were teething."

Ava looked shocked and Travis smiled.

"They get a little older they could gnaw on chicken bones, if'n you got 'em."

"Times change," Travis said.

"That's a fact," Hogan said, pouring up glasses of iced tea. "We can catch up, or you can cut to the chase and tell me why you're here. I got a feelin' it ain't tell me you're a dad."

"No," Travis said. "But it has to do with family."

"Never had one," Hogan said. "Always thought that was easier for a lawman."

"We all come from somewhere," Ava said.

"True," the old man replied, handing her a glass of tea. "My parents passed when I was young. That kinda loss stays with a man. Makes you a little standoffish when it comes to getting close to people. That was always my rule, till I met Travis. He wormed his way in."

"I didn't realize he was treating me bad," Travis admitted. "Compared to the way I grew up; Hogan was a saint."

"What family has brought you here?" Hogan asked, settling himself into one of the recliners. "Ain't nothing here that's good."

"Leon broke out of Lucerine," Travis said.

"You losing your marbles, kiddo? That's impossible."

"Chief Inspector of the GCIB told me about it. It's on the site too. Leon and a gunslinger Augustine Ward. They had help, but the guards won't say who paid them."

"And you think he's here?"

"Always said he would come here if the heat got too high," Travis said.

"Only one way to find out," Hogan said. "You riding or flying?"

"Riding, if you've got a mount I can borrow."

"I do," Hogan said. "Let's make a plan."

There were three compounds within a day's ride. Each one was run by a different organized crime syndicate. If Leon was smart he would be off grid, laying low outside the settlements. But for most outlaws, the appeal of DR was the lack of law. They made their plans. Travis would go to the compound controlled by Infada Hardliners. Hogan would go to the closer settlement controlled by the Incendius Organization. If they both struck out, they could check the third settlement run by Hardboyz. That night, Travis caught his mentor up on how his life had radically changed since getting the *Purgatory*.

"Now you're here, penniless, with very few prospects, and a bounty on your head."

"It appears so," Travis replied.

"I should have known it. You're a hard man, Travis. You don't know when to let a bounty go."

"I don't hunt bounties," Travis said.

"You sure as hell are now," Hogan said. "A million credits? I never saw that much money at one time in all my life, kid. The GCIB has you over a barrel, and unless I'm very much mistaken, you're going to end up dead."

"Maybe," Travis said, handing over his data slate to the older man. "Recognize any of these outlaws?"

Hogan chuckled. "These are the worst of the worst. I recognize a few. You start putting people in chains and the entire planet will be out to get you."

"Yeah, we have to be discreet," Travis said.

"Or maybe you just go back to the GCIB and appeal the fine," Hogan said. "Better to be bankrupt than dead."

"If I don't pay it, they'll yank my license."

"So let 'em," Hogan said. "There's a lot a ways to make a living finding people other than fugitive recovery. If I told you once, I've told you a million times, fugitive recovery is a dangerous game."

"Which is why I do it," Travis said.

"'Cause you've got a death wish?"

"Because I can do it, and not many people can. I've made a difference in the galaxy, Mick. There are bad guys behind bars because of me."

"And there's a price on your head too," Hogan replied. "Don't forget that."

"I never do," Travis said. "How's your aim with the long rifle?"

"I can still shoot the wings of a housefly at a thousand yards," he bragged. "That how this works?"

"No," Travis said. "I take my prisoners face to face."

"You're just asking for trouble."

"Maybe," Travis said. "Seems like the best way to go about it."

"It's not," Hogan said. "But to each his own. Morgan Black comes looking, I'll give him a few extra holes to bleed from."

"Thanks, Hogan," Travis said. "You sure you don't mind Ava staying here in the ship?"

"She can stay in the cabin, but I don't share my bed," he said. "Usually sleep in this chair, but I'm territorial, and set in my ways."

"She'll be more comfortable on the *Purgatory*."

"Great name by the way."

"I thought you might like it."

"I'm sure your prisoners do too."

"Not so much."

"She's welcome. And if she wants to feed the horses while we're gone, all the better."

"She won't mind it," Travis said. "She's not the type to sit around all day."

"I have to admit it, Travis. I think it's great. She's a beaut. And that baby is sweet as honey. I think you're a fool for not taking them some place safe and forgetting all about your father and fugitive work."

"That's still on the table, once Leon is locked up."

"Why do you care about him?"

"He's a plague, Hogan. A one-man wrecking crew. Destroying lives is all he knows. The Marshals won't find him. They probably think he's just an old man that can't hurt anyone anymore, but I know better. Wherever he is, whatever he's doing, Leon Hurts is living up to his name."

"So you track him down, and then what?"

"I take him in."

"And if he won't go?"

"Then I have no choice."

"You'd kill your own father."

"It'll come down to who kills who first," Travis said. "He'll kill me in a heartbeat if I give him the chance."

"Then don't," Hogan said.

"I don't plan to," Travis insisted.

But in the back of his mind there was a nagging doubt. He had never frozen in a fight before. He had never hesitated to pull the trigger, but he couldn't help but wonder if facing his own father would be harder. All he could do was trust his instincts, and every fiber of his being was telling him he had to go hard and not rest until Leon Hurts was back in prison. Or dead, either option worked for Travis. He wasn't picky, but he was leery. It was going to be the hardest fight of his life. He just hoped it wasn't his last.

21

Sanada Soto set a course for Dur Rohstoff in the Leuchtend system. Black had wasted no time upon arriving near the Putnam Exchange. Soto barely reached the trade route in time to identify the *Dymetr* and track its secondary jump. But he felt no compulsion to hurry after Morgan Black. Maybe the assassin would jump from the Leuchtend system, but it was much more likely that he sought refuge on a world known for harboring outlaws. It was exactly the kind of place one would expect to find a notorious assassin.

Once the nav computer was set, the autopilot made the jump into hyperspace. Soto was not a proponent of using technology all the time, but there were tasks for which it was ideal. Piloting a ship through space was one such task. It required precision, not intuition, and Soto preferred to let the autopilot do what it was designed for. The happy byproduct of his space yacht with advanced AI autopiloting capabilities, was that Soto had time to tend to his wounds. The cut on his stomach was minor. He simply sprayed it with anti-bacterial and let his body do the rest. But his shoulder was another matter. Morgan Black had reopened the wound and caused trauma to the deep cut. Soto had to refill the opening with synthetic flesh that stopped the bleeding and encouraged healing. It did nothing to stop the deep ache in his shoulder, or the feeling of weakness in his left arm.

With his body seen to, Sanada looked to his sword. The blade of the Kodachi was covered with blood. It was all in the wooden scabbard too. He removed the weapon and wiped it down. Then he sprayed the blade, guard, and handle with a natural cleaner, and wiped it all down again. Finally, he applied pure beeswax to the blade, just a thin layer, to ensure that no moisture corrupted the steel.

The scabbard had to be taken apart. It was made from two pieces of magnolia wood glued together. It was a perfect fit. After heating the scabbard, he managed to pull it apart. It took two hours of careful work to remove the blood and the old glue before he could put it back together. It was tedious work, but his sword was without equal, and he cared for it as such. There was a sense of purpose in the task of keeping his weapon clean and exceptionally sharp. He didn't think of his life as having a holy calling, but rather his financial and business success had afforded him the opportunity to be of service to the greater good. It was his task to help harmonize the galaxy by bringing the yin-yang of light and darkness into balance.

Only after his weapons were properly seen to, did Sanada sleep. It was a bit of a surprise when his dreams were disturbed with nightmares. Soto didn't fear death, but he couldn't help but be frightened when Morgan Black appeared in his dreams. In his sleep, the tables were turned. Morgan Black became Soto's hunter, tracking him down, chasing him through an endless series of rooms, always on the verge of slaying the silent assassin. Unable to return to sleep, Soto tried to meditate. But that too was difficult. Normally, he had no trouble clearing his mind, but the presence of his enemy was strong. It could not simply be willed away. It was as if Morgan Black was all he could think about.

Evolving Threat

For the first time in years he thought of getting drunk. It was an understandable reaction to an unwanted thought or memory. Soto had fought Morgan Black twice, and twice he had failed to end the other man's life. Never before had he encountered an enemy that he was unable to kill. Failure was a terrible burden. Perhaps it would have been better to die on Expanse than to live with having failed. Of course, at the time he hadn't thought of it as a failure. His task, as the lawman had requested, was that Soto distract Morgan Black from hurting the pregnant woman long enough for Travis to recover from getting shot by the infamous assassin. Technically, it was Travis' failure, not Soto's. But who could he blame for what happened on Luxor? It was not the outcome that Soto had envisioned. And while his enemy hadn't actually escaped from Soto, he still felt burdened by fear. Whether it was fear of death, or fear of failure, Soto wasn't exactly sure.

But he did know that getting drunk would allow him to forget his failures for a short time. It was the weak man's escape. Drinking, drugs, any type of vice really, was just a way to put off doing what one didn't want to face. And Soto wasn't the type to run from his reality, or to hide his mind from the truth through alcohol. Besides, if he got drunk, it would give Morgan the chance to escape, and that would be true failure. Soto had no way to track the assassin's ship. He might be able to track Morgan down through the alias he had used on Luxor, Everett Hitch, but it was probably only one of many alter-egos the infamous assassin used. And he would not be so foolish as to use it again after the debacle on Luxor.

Instead of getting drunk, Soto put himself through a rigorous workout. It was the best way to clear his mind, and in the process, he discovered what his wounded shoulder was capable of. It wasn't much. The pain was bone deep, a throbbing ache that didn't ease up or go away, especially as Soto worked his body in the dojo on his ship.

A shower helped refresh him. After getting dressed in his traditional clothing, and tying his hair up in a topknot, he ate breakfast.

He kept a variety of fruits and berries in the galley of the *Rising Sun*. He also drank a high protein shake to help restore his body after the workout.

Finally, he went to the cockpit of the yacht. The ship was in a high orbit around Dur Rohstoff. The planet had no flight control. It was an open world. The surface was unstable, but it still had an atmosphere. His ship had immediately located the *Dymetr* upon dropping from hyperspace. As expected, the ship was making straight for the planet. It had gone down in the northern hemisphere, toward the largest continent. Soto would follow, but he couldn't go without a disguise.

In one of the converted passenger cabins Soto kept a wide range of clothing. He put on boots, black denim jeans, a plain white button-up shirt with no collar. A black leather vest with laser absorbing fibers that would protect his vital organs. He tied a long bandana around his neck, and put on a long coat that would hide his Kodachi. A short-topped, wide-brimmed hat covered his topknot, and a showy laser pistol went into a thigh holster on his right leg. Soto could use the pistol, but preferred the sword. He wasn't a shootist, and didn't bother with a Slinger or lightweight pistol. Instead, he carried a Heisenburg Classic. It looked like a revolver, but fired laser bolts. It had an arching grip made of pearl. Inside was a Voltex Lithium fast charging power cell capable of firing eighteen shots at full power. It was an elegant, perhaps sentimental type weapon, the kind gentlemen who had no intention of using the weapon wore.

Soto looked the part and was ready to venture out in search of his quarry. He could have flown at high altitude in search of the *Dymetr,* but he guessed that sort of search would be futile. Morgan Black would have hidden his ship. And that meant Soto would need to search the old-fashioned way. He landed on a wide patch of grassy land and went into the space yacht's auxiliary compartment. Inside was a four-wheeled electric vehicle with solar cells on the roof to recharge the batteries. He climbed inside and settled behind the wheel. A voice command was enough to open the auxiliary hatch. It lowered, creating a ramp he could drive off of. The world outside his ship was pale, dusty, and barren. A hardy, weedy grass covered the ground. Small, stunted shrubs could be seen in the distance, but no trees were visible. The sky was tainted yellow with smog. Dust devils swirled in little cyclones. It wasn't a very hospitable looking place, but he didn't expect his quarry to be hiding in the lap of luxury. Not after nearly getting killed in Luxor. Soto had been seconds away from ending Morgan Black's reign of terror. And it was time he finished the job.

The wheeled vehicle started silently, and made no noise as he pressed on the accelerator and drove out of his space yacht. The ship sealed itself off and awaited its lone occupant with a variety of security systems. Anyone trying to get close to the vessel would be met with lethal force. Soto had no concerns for his escape from the dying planet. His focus was on finding his quarry, and ending the infamous Man In Black's life. Once that was done, Soto could return to his ship and fly safely away from Dur Rohstoff. Until then, nothing else mattered but finding Black.

22

At daybreak they set out. Travis rode a roan gelding that was happy to get out of the corral and eager to stretch its legs. It hurried along until it was eventually at a gallop. Travis knew better than to fight the creature. Riding a horse wasn't like piloting a ship, or driving a hovercraft. It wasn't a mechanical device that could be controlled. It was better to harmonize with it. If the roan wanted to run, Travis would accommodate the animal.

It ran for a full mile before slowing down, eventually settling into a walk. But the horse kept its head up as it looked all around. It was almost as if the animal could tell they were on an adventure. Travis loved the freedom of the wide-open spaces on Dur Rohstoff. It was a dangerous planet, from the people to the environment, but it was also a place that was full of potential. The air had a metal tang to it thanks to the heavy industrial work that had been done there in the past. There were still cities and factories on Dur Rohstoff, but they were dangerous places that had been ravaged by almost daily earthquakes. Buildings that weren't designed to withstand the constant tectonic activity soon fell. Just riding through a town was dangerous for that reason alone. No one wanted to be caught in the collapse of a structure, and for that reason the mountains and even tall hills were avoided. Landslides and avalanches were common. In fact, many of the mountains themselves had been ripped apart and leveled by the constant quaking.

It was a full half day's ride to the Infada camp. They were a militant criminal organization built around a religious belief that included slaughtering nonbelievers. But, like every other organized crime group on Dur Rohstoff, they traded goods with one another. An hour out from their camp, he started to see other travelers. Most walked, but some rode horses or drove land vehicles. Hovercraft would have been more practical for traversing the unstable terrain, but they required much more power than a rolling vehicle. Dur Rohstoff had many things, but it couldn't sustain a reliable power grid. Solar generators kept the OC compounds running. Very little was produced on the planet. It was either stored on DR or consumed. Anything else required too much stability, and was impractical.

The Infada utilized geodesic domes to house their stolen goods, and for shelters. They were mostly made of lightweight metal frames, with layers of plastic pulled tight around the domes. The compound was laid out in a massive circle. Travis had to ride around the outskirts until he came to the portion of the compound where visitors were welcome. He tied the roan to a hitching post after getting water for him at a trough near a saloon. Then, he casually entered the dome. Inside the simple structure a bar sat in the center. It was a triangle-shaped structure, three solid pieces bolted together. The woman behind the bar had one eye, and half her face was mangled with burn scars. She had the Infada tattoos on her neck, and wore a black sleeve over one arm with scrawled white letters in a language Travis couldn't read.

He walked to the bar and leaned against it. "You sell whiskey?" he asked.

"Rum," she replied.

"I'll take that," he said. "And a beer too."

She nodded and began making the drinks. Travis looked around. The bar was surrounded by mismatched tables. Some were low, others tall. Each had a little lamp on the surface, but there was plenty of sunlight penetrating the plastic cover on the dome so that it was nearly as well-lit as being outside.

There were only a few patrons. Most sat in pairs, talking in low voices. Travis saw plenty of rough-looking individuals, but didn't see his father. The bartender set his drinks on the polished surface of the bar just as a tremor shook the compound. Travis didn't react. He continued leaning on the bar and watched the beer tremble in its mug, which made it foam and overflow the glass. Travis picked up the smaller tumbler of rum. He thought it smelled like engine cleaner. He took a sip, and let it burn through the dust in his mouth and throat that had accumulated on the long ride. The tremor subsided. The bartender swiped up the beer that had been lost from his glass, but didn't offer to top it off. Travis took another sip of the rum, then chased it down with the beer.

A man in black clothing who looked like he belonged in a desert approached. The woman fixed him a drink. It wasn't rum, and it wasn't beer. Travis didn't know what it was, but the man took it, and slugged it down, before turning toward him.

"I am Naftali Zinestra," he said. "You're not from around here."

"Just passing through," Travis said.

"Looking for something in particular, stranger?"

"Just enjoying a little civilization," Travis said.

"You want company?" Naftali asked. "A woman perhaps?"

"You never know what the night might bring," Travis replied.

"I have the best pleasure women in the area," he said. "Ask anyone. Naftali's is the finest pleasure house."

"I'll keep that in mind," Travis said.

He walked over to a table and sat down where he could see anyone that entered the dome. He nursed his drinks for nearly an hour. It was mid-afternoon when he went for a walk through the little community. There were a variety of businesses, including a barber and bath house. A mechanic who kept his tools and parts inside a vehicle with big wheels was working on an old pick-up truck near a small dome selling weapons. There were several places to eat, and several more that sold drinks. Gambling with hard dice was the game of choice. Travis saw several games in progress inside the taverns he visited. He did his best to pace himself and eat between visiting the various bars and saloons. The Infada Hard-liners didn't drink fermented beverages, but didn't count gambling or prostitution as sin. By nightfall Travis had been in all the saloons, and was settled in what he considered to be the most popular establishment. He sat at a tall table that was only big enough for two people, and not large enough for placing dice, watching the dome fill up with people. It was mostly men, but there were some women too. Most were hard-looking folk. They wore sweat stained, often threadbare clothing. Everyone carried weapons, mostly laser pistols. He saw some Slingers, but most of the people carried larger, heavier weapons that could handle larger power cells.

Eventually a person of interest came into the dome. It wasn't Leon Hurts, or Augustine Ward. Travis had seen no sign of either of them. But he did see Roman Jacowski, better known as Jaco. He was on the list that Travis had gotten from Chief Inspector Logan Brand on New Salem. Jaco was wanted for a string of murders across several worlds. Travis watched him. Jaco was a hard drinker, throwing back rum cocktails with an aggressive style. The reward for him was two hundred thousand credits. And he wasn't the only person on Logan's list to come into the bar that night.

Falisha Willcott was wanted for kidnapping and assault on Pluxo Four. Her reward was seventy-five thousand credits. She was a thick woman, both through the hips and in her arms. She had long braids with little shells tied into the bottoms that made clacking sounds when she moved. She carried a blaster butt out on her left hip, and a huge knife on her right. She wore them both high on her hips, and the weapons were like arm rests for her.

Jessup Cunningham Lucas was also known as the Mannak Mangler. Wanted on Mannak Major for a series of brutal slayings for the Infada Hardliners. He wore dark robes, and a turban on his head. Unlike Jaco who was drinking like it was his job, or Falisha who was holding court with a group of loud followers, Jessup was busy gambling. His thick mustache was wide across his face and came down to his chin. Travis wasn't certain how much Jessup's reward was, but over a hundred thousand he guessed. It wouldn't do him any good to go looking the list up while he was in the Infada saloon.

It was a night rich with opportunity, but not the one Travis wanted. He knew it would be better to fill the *Purgatory* with wanted outlaws before confronting Leon. But his father loomed large in Travis' mind. His father, wife beating killer, con man, abusive parent, and wicked narcissist. Of all the outlaws and desperados that Travis had gone against, no one had a deeper personal connection. It was one of the things he thought that made him good. He could be completely unbiased. Yes, he knew what they were wanted for, but that was just information to Travis. It was a bit like knowing what a cake was made of, but without having done the baking and mixing the individual ingredients personally, there was no connection. But Travis knew the things his father had done. He knew it, and hated it, and wanted to see his father dead or back in prison. It wasn't just a job with Leon Hurts, it was personal. And Travis didn't know if that would make him better or worse.

As the night wore on Jaco continued drinking. The rum didn't seem to impair him in any discernible way. Jessup won big at the dice tables, and moved on. Travis kept tabs on Jaco and Falisha, waiting to see who would leave first. It was Falisha. She had drunk enough, and staggered from the dome. Travis followed at a distance. She went to the latrines and Travis waited in the shadows. Eventually, she came out, wiping her mouth on her sleeve. She looked shaky and weak as Travis followed her. She made her way toward a cluster of small domes that were clearly living quarters.

Travis had already made up his mind that he would take Jaco and whoever else he could get. If he didn't have to wait too late, he could walk his prisoners back to Hogan's cabin by morning, he guessed. The only really dangerous part would be leaving one unconscious while he went back for the other. If that person was found, and an alarm was raised, he could be in serious trouble.

"Hey there," he called out. "Could you help me, ma'am."

"What the hell did you just call me?" Falisha said as she spun around with her knife drawn.

There wasn't much light in the compound at night. The smog hid the moon and stars behind a glowing pall. The spaces between the domes were gloomy. There were enough lights in the bars and taverns and pleasure houses that their domes glowed yellow in the darkness, but they did little to illuminate the dark places between them.

"Sorry?" Travis said. "Just looking for a place to piss."

"You think I care where you drain it?" Falisha said. "You come near me and I'll cut it off for you."

"No thanks," Travis said with a chuckle. "Think I'll keep it."

"Drunk fool," Falisha said.

Travis couldn't help but smile. Falisha Willcott could hardly stay on her feet, but Travis was the drunk. He drew his Slinger and made sure it was powered all the way down, then returned it to his holster. There was no need to shoot the drunken woman. Instead, he took his stun wand and extended it with a flick of his wrist. The device made a peculiar sound when it extended and locked in place. Travis had just powered it on when Falisha turned back around.

"I done warned you, fool," she snapped as she drew her knife. "Now you're gonna pay."

She bent her knees a little and leaned forward. The big blade caught what little light there was around them as she waved it in a menacing fashion. Travis saw the tiny bolt of blue energy crackle like lightning between the nodes of the stun wand.

"Falisha Willcott," he said softly. "I'm here to take you in for assault and kidnapping."

"Done heard that threat before," she said. "Ain't no one been able to carry it out. I doubt you'll be any different."

"You can drop the knife and surrender," he said.

She laughed. It was loud, and so contagious Travis found himself grinning.

"Oh, that's rich lawman. I ain't gonna make it easy on you. Best come on and get some if you're gonna. I done got me a taste for blood."

Travis nodded, and took a step forward. That was all Falisha needed to spring into action. Travis knew that some people could, under the right circumstances, sober up instantly, or while so inebriated they could barely walk, still play a musical instrument better than they could sober. For Falisha, her skill was fighting. She had been slow and unsteady before the fight started, but once it did, she moved with speed and strength. Travis was barely able to jump out of the way of her charge, and even though he thrust his stun wand at her, somehow she managed to avoid it.

"Oh, I'm gonna enjoy carving you up, baby," she said.

"Somehow, I doubt that," Travis replied.

She held the knife up and licked the spine of the blade. It was strangely intimidating. When she came at him again, she slashed the big knife like she was hoping to spill his guts. Travis didn't give her the chance. He danced backward, and brought the wand down hard across her forearm. There would be time to stun her soon enough, but first he needed to get her on her heels.

She grunted in pain, but managed to snatch up the knife with her other hand instead of dropping it.

"Gonna make you pay for that one lawman," she snarled. "Falisha done playing now."

She growled like an animal as she came forward. She moved slower, anticipating his defense. Travis considered simply drawing his

Slinger and putting her down before she got past his guard and caused damage with her knife, but he didn't want to alert the camp to his presence. He backed up slowly, waiting for a chance to use the stun wand.

Falisha feinted one way, then slid forward, jabbing at him with the knife. Travis dodged back, then lashed out with a kick that landed just inside Falisha's right knee. She howled in pain and stumbled back. Travis attacked, moving forward. Falisha waved her knife to fend him off, but he sidestepped and thrust the stun wand into her shoulder. The current, fifty thousand volts, rushed through her body. She stiffened, her eyes bulging for a second, then she dropped to the ground.

Travis looked around. No one was watching that he could see. He kicked her knife away, then bent down to check her for hidden weapons. But Falisha wasn't unconscious. She was just pretending. She grabbed the front of his coat and pulled him down on top of her.

"Got you now!" she crowed.

Travis slammed the handle of the stun wand into the side of her head. He didn't like hurting his prisoners, but when his own safety was in jeopardy, he didn't hesitate. Falisha grunted in pain. He saw her eyes roll in their sockets. It was a creepy sight, but she fell limp. Travis got to his knees beside her, checked her body and found several other small blades. And it was possible he had missed some. He rolled her over and bound her wrists with plastic restraints. Then he waited. Carrying her wouldn't work. It only took a few minutes for Falisha to regain her senses. She was furious, but fully conscious. Travis pulled her to her feet, staying behind her, holding her restraints. It was the easiest way to control an unruly captive.

"Do as I tell you and I'll let you walk out of here," he said.

"You'll cut me loose?"

"No, but I won't stun you either, Falisha," he said. "You ever been stunned?"

"Time or two," she said. "I think you concussed me, lawman. Everything's blurry."

"That might be from all the rum you were drinking," he said, leading her toward his horse at the edge of the compound."

"Yeah, I can throw it back," she said. "And I know how to have fun too. What say you take these restraints off and I'll show you how fun I can be."

"No thanks," Travis said. "You're too much woman for me."

"Oh, I know that's true, baby. Where you taking me?"

"Back to Plexo," Travis said.

"It ain't true, what they accused me of," she said. "I was railroaded. I'm innocent. I was just defending myself."

"That's not my concern," Travis said. "Take it up with your lawyer."

"Ain't got no lawyer," she said. "Are you for real right now?"

"I take you in," Travis said. "What happens after that is up to the system."

"It's a broken system," she insisted.

"Maybe so," Travis said, thinking of his million credit fine for having lost Grant Stevenson. He agreed that it wasn't fair. Nor was it always right. But what happened to a prisoner after they were turned in to the authorities wasn't Travis' concern. "Keep walking."

They moved a mile outside the compound. Travis pushed Falisha toward a jumble of boulders. "You can stay right there," he told her. "I've got business in town."

"Just gonna leave me out here in the dark?" she snarled, turning around.

Travis already had his Slinger out. The shot was quick and took Falisha down. He didn't like not being honest with his prisoners, but he knew they weren't honest with him. He would have tied Falisha up if she weren't a blade fighter. The odds that she would get to a blade hidden somewhere he hadn't found in her clothing or on her body were too high. He rolled her onto her side just in case she woke up vomiting. He knew she would have a massively terrible hangover when she came to. But that was just as much from the rum as from his stun shot. He had to hurry back to town and try to get Jaco before that opportunity got away.

Despite the danger, and the work of wrangling prisoners, Travis was starting to feel like maybe he could get enough fugitives into custody to pay off the fines. It might be possible, he thought, to get his life back. And with a fresh start, create something with Ava that was better than anything he had ever hoped for.

23

organ Black had a broken nose and a concussion. There was no need to disguise himself on Dur Rohstoff, his swollen nose and black eyes would have made him unrecognizable anyway. He had landed the *Dymetr* five miles outside of the Incendius compound. Long before he had taken the job to kill Travis Hurts, Morgan Black had a relationship with Mallorie McSwain. The two remained friends, and he occasionally visited her on Dur Rohstoff. She had no idea who he really was. To her, he was Charlie Postle, an independently wealthy businessman. She had never seen him fight, or kill anyone. And when he sent word that he was in the system, she was delighted to come and pick him up.

"You took like hell," she said as he climbed into her vehicle. "What happened?"

"I was attacked," he said. "Mugged by common thieves. I'll never go anywhere without a weapon again."

"I'm so sorry," Mallorie said.

She had no idea that he knew she was part of a criminal organization. And for over a decade she had been in charge of the

Incendius compound on DR. Even when he visited they didn't discuss much about their lives. They just enjoyed one another's company, without digging deep or getting attached. Theirs was a romance of convenience.

"Are you on anything for the pain?"

"No," he admitted, although he didn't say why he had cut the painkillers cold turkey. Secretly he had vowed to never let himself get caught with his faculties impaired. He couldn't point directly to anything that had happened in the fight on Luxor that was a result of the narcotics, but he knew he could have been slaughtered in his sleep, or chopped into little pieces, because his reflexes were slowed by the drugs. His chest still hurt, but not as much as his head. It throbbed terribly.

"Well, let's get you a drink. Have you eaten yet?"

"No," Morgan replied.

"Good. Are your teeth okay?"

"They're intact," he said. "I can eat."

"We'll go to the cantina," she said. "I've got a few loose ends to tie, and then I'm all yours."

"Good," he said. "It's been a long time."

"Too long," she agreed.

They ate enchiladas with refried beans, and rice. It was flavorful and spicy, which was ideal with the local punch. Despite his pain, Morgan enjoyed their meal. And while Mallorie McSwain went to tie up her loose ends, Morgan relaxed in the cantina with a cool drink. At least until Augustine Ward arrived. Fortunately for Morgan, he was seated in the back corner of the cantina's shipping container where the shadows were deep. If not for the little lamp on the table, they wouldn't have been able to see their food. But his face was shrouded in gloom, hiding his swollen features.

Augustine Ward was drinking. He had a woman on his arm and look of delight on his face. The woman kept whispering in his ear, but Augustine refused her suggestion. She was probably hoping to do what she got paid for. It might have been fun to drink and gamble, or at least watch Augustine gamble, but she didn't get paid for that. When the server came back to his table and refreshed his drink, Morgan asked about Augustine.

Morgan put a gold coin on the table. "Who is that man over there? The skinny one, with the pretty girl on his arm."

The server looked across the room, and nodded. "Can't say for sure," the server said. "Rumor is he and another fella broke out of Lucerine."

"Is that a fact?" Morgan asked.

"That's the word around town," she said. "I haven't seen the other guy, but that one is a big spender. You want me to make an introduction?"

"No," Morgan said. "That won't be necessary. Do you happen to know who the other fella was?"

"Just by name," the server said. "They say he's Leon Hurts. That name mean anything to you?"

It did, but Morgan lied. "No, it doesn't," he said, pushing the gold coin to the server who snatched it up.

"You need anything else? The bill still on Ms. McSwain's tab?"

"Everything but the information," Morgan said. "Thank you."

"My pleasure, mister," the server said.

She sauntered away, but Morgan didn't notice. His mind was reeling. Augustine Ward had been Travis' prisoner and a wanted man. There was no doubt in Morgan's mind that Travis would have taken Augustine in for his crimes after escaping P2. And there was simply no way that Augustine Ward could have planned an escape from a supermax penal colony. Lucerine was a barren rock. No one got close to the planet without being fully vetted. It would take major resources to get someone out, and yet there he was. Morgan wouldn't have believed it if he hadn't seen the man with his own eyes. They had history. Morgan looked specifically at Augustine's left hand, the one that Morgan had shot when they faced off. Of course, Augustine had no idea who Morgan really was. He was going by the alias Rooster, and stepped between Augustine and a miner. The gunman had been showing off, and said he would shoot with his left hand. So, Morgan had shot the gun from Augustine's hand, critically injuring two or three fingers in the process. But from where he sat, it appeared to Morgan that Augustine's left hand was just fine.

Of course, none of that was as interesting as the fact that Leon Hurts had escaped from prison. Morgan had gotten close to Travis on P2, but the bounty hunter never mentioned his felonious father. But Morgan had done his homework. It wasn't hard to look into Travis' past and discover his father was locked up on Lucerine for life. The fact that Leon had escaped prison and was on Dur Rohstoff could mean only one thing. Travis Hurts would soon be here too.

Augustine didn't stay in the cantina long, before moving on with his entourage of friends. They weren't really his friends. They were just around for the money, to party with Augustine. He was paying them to pretend to think he was great. They were no different than a whore in that respect. When the money was gone, they would be too. But as long as Augustine had coin, the group would listen to his stories and pretend he was the greatest shootist to ever live.

Morgan was only slightly concerned that Augustine Ward could recognize him. He had been on Travis' ship when Morgan freed Frank Lee Voss. How a hardened criminal could be bested by a pregnant woman Morgan didn't know, but he had. And while that seemed incredible to contemplate, the more pressing concern was that Ward could out Morgan. That would be an issue. Morgan was careful to keep his identity as the Man In Black concealed from the galaxy at large. But Augustine had an axe to grind. If nothing else, Morgan needed to make it impossible for Ward to talk about him ever again.

"All done," Mallorie McSwain said, hurrying back to the table where Morgan sat. "You ready to head back to my place?"

"More than ready," Morgan said.

"Good," she said. "Let's get out of here."

"Just lead the way, my sweet."

She took his hand, and they left the cantina. It was dark when they stepped outside, but Morgan couldn't resist the temptation to look around. He didn't see any sign of Augustine Ward. But his little getaway had been radically altered. He would have to put in some work before he left Dur Rohstoff. If he was lucky, Travis Hurts would come to him. Fate, it seemed, was keeping them together. Of all the worlds in the galaxy, they continued to meet on the same ones. Morgan wasn't drunk, but his head was buzzing. He just wasn't sure if it was from the hard punch in the cantina, or from his destiny calling him to greatness.

24

Travis got back to the compound and found Jaco in the same saloon. Somehow, the man was still drinking. Travis hadn't even seen him get up to go to the bathroom. Travis could nurse a drink for a long time, but Jaco was throwing them back with reckless abandon. As he approached, Travis could see that Jaco had a laser pistol on his hip. It was a utility weapon, and there were no additional power cells on his gun belt.

Under different circumstances he would have waited until Jaco left the saloon. It wasn't his intention to make a scene. By getting the fugitives out of the compound quietly, he remained free to keep collecting them. But he hadn't seen Jaco leave his seat all evening, and the bars in the Infada compound didn't close. Plus, Travis needed to get back to Falisha before she woke up and cut herself free of her bonds. That left him no choice but to go right at Jaco.

He was still a few paces away from the outlaw's table when he smelled the piss. It was strong and fresh. Travis looked down. Pee was dripping from the little metal chair Jaco was perched on. The geodesic domes had no flooring, just hard packed earth. The ground under Jaco's seat was dark with moisture. And the man was still drinking the rum shots as fast as the server could carry them out to him.

"I guess that's why you didn't need to go to the bathroom," Travis sighed. He reached out and put a hand on Jaco's shoulder. The wanted fugitive was trembling. He had both hands on the table where Travis could see them. He bent down close to Jaco's ear and whispered, "Time to go."

Jaco slowly turned his head and looked up at Travis, who had one hand on his Slinger. The outlaw nodded, tried to stand up, then toppled over.

"Bout time someone got that old drunk out of here," the server said. "Take the chair with you. It all smells. Last time he was here he messed himself and we had to carry him out."

"We're going," Travis said, as he pulled Jaco to his feet.

Normally, he was extremely wary about getting close to fugitives. Mack Hogan had taught him there was never a reason to let a killer get his hands on you. And Roman Jacowski was a murderer, there was no doubt about it. Yet something had happened to the man. Travis had seen him trying to drink himself to death. He was way beyond drunk, and could hardly stand up even with Travis supporting him. Somehow Travis managed to get Jaco out of the saloon.

It was nearly midnight. Travis guessed there was just enough time to reach Hogan's shack by morning if he left right away. But it was slow going with Jaco. When they reached Travis's horse, Jaco got sick, which made the horse nervous. Travis was afraid to stun Jaco. The man had drunk so much he feared it might stop the outlaw's heart. But after he finished emptying his stomach, Jaco passed out. It took Travis several minutes to get Jaco up and onto the horse. But with that managed, Travis felt confident he could leave the compound. He took Jaco's laser pistol and stuck it into one of the saddlebags, which were filled with emergency supplies. Then he led the horse away from the compound. He had gotten right to the edge of the little business section when someone called out to him.

"Hey, what are you doing with him?"

Travis turned around, and found himself face to face with Jessup Lucas and two of his companions. Travis didn't recognize the other men, but they were all heeled. He had been in enough scrapes to know when a person was spoiling for a fight. Jessup and his friends were looking for trouble, and thought they had found it.

"Taking my friend home," Travis said. "He's had too much to drink."

"Or you bushwhacked him," Jessup said.

"Who is he?" one of Jessup's companions asked.

"Roman Jacowski," Travis said.

"Oh, ain't this beautiful," Jessup said. "Now, I know you're lying, stranger. Jaco ain't got no friends."

"I knew him from Kingston," Travis said. "We did some work there together."

"Nah, we ain't buying it," the third man said.

Travis spread his hands in a placating gesture. "Well, that's the truth. He needs help."

"Jaco don't need nothing," Jessup said. "Take him down off that horse, and leave him in the street. That's where he belongs now."

"I'm not going to do that," Travis said.

"Looking for a beatdown stranger?" one of the companions threatened.

"I think maybe you ain't his friend," Jessup said. "I got a feeling maybe you're after something else, stranger. You a lawman? You here looking for bounties on honest men?"

"Like I said, he's my friend, and I'm here to help him," Travis insisted.

"And like I said, pull him off the horse, or you'll be joining him in the dirt."

"Maybe that's what he wants," one companion said.

Travis flipped the front of his poncho over his right shoulder, freeing his gun hand. He let it hang over the Stinger.

"I ain't looking for trouble," Travis said. "But if you boys want some ..."

"That a threat, Mister?" Jessup asked.

"It's a promise."

"I guess he thinks we're scared," Jessup said. "There's three of us, and one of you, Mister."

"I'll take my chances against three chumps like you," Travis said.

"That's a fancy shooter," Jessup said. "But you can't beat all three of us."

"Maybe, maybe not," Travis said. "But I know this for sure. You'll go first."

"Then we'll kill you," one of Jessup's companions threatened.

"Won't matter much to him," Travis said. "Your call. You pull on me, and I'll take you down. All three of you."

"He can't do it," one of the men said.

"He's just trying to get in your head," the other companion said.

Jessup turned his head and grinned. "As if," he said.

Travis drew his Slinger in a single fluid motion. Jessup and his friends didn't even notice until the first shot was fired. The stun beam wasn't as bright as a laser blast, but in the dark compound it was noticeable. It hit Jessup in the left side of his chest. He fell backward and Travis shot the man on his right. If Jessup's other companion had been a fast draw he might have taken Travis out. But he panicked, took a step back, and fumbled with his heavy pistol. Travis shot him down.

Three bodies lay in the street. Travis popped out the half-spent power cell on his Slinger and looked around. If anyone had even noticed the shooting, they didn't seem to care. No one came running to see what had happened. With his Slinger reloaded, he slid it back into the holsters, and turned to the horse. Hogan's animals were well trained. The roan hadn't moved when the shooting started. Travis pulled out a tarp and some rope. He tied the rope to the tarp, which spread out on the ground. Then he picked up Jessup and put him on the tarp. Next, he laid Jessup's companions beside the outlaw, one on either side. Finally, Travis tied the rope to the horse's saddle horn and let the animal pull the three unconscious men out of town.

It took half an hour to reach Falisha. She was still unconscious. In the darkness, Travis pulled his data slate and did a simple facial recognition scan of Jessup's two friends. They weren't on Logan's list, but they were wanted men. Each of them had a reward, Coby Redman for fifty thousand credits, the other, Zane Hicks, for forty thousand. By Travis's estimation he was well past the halfway mark for the seven hundred and fifty thousand credits he owed the GCIB after they stole his reward money for bringing in Victoria Hennings-Mabry. And he had done it all in one night. All he had to do was get his prisoners back to Hogan's cabin and locked up on board the Purgatory. But that wasn't going to be easy. The tarp was already torn from being dragged over the rough ground.

Travis searched all three men. They each had a couple of different weapons on them. He put everything into plastic baggies he found in the gear that Hogan had sent him out with. Travis pulled Jaco down off the horse and searched him too. The man had no other weapons, and no money. How he was going to pay for all the drinks he consumed was a mystery to Travis.

He got them all in restraints, then tied them to one another with the rope. He looped it around their necks, then tied it to the horse's saddle. There was still an hour of dark before sunrise when he broke open a cartridge of smelling salts to rouse the outlaws.

They all complained. He knew they would. They were sick too. It was part of getting stunned. Weak, sick, and completely helpless to do anything about their situation, Travis led them through the wilderness toward Hogan's cabin.

The first hour was hard. Then the sun came up and with it a heat wave. They were all dehydrated from their night of drinking.

Travis pushed them for another hour, before deciding to stop and let them rest near a spring. Travis collected a canteen full of water and dropped in a couple of old fashion iodine tablets. He shook the canteen as the tablets dissolved, then took a sip. The water had a strange, chemical taste, but it was cool and wet. He drank his fill, then poured up a small cup and let Falisha drink.

"Naw, that ain't right," she said after taking a sip. "That's bad water.'

"It's been purified," Travis said.

"No way, that's scabby water right there, now. I know it is."

"Suit yourself," Travis said. "But you fall, and we'll drag you to the ship."

He took the cup of water to Jaco, who drank eagerly. The man was barely conscious. If Travis didn't know better, he might think Jaco was on Zomlollipops or Dreamers. He refilled the cup and let Jessup drink.

"Why's it taste like that?" the outlaw complained.

"Iodine," Travis said. "It kills any bacteria or micro-organisms."

"Tastes bad," Jessup said.

"I'm surprised you can taste anything at all."

"This isn't humane treatment," the desperado complained. "You can't do this to us."

"Is that what the people you killed said?" Travis replied. "Did you listen to their pleas?"

"I never killed nobody," Jessup said. "It's a frameup."

"Sounds familiar," Travis said, looking at Falisha, who turned away angrily.

After giving everyone water, including the horse, they set out again. But they didn't go far before a cloud of dust in the distance got Travis' attention. It might have been a storm, but it was too small. If it was being kicked up by a vehicle, Travis thought he would be able to see it, or hear it. But deep in his gut he knew the truth. It was either a band of natives, or a wandering horde of Scabbies. Neither was a welcome sight. If it was just Travis, he might kick the horse into a gallop and have the roan outrun the approaching danger. But with his prisoners, running was an impossibility. Instead, he started looking for shelter.

"Hey, lawman," Jessup snapped. "You see that dust cloud. You gotta cut us loose or we'll all die."

"That's gotta be a band of natives," Coby Redman said. "They'll kill us and eat us."

"You're one sick bastard, you know that," Falisha said.

"Just keep moving," Travis said.

Fear was gnawing at Travis with every passing minute. There was no safe space in the wide-open prairie. Travis put his comlink in his ear and tapped it to activate.

"Ava, do you read me?"

He waited, hoping and praying that she was listening.

"Ava, are you there?"

Another minute passed. Then a voice sounded in his ear. "Yes, Travis, we're here. Sorry. I was in the middle of a very messy diaper, wasn't I. Yes, I was. Yes, I was, but she's all clean now."

"Ava, listen to me. I need your help."

"Is everything okay?"

"At the moment," Travis explained. "I've got five prisoners in tow."

"Five?"

"Yes, at least half of what we owe."

"Oh, Travis that's wonderful news."

"There's a problem though, Ava. Looks like a band of natives is tracking us. I can't outrun them."

"How can I help?"

"Come and get us."

"We might get seen," she reminded him.

"Can't stop that now," Travis said. "Besides, I'm leading five people with ropes around their necks. If anyone sees us they'll know I'm a Fugitive Recovery Specialist whether you pick us up in the ship or not."

"Okay, I'm on my way," she said. "But Travis, if you have to, just cut them loose and ride hard."

"I hear you," Travis said. "Hurry."

It was a relief knowing that help was on the way. But Travis knew the ship coming to get them was in many ways an even greater risk. Ava might rescue them all, but she might also get caught in the fighting. If the natives damaged the ship, they would find a way in, and kill everyone on board. Even little Kaylee. Travis had no firsthand knowledge of the native people, but he knew they weren't friendly. The stories of the roving bands of raiders had most likely been exaggerated, but Travis had no intention of betting his life on that.

"Come on!" he snapped at the prisoners. "Let's move."

"We could go faster without Jaco," Jessup complained. "Why don't you cut him loose?"

Travis ignored the suggestion, and searched the sky for signs of the *Purgatory*. It only took Ava ten minutes to reach them. But as soon as the ship appeared the natives came rushing forward. They were in ragtag outfits patched together from a variety of clothes they had stolen over time. Their bodies were streaked with red and blue paint. They had guns which they waved over their heads as they ran.

"Setting down, Travis," Ava said, her voice tense over the comlink.

"We're right on your six," Travis said. He slid down off the horse, and dropped to one knee while pulling his rifle around on the sling he kept it on. The weapon came up against his shoulder and he started shooting. The natives were still over a thousand yards away, but the ship needed time to land. The rear hatch was opening. Travis needed to slow the natives. Several of them fell under his laser fire. The Ranger was a long-distance weapon, with a powerful laser. But his battery would only give him forty shots. After that, he would have to use the Kicker, which had a fraction of the distance.

"All right," Travis said to his prisoners. "Let's go. Move! Onto the ship, now!"

He led the horse into the ship. It was nervous and didn't like walking on the metal deck.

"What is this?" Jessup demanded. "A prison ship?"

"Get on board or get left behind," Travis said, standing at the rear hatch control.

"No, we ain't getting on that thing," Jessup said angrily. "No way."

Travis drew his Slinger and zapped the outlaw. He dropped to the ground, pulling Coby Redman and Zane Hicks down with him.

"Get him on the ship, or I'll leave you all here," Travis said.

They grabbed Jessup and pulled him up the ramp. Gunshots sounded from the natives. They fired old-fashioned projectiles. Some hit the ground, kicking up little clouds of dust. Others flew past the ship. A couple even hit the *Purgatory* with resounding pings.

"Oh, hell," Falisha shouted. "I'm hit. I'm gonna die."

Travis glanced over and saw that she had been shot. Blood was running down her leg. He hit the button to raise the rear hatch.

"Ava, go!" Travis said as he fired back at the band of natives with his Ranger.

The ship lifted slowly upward, then gently began to move forward. Travis was thankful Ava was being careful. The roan was neighing and stamping its hooves on the deck. Travis watched the rear hatch close, then breathed a sigh of relief, just before Jessup's friends slammed him into the wall.

It might have been a disaster, but they weren't very smart. They tried to get the rifle, which was attached to a strap that went over Travis's shoulder and around his back. They were tugging and he was pushing. He had one hand on his Slinger, but wasn't able to yank it out before Coby got hold of his arm. Zane let go of the rifle and threw his forearm into the back of Travis' head. His face hit the unyielding metal of the hull, and split open the skin above his left eye. Then he tried to pull Travis' Kicker free of its holster. Travis managed to grab Zane's wrist. They started to push him against the wall again, but Travis got his right leg up and pushed off the wall.

Then the horse panicked. It jumped forward, yanking the prisoners as it went. They all fell to the deck. Travis got to his knees quickly, wiped the blood out of his eye, then drew his Slinger.

"Don't!" Zane shouted.

Travis shot him, and Coby Redman. He was tempted just to keep on shooting until they were dead, but he knew they wouldn't be worth anything to him then. And like it or not, he needed the reward money.

"Don't shoot me," Falisha shouted. "I'm bleeding out."

"You've got a flesh wound," Travis said. "Did the bullet come out the back of your leg?"

"It's bleedin' bad," she replied. "Blood's on both sides."

"That's a good thing," Travis said, wiping more blood off his forehead.

He had to cut Jessup, Coby, and Zane loose from each other before dragging them into separate holding cells and closing the door. Then it was Falisha's turn. She acted like she couldn't walk, so Travis pulled her in, just like the others. After cutting Jaco loose, he was the only one of the group to go willingly into his cell.

"I'm going to die in here," Falisha complained. "You gotta get me to a hospital."

Travis went past the horse to the wall that separated the cargo hold, from the engineering compartment. There was a first aid kit on the wall. He opened it, ripped open a gauze pad, and pressed it to his head. He was angry for being bushwhacked by Jessup's companions, but also glad to be alive. He felt the ship descending before Ava's voice sounded in his comlink.

"We're back at the cabin," she said.

"Good," Travis said. "I need to get the horse out of here."

"What should I do?"

"One of the prisoners needs some medical attention," Travis

said. "She got shot in the leg. But don't feel sorry for her Ava. Felisha will cut your throat to get free if she gets the chance. Don't remove her restraints until we get a chance to do a thorough search."

"Okay," Ava said.

Travis lowered the ramp and led the nervous horse out of the ship. The roan was happy to be back home and went straight into the corral. Travis got the saddle and blanket off, then went back to the ship and let Ava doctor his forehead.

"How did this happen?" she asked.

"A couple of them jumped me," Travis explained, "while I was holding off the natives."

"I can't believe you got five prisoners!"

"Me either."

"Are they all wanted?"

"Yeah, but they're not all on the list."

"So, what happens now?"

"Depends," Travis said. "Word's bound to get out. Five people missing from one compound is too many to be random. They'll put two and two together."

"And know that there's a lawman rounding up fugitives," Ava said.

"Most likely. It won't make our job any easier."

"We could just leave," she said. "Fly out of here now. We could round up another batch of fugitives somewhere else."

"Have you heard from Hogan?" Travis said, knowing the old man wasn't back or he would have met Travis in the corral.

"No," she said. "Is that bad?"

"Might be," Travis said. "We can't leave without knowing he's okay, that's for sure."

Ava had cleaned out the gash above Travis' eye. She filled it with flesh glue and pinched it closed. He winced.

"Sorry," she said.

"It's okay. I know you've got to do it."

"Smarts though, I bet."

"Like you wouldn't believe," he said.

"Lie down, Travis. I'll see to the prisoners and wait for Hogan."

"He might not come back," Travis said. "If he doesn't, you wake me up in four hours."

"Just four?"

"That's all I can afford. I'll need to go after him."

"All right," she said. "But this time we stay in contact."

"Agreed," Travis said. "That's the third time you've saved my life."

"I know," she said. "But who's counting?"

25

"Travis, wake up," Ava said.

There was a tone to her voice that Travis had rarely heard. He came awake suddenly, shaking off the sleep as his adrenaline began to pump through his system.

"What is it?"

"The natives," she said. "They're headed straight toward the cabin."

"Any word from Hogan?"

"No," she said. "Haven't seen anything, or heard anything."

"Get the ship ready to fly."

"Won't they take everything he's got?"

"Probably," Travis said.

He hurried from the living quarters to the cargo hold. The prisoners were in the holding cells, still bound. They all appeared to be sleeping, and Travis didn't have the time or the desire to check on them. Instead, he hurried out the back of the ship. He could see the natives moving across the grassy prairie. They were outside of rifle range, but wouldn't be for long. The sight of the cabin and the ship had probably excited them.

Travis ran back in the ship. "How's Kaylee?"

"Fine," Ava said. "What are we going to do?"

"Gotta find Hogan," Travis said. "I know where he keeps his money. I'll get it, and lead the horses out of the corral."

"We can't carry five horses, Travis," Ava said.

"I know," he told her. "I'll have to ride them out."

"Can you do that and stay ahead of the tribe?"

"My guess is they'll stop at Hogan's cabin for a bit to see what they can steal."

"Oh, no," Ava said.

"Nothing we can do about that," Travis said. "There's too many to fight. They're probably on their way to the Incendius compound. That's where Hogan went. We'll find him there."

"All right, but you stay in comms range," she said.

"And if anything happens to me you get off this world," Travis said.

"What about the prisoners?"

"Take them back to the New Salem. Let the GCIB sort them out."

"All right," she said. "Don't die."

"Don't plan to," he said.

They kissed. It was quick and fierce, then Ava turned to the ship's controls and Travis collected his weapons on his way out of the ship. He had spent time with Hogan on DR in the past. He knew the older man liked his independence. And that Mack Hogan kept his money in a little metal coin box that fit in a slot under the cabinet. Travis ran in, dropped to his knees, and yanked the baseboard out of its place between the cabinet and the floor. The box was there, covered with dust. Travis pulled it out. If there were keepsakes Travis didn't know where or what they were. He tucked the coin box into his coat pocket and ran back out to the corral. The horses were getting nervous. The tribe was testing the distance with their projectile weapons. They were aiming at the *Purgatory*, which was about to lift off. Travis threw a blanket over the back of the roan, and then put his saddle on the horse. The others all had bridles but no bits, and no saddles. There were a couple extra saddle blankets in the tack room. Travis put them on the other horses, and ran a rope to each of their bridles. Then he left everything else, and climbed onto the roan.

"Travis," Ava said via the comlink in his ear. "Get out of there."

"We're going," Travis said.

It didn't take much coaxing to get the roan moving, and the other four horses to follow. Travis pulled the lead rope at first, but soon the horses were cantering on their own, anxious to put some distance between them and the tribe of natives. Travis rode well away from the cabin and looked back. There were at least two hundred people in the roving band. At least a third of that number were adult men of fighting age. He could see them still headed straight for the cabin, even with the *Purgatory* and the horses gone.

"Looks like we made it," Travis said.

"For now," Ava said. "That cabin won't keep them occupied for long."

"Agreed," Travis said.

He kept the horses moving. The Incendius compound was a three-hour ride on horseback from Hogan's cabin. He sent Ava on ahead, with instructions to land on the far side of the compound. After checking his weapons, he settled in for the ride, but kept the horses moving at a quick, sustainable pace. There was a good chance that Hogan might have run into trouble in the compound. The old man was known as a horse breeder. And he had spent a long career working around criminals. He knew how to get the information he wanted without getting into trouble, but sometimes trouble found a person whether they were looking for it or not.

When the compound finally came into sight, Travis breathed a little easier. There was no sign of the natives behind him. He rode right into the compound and tied up the horses to a rail along one of the cargo containers. It was getting late in the day. The sun was headed for the western horizon, and Travis went straight into the nearest saloon. The long, narrow confines and gloomy interior felt a bit claustrophobic after being out in the open all day. Travis preferred the geodesic domes of the Infada Hardliners, but the Incendius Organization hadn't asked for his opinion. And if they knew who he was, they would kill him just for being a Fugitive Recovery Specialist.

"What'll it be?" the man behind the bar asked.

"What do you have?" Travis asked.

"Tequila, Whiskey, beer, and if those don't suit you then you best keep riding."

"Beer," Travis said. "Thanks."

He took the glass mug the bartender gave him and carried it back into the saloon. There were a couple of card games being played, and a couple of shifty looking couples that eyed Travis suspiciously. But there was no sign of Hogan. Nor was it the type of situation where a man could just ask about his missing friend.

Travis drank his beer quickly. It was the only food or drink he'd had in a while, and helped settle his nerves a little. He knew there wasn't time to dawdle. Finding Hogan before the native tribe showed up was the key.

"Any luck?" Ava asked in his comlink as he walked out of the saloon.

"Not yet," Travis said. "You in a good spot?"

"North of the compound, about two miles. Is that okay?"

"Can you see it from where you're sitting?"

"No," she said.

"Then it's perfect," Travis told her.

He went into a cafe, bought himself a burger, and ate it quickly. Hogan wasn't in the cafe either. Travis' third stop was an outdoor cantina, situated between two storage containers with sails stretched out to form an awning over the wide sitting area. Travis got himself a beer at the bar, then turned to look around. Hogan was there, but so was Augustine Ward. When Travis turned and saw the gunman, it was too late to hide.

"Hey!" Ward shouted.

He was surrounded by a group of people. They were all drinking and eating. There was a lot of laughter and loud voices.

"I know you!" Augustine shouted.

"Know you too," Travis replied. "I guess the rumors are true."

Augustine laughed. "I didn't believe it when Leon said you'd come, but here you are."

Travis glanced at Hogan, who shook his head slightly. It was a signal. He hadn't seen Travis' father. There was a slight sag in Travis' shoulders. Disappointment weighed heavy.

"Too bad he's not with you," Travis said.

"Who the hell is this guy?" one of Augustine's onlookers asked.

"That there is Travis Hurts, the bounty hunter," Augustine Ward declared. "And I'm gonna kill him."

26

Morgan had spent the night with Mallorie McSwain, and most of the following day. They had gone together to the open-air cantina for an early dinner, but McSwain was called away. Morgan wasn't surprised when Augustine Ward showed up. Morgan's face was swollen across his nose, both cheeks, and around his eyes, which were bruised a dark purple. When he looked in the mirror he hardly recognized himself, and doubted that anyone else would recognize him. And Augustine Ward wasn't paying attention to anyone but himself. He loved being the center of attention, even if it was because of his money. The man craved the spotlight more than anyone Morgan had ever met, and he had met some of the most famous people in the galaxy.

So it wasn't surprising when Augustine showed up with an entourage of onlookers. They were loud and obnoxious. And it wasn't surprising that Augustine paid Morgan no attention, and didn't recognize him. Morgan was surprised when Travis Hurts walked in. The man was unstoppable, Morgan thought. He had expected that Travis might show up sooner or later, but to see him come walking confidently into the cantina was a shock. Morgan pulled the brim of his dark hat down a little, and shifted in his seat to ensure he could get to his pistol if need be. But Travis didn't recognize him either. Perhaps that was because of Morgan's swollen face, or perhaps it was a result of the fact that Augustine was calling the bounty hunter out. It was a bold move by Ward, but a dangerous one. Of course, running wasn't much of an option on DR. It wasn't the kind of world one wanted to get lost on. And there was no place less remote than a dead planet.

"Outside," Augustine said. "Meet me in the street or I'll come looking for you, Hurts."

"I'll be there," Travis told him. "Soon as I finish my drink."

"A little liquid courage?" Augustine said. "Can't say I blame you. If I had to throw down against myself I'd be scared too."

"Oh, I don't know," Travis replied coolly. "Last time I seen you fight; you ran off like a coward with your tail between your legs."

"I'll make you regret saying that," Augustine snarled.

"I'm sure you'll try."

"In the street!" the gunman screamed.

Travis lifted his glass and turned his back on Ward, who was trembling all over with anger. Morgan watched the bounty hunter keep his eyes on Augustine Ward via the gilded mirror behind the bar. Augustine left the cantina, as did his entourage. Soon there was shouting in the streets.

Morgan didn't move. He just kept his head down and watched Travis from a distance. An older man joined him at the bar. Travis drank his beer, then set the empty bottle on the bar. Morgan saw him say something to the older man, then he turned and headed for the street.

Morgan Black couldn't help but smile, even though it hurt. He loved a good showdown, and if Travis managed to win the gunfight, Morgan had a surprise for him.

✝✝✝

Sanada Soto had just reached the Incendius Organization's compound on Dur Rohstoff. After searching a few of the others, he was beginning to feel the net closing in on his quarry. It was possible that Morgan had left the planet while Soto searched. But it seemed very unlikely that Morgan Black would run so far just for a quick layover. He had come to a dead planet to hide out, off the grid, hoping Soto wouldn't find him. But Soto was there, drawing inexorably closer moment by moment, until they met again.

The compound was full of excitement. Soto followed a group of people toward the strip. There was talk of a showdown. It was almost festive, like fans gathering before a sporting event. Soto had seen duels take place on dozens of worlds. Each one was different. The people on Dur Rohstoff seemed invigorated by the prospect of death.

Soto followed the locals to the main street, if it could be called that. There was no street to speak of, just the area between two rows of shipping containers that had been converted to businesses. Some were divided in booths, with the sides cut out where customers could walk up and inspect the goods being sold. Others were converted into buildings, cafes, taverns, and brothels. The light of day was starting to fade to a soft, golden yellow as the sun sank toward the horizon.

Soto passed horses, and wheeled vehicles. The people gathering in the street aligned themselves along the sides. Only one man was in the center of the street. He was a short, thin man with wrinkled clothes, and short-brimmed hat. His gun belt was thick, and angled down on his right side. He had a quick draw holster tied to this thigh, and he was flexing his hand over the butt of the firearm.

People were coming from all over the compound to see the showdown. Most had drinks in their hands. A breeze was blowing softly, and people were talking, their voices swirling together into a dull roar that was carried on the wind.

And then the gunslinger's opponent walked out into the street. The crowd booed savagely. Soto heard someone say it was a lawman. Soto leaned out and gave the newcomer a good look. He was surprised to recognize Travis Hurts. The man was a bounty hunter, and Dur Rohstoff was filled with outlaws, but it was still surprising for Soto to see someone he recognized. But it only confirmed that he was in the right place. Soto was fully convinced that if Travis Hurts was there, that Morgan Black was somewhere close by. He turned his attention from the gunfight to the crowds. He was no longer a spectator, he was a predator, and he was on the hunt.

✝✝✝

Leon Hurts was smoking a cigar not far from the brothel he had just left. The cigar was good, and he was feeling good. The rich smoke was pleasant and the kick from the nicotine was giving Leon a head rush. He felt almost giddy.

"Someone's having a showdown," a man running past the booth selling the cigars called out. "Come on!"

"Pardon me," the proprietor of the cigar booth said, as he hurriedly closed the window that opened into the end of the shipping container.

Leon could see people streaming in from all over, gathering in the street. He followed. When he saw Augustine he wasn't surprised. The young fool had been rushing headlong toward a bad end since they arrived on Dur Rohstoff. Leon had been pacing himself, and mentally adjusting to the fact that he was no longer a prisoner in penal colony. The change had come close to breaking him. Then fortune smiled on him with the two bumbling thieves who tried to bushwhack him. Hurting those men had reminded Leon Hurts of what he was capable of. After that, accepting the hedonistic pleasures of the compound had been a little easier. The open spaces of the dead world seemed a little less daunting.

He had eaten and had his first sip of good whiskey, before spending time in one of the many brothels along the strip. There were times when he thought he must be dreaming. There was no kindness on Lucerine, no pleasures at all, and nothing good. Yet somehow, someway, he had escaped that hellhole and found himself in a place where there were good pleasures to be had for the asking ... and a few coins. Leon didn't mind the cost. He was flush with hard credits, and starting to enjoy himself.

Augustine, on the other hand, had run from place to place like a child in a toy store. Leon didn't mind giving the younger man space. He wasn't much use to Leon anymore. The time would come when Leon might need associates, either to help him achieve some goal, or to con someone out of something he wanted, but for the time being he had no plans and didn't need anything.

Then Leon saw his son. Travis was wearing a poncho and a flat-topped, wide-brimmed hat. He moved with confidence, even though the crowd was booing him. All around Leon he heard people saying that Travis was a lawman. But Leon didn't care. He was filled with a strange sense of nostalgia and at the same time, a sudden, burning need for revenge.

"Surprised you showed, lawman," Augustine cried, playing to the crowd. "This here is Travis Hurts, bounty hunter. He's here to take you to prison. Well, you ain't taking nobody nowhere, lawman. I'm sending you to hell."

The crowd cheered their champion. Leon ignored them and stalked down the street toward the two combatants.

"Big talk, Augustine. Tell you what," Travis said. "I've got one cell left in my ship that isn't already taken. What do you say I haul you back to prison where you belong?"

"Hell no," the gunslinger said. "I ain't never going back."

"Never's a long time," Travis said.

"You got the jump on me once," Augustine called out. "But this time you'll have to face me, man to man. And I don't think you've got it in you, lawman. I know you ain't as fast as me."

"Always been fast enough, Ward. How are you gonna feel when you wake up in Purgatory?"

"I already said I wasn't going back," Augustine said. He cleared his throat and spit in the dirt. "I've heard you yakking about as much as I care to."

"You draw on me Augustine, I'll put you down," Travis said. "I didn't come here for you."

"Who'd come for?" Leon shouted as he approached Augustine from behind.

The gunman looked over his shoulder, but Leon was staring down his son. And Travis looked like he was seeing a ghost.

"Bet you never thought you'd see me again," Leon said. "In fact, I think you were counting on it."

27

Travis felt sick. His stomach was suddenly gurgling, and his legs felt weak. In all his life, no one had ever frightened him as much as his father. And seeing him after nearly twenty years of facing outlaws and gunslingers, he still felt a deep sense of terror.

"I'm here," Travis said. "But you knew I would come."

"Been counting on it," Leon said.

"This is my fight old man," Augustine said.

"Oh, be my guest," Leon said to the gunman, then turned and looked at Travis. "We'll finish our business when you're through."

Leon stepped aside and Augustine looked around.

"This crowd big enough for you?" Travis asked him.

"I want to make sure everyone sees you die."

"Jerk that pistol and we'll see who goes down."

Travis folded back the right side of his poncho, flipping it up over his shoulder. His right hand was poised just above the handle to his pistol. He had been called out, which gave him the right, legally, to draw first. But Travis wasn't concerned about legal or illegal. He didn't care that the entire crowd wanted to kill him, or

216

that even if he won the gunfight he wouldn't have any way to escape.

He reached up and tapped the comlink in his ear.

"Ava, can you hear me?"

"Yes, Travis. Did you find him."

"Yeah, I found everyone. Things are a bit testy here."

"Testy? What's that mean?"

"Means if you don't hear from me in ten minutes, you leave and don't look back."

"Travis, you're scaring me."

"Sorry about that. I love you, Ava, but I can't talk anymore. I've got business with some bad men."

"Don't you die on me, Travis Hurts. I mean it."

"Do my best. Talk to you soon."

He tapped the comlink again, and focused on Augustine Ward. The gunman was fast. Everyone knew he had a reputation. And Leon watching him felt like a lead weight on Travis' gun hand, but there was nothing he could do about it. The fight was on, and he would live or die. He had always expected his life to end at the hands of a fugitive. He was afraid, but he was also a little relieved. If he had reached the end of the line, he was going out with his boots on and facing the danger head on. A man couldn't ask for much more than that.

"You ready to die, lawman."

"I am," Travis said. "What about you? Are you ready to go back to Lucerine?. The inmates there will be happy to welcome you back."

"Told you," he snarled. "I ain't going."

With that he went for his gun. Augustine was fast. He snatched up the Slinger and cleared leather in one swift motion. Travis was fast too. He pulled his pistol out and brought it level, firing just a split second before Augustine Ward. The stun shot knocked the gunman backward, his pistol flying out of his hand.

The crowd fell silent. Travis glanced around to make sure he wouldn't get buffaloed. Every man in the crowd had a weapon. Most were wanted outlaws; the rest were desperate ruffians and criminals who worked for the Incendius Organization. Travis had no friends in the throng of people. No help. Hogan was there somewhere, but Travis had warned him what was coming and sent him for the horses.

"Not bad," Leon said, stepping from the crowd and walking toward Travis. "You're quick with that Slinger, and tenacious, I'll give you that. I like to think I gave you a little of that starch in your backbone."

"You never gave me anything but sadness," Travis said.

"You were always such a baby," Leon said. "Always crying about your mother."

"Because you killed her," Travis said, ignoring the crowd who sighed in shock at the revelation.

"You wouldn't have liked her, son. She was a taker."

"You would know," Travis said.

"You're damn right about that," Leon said. "And I've been waiting a long time for this."

He stopped just a few feet away.

"For your revenge," Travis said.

"You betrayed me. You turned your back on everything I tried to teach you. And why? So you could run off and become a lawman. Are you making up for the wrongs I made you do as a kid? Are you trying to make the galaxy a better place?"

"You taught me how lowlifes and scumbags like you think," Travis said. "And I've used that to my advantage."

"I taught you to be a man, to be a free man. But you became a slave."

"You can surrender, Leon Hurts. But one way or another, I'm taking you in."

"You plan to gun me down?"

"If I have to," Travis said.

"Tell you what, big man. I'll take off my guns, and you take off yours. We'll have it out, right here in the street. You win, you take me back to prison. I win, well ..."

"Fight! Fight! Fight!" the crowd chanted.

Leon Hurts pulled his pistol from his holster with two fingers and flung it away from him. Then he pulled out the little Sixer in his coat pocket, and threw it too. Finally, he took off his coat and hat. Someone came and took them from him. He rolled up the sleeves of his shirt and Travis could see the veins and scars on his forearms. Leon Hurts was older, but he was not elderly, not infirm.

Travis took off his hat, drew his Slinger, and put it inside the hat. He walked over to the side of the cantina. An empty chair was left near the street. Travis took off his poncho, and his Ranger rifle. He folded the poncho and laid it in the chair. The rifle was propped against the chair. On his left hip was the Kicker. He pulled it free of the backward facing holster, and set it on the chair on top of the poncho. His hat went on top of that, and he hoped that maybe Hogan would get it if he died.

When they turned back to the street, the crowd had moved closer. They formed a ring of sorts. Travis moved his head from side to side, loosening the muscles in his neck and shoulders.

"You sure you're up to this, old man?" Travis asked.

"I think I'll manage, son," Leon replied.

"Don't call me that. You were never a father."

"Who clothed you, and fed you, and put a roof over your head?"

"I did," Travis replied. "You were too drunk, or too high, or too busy plotting your schemes with the trash you associated with."

"And it taught you self-reliance."

"It taught me that I couldn't count on you."

"Can you count on this?"

Leon stepped toward Travis and threw a looping haymaker. It wasn't his best punch. There was no speed on it, and he telegraphed it so that Travis easily stepped back to avoid the blow.

"See there, I taught you some things, the important things," Leon said.

"Last chance," Travis said. "Surrender, and I won't have to hurt you."

"What's a little pain between family?"

Leon threw a quick little jab, which Travis avoided. He couldn't believe he was fighting his father. It seemed cliché but also surreal. Leon Hurts had escaped the prison colony on Lucerine and he wanted to fight Travis. Actually, Travis knew he wanted more than that. He wanted to hurt Travis, to have revenge for Travis getting him arrested and thrown in prison. He wanted to make Travis suffer, and that thought really scared him.

"You going to fight, or just run away?" Leon said.

"You don't want to fight me," Travis said.

"You're right. I want to kill you."

Suddenly, Leon exploded in rage. He dove forward, grabbing Travis just below his arms and lifting him off the ground. The older man's strength was surprising. Travis couldn't breathe, and for a split second didn't know what to do. Then Leon flung Travis to the ground. He landed hard, his head smacking the ground. But the pain spurred Travis into action. He knew he didn't want to be on the ground. He rolled to the side, coming up on one knee. But Leon was still coming for him. He threw a hard hook. Travis had to raise his arm to protect his head, but the punch still rocked him. Then Leon threw a knee at Travis' face, and he barely managed to slip to the side and avoid it.

Travis countered with an upper cut to Leon's groin. But the older man was thick through the body, and strong. He grunted with the pain of the punch, but didn't fall back. Instead, he countered with a punch that landed on the side of Travis' head. It hurt. The gash above his eye that his prisoners had dealt to him in the cargo hold of the *Purgatory* started bleeding again.

Leon grabbed a handful of Travis' hair to yank him upward. Travis didn't resist. Instead, he leaped forward, throwing his shoulder into Leon's chest. The unexpected shoulder check knocked Leon backward, and Travis followed up with a kick to the side of his father's knee. It was like kicking a tree. Leon regained his balance, absorbed the kick, and then launched himself at Travis again. They collided. Leon had more mass, and Travis was knocked backward. They fell together hard. Travis felt his back spasm, but there was no time for pain. The fight had turned into a brawl for survival. Both men where punching and kicking. The blows didn't have enough leverage to cause damage, but they were searching for their chance. Leon bent his head close to Travis, and bit him on the shoulder. Travis thrust his thumb into his father's eye. Leon roared in pain, rearing back. Travis landed a punch on the older man's chin, but it didn't even faze him. Leon dropped an elbow down onto Travis' forehead. The gash from the day before split open, and blood gushed into Travis' hair.

Twisting his body around, Travis got a leg in front of his father's face, and pushed him back. He grabbed the big man's arm, and got both legs across the front of Leon's body. Travis was just about to flex his back and hyperextend Leon's elbow. But the big man fought dirty. He bit the back of Travis' leg, and managed to land a blow to his son's groin. Travis groaned as he rolled away, but Leon was like an animal. He jumped onto Travis' back, using his weight to smash Travis on the ground.

The compound had been built on what had once been some kind of large, paved lot. The asphalt had been cracked by thousands of earthquakes, the pavement shattered and ground up into tiny bits of gravel. The shards pressed into Travis' body. He raised his head. It was an instinctive reaction, but it left his neck vulnerable. Leon wrapped a thick arm around it and squeezed. For a moment Travis felt as if his head was going to be ripped from his shoulders. He grabbed his father's arm and pulled it down. Air rushed back into Travis' lungs. But Leon smashed his own forehead into the back of Travis' skull. His face crashed against the gravel, and Leon didn't let up.

"I'm going to kill you," he snarled. "You betrayed me, Travis. You think you're better than me. I'll make you wish you had never been born."

He lifted his big body to strike another blow, but Travis turned suddenly beneath him. The younger man brought his hand up and pressed his thumb into the underside of his father's jaw. Leon immediately let Travis go and pulled back to escape the painful pressure point. Travis hit his father with a hard palm strike to the nose. The cartilage crumpled and blood sprayed from both nostrils. At the same time Leon's eyes watered hard. He didn't see what Travis was doing.

The crowd was shouting and cheering. Travis rolled away from his father and got to his feet. Leon was still on his knees, clutching at his ankle. Travis threw a kick, driving his shin into the side of his father's head. Leon went down. In a regular struggle Travis might have dived on top of his father and tried to pin his arms behind his back, but before he could, someone from the crowd threw a canned drink at him. The can was open, and only half full, but it hit him just above the ear and sent Travis staggering.

The crowd had closed in tight around the fighters. Travis staggered into someone who drove a fist into his kidney. The pain sent Travis forward a step, his back arching from the blow. Someone else spit on him, a great flood of tobacco juice. It hit his face, spattering into his eyes and burning them. Travis bent over, wiping the spit and blood away from his eyes.

When he could see again, Leon's face was red with rage. He had just pulled a pistol from his boot. There was nothing wrong with his ankle, he was getting a weapon. Travis knew he was going to die. There was nothing he could do to avoid getting shot. But then someone from the crowd stepped forward and kicked the gun from Leon's hand. It went flying away. Travis saw a man with two black eyes dart back into the crowd, and he dove toward his father.

He landed on his knees in the middle of Leon's body, driving the breath from the older man's lungs. Travis then threw an elbow at Leon's face, opening a gash between his father's nose and eye.

"You ingrate," Leon snarled, his hands reaching for Travis' throat. "You're worse than that bitch you came from."

"No!" Travis shouted, as he pounded down onto his father's face with another elbow that split Leon's lips and knocked two teeth out.

The older man spit blood and teeth, but got his hands on Travis' throat. His fingers squeezed hard. Travis hit Leon with all his strength, and felt the older man's jaw snap. The hands on his throat loosened briefly.

"Let go or I'll kill you," Travis said.

Leon couldn't talk, but he growled like an animal and dug his fingers into Travis' neck. Travis hit him again. The pain was so intense that Leon twisted hard to get away from Travis. The younger man nearly fell, but he grabbed onto the thin, stringy hair of his father's head. He pushed the top of Leon's head one way with his left hand still tangled in his father's hair. With his right he grabbed the bottom of Leon's broken jaw and pulled. The older man wailed in pain, his head twisting awkwardly. It wasn't a fast movement, but slow. Leon's head twisted; his scream was terrible. For a moment Travis considered stopping, but he knew his father would never stop. He thought about the gun he pulled from his boot. He thought about the fingers around his throat. And then suddenly there was snap that was loud enough that the crowd heard it and fell silent. Leon went limp, his neck broken. He was a big man, and still strong. But over the years his bones had lost density and grown brittle.

Travis felt a sense of relief and regret at the same time. He set his father's face down gently on the gravel. His eyes were flooded with tears. Travis wiped them away, along with the blood from the gash in his forehead, and stood up on trembling legs. It was a terrible thing to realize that a parent doesn't love their child. It's even worse when the parent habitually abuses that child. But

Travis had endured the lack of love and the constant abuse. He had risen above and made a name for himself despite it all. And yet, none of that pain had prepared him for the crushing guilt and shame of having to kill his father. He screamed in frustration and rage.

The crowd screamed with him, some laughing, others applauding. They didn't know what Travis had done. They didn't understand or care. But it was over. Travis didn't care what happened to him. All he could think was that he had killed his father, and what did that say about him as a man?

"Guess it's my turn," someone said.

"Yeah, he ain't getting out of here alive," someone else said.

"He's a lawman."

"Send him to hell."

"I say we hang him."

"Let him rot."

Then a familiar voice spoke up. It broke through Travis' fog of guilt and shame. "Hello Travis."

He looked up and saw a face he could barely recognize. Morgan's nose was swollen, his eyes mere slits in the blackened skin. But his voice was the same. It was one he had heard in his nightmares many times since their showdown on Pergamum Prime.

"Black," Travis said.

"Everyone back up," Morgan shouted. "This man and I have unfinished business."

Travis was exhausted and had no weapons. There was no way for him to escape, and the crowd began moving. They went from encircling the combatants, to forming a narrow corridor so that when the shooting started, they couldn't get hit in the crossfire. The only problem with that was that Travis was unarmed.

"How'd you know I was here?" Travis asked.

"I've got a tracker on that ugly ship of yours," Morgan said, "since Las Brazzas."

He did have a tracker on the *Purgatory* but he hadn't checked it since nearly getting himself killed on Expanse. Morgan felt that Travis had cheated him by wearing body armor, but it seemed that his luck had finally broken in Morgan's favor. He had run to Dur Rohstoff to escape his own silent assassin, only to discover that Travis was in the same place.

Travis realized what a huge mistake it had been not to take Morgan's threat more seriously. It had crossed his mind to check the *Purgatory* for a tracker, but something always came up.

"I should have killed you on Expanse," Travis said.

"But you didn't," Morgan replied. "You failed on P2, you ran like a coward on Las Brazzas, and you failed again on Expanse."

"You were the one with a contract to kill me," Travis said.

"And now I'm going to fulfill it," Morgan said. "Normally, I wouldn't draw on an unarmed man. But since you didn't play by the rules the last time ..."

Morgan was wearing a jacket. He pulled it back and tucked it behind the holster on his right hip. Travis recognized the Ripper he had been shot with on Expanse. Even with body armor on that had been a horrible experience. At least he would be dead, he thought, and wouldn't be in pain once Morgan shot him with the powerful blaster.

But before anything could happen between them an alarm sounded. A voice carried on a public address system sounded frantic.

"Natives approaching. Natives approaching. Prepare to fend off a raid!"

The crowd reacted instantly. The Incendius people ran to get into position to hold off the tribe of natives approaching the compound. But at least half of the crowd were people from outside the compound who were there for business or pleasure. Many of them ran to escape. A cloud of dust rose up around Travis and Morgan. When he looked over he saw the chair with his poncho, hat, and weapons. They seemed untouched, but he had no chance of getting to them before Morgan shot him down. All around the

Strip the merchants were closing up their shops and locking things down in case the natives got past their defenses.

"Maybe we should help them," Travis said.

"Who cares about this place?" Morgan replied. "If the savages want to die trying to get their hands on a few trinkets, what difference does it make?"

"Let me get my gun and we'll finish this business between us."

"It's already finished, you just don't know it yet," Morgan said. "And you can go to your grave knowing that the widow woman and her pup will be joining you soon."

"Leave them out of this," Travis said.

Morgan touched his swollen face. "She asked for it when she shot me, remember?"

"There's no profit in it," Travis said. "You'll be hunted down like a dog."

"I've killed hundreds of people, and no one even knows who I am."

"I know," Soto said, appearing out of the rushing crowd and dust like an apparition.

Morgan whirled. He drew his Ripper as he turned but Travis saw Soto's blade come to meet the weapon. It severed Morgan's hand cleanly at the wrist, but at the same time the gun went off. It knocked Soto backward.

"Got him!" Morgan shouted, as he held up his arm.

Travis saw the blood spurt upward, and then he turned and ran for his own weapons. He couldn't imagine losing a limb, or the pain Morgan Black was in. But he wasn't surprised when the infamous assassin found another weapon and began shooting at Travis. He grabbed his Ranger rifle and dove for the corner of the shipping container that made up one half of the outdoor cantina. Laser beams ricocheted off the sturdy metal siding, but missed Travis. He brought the rifle to his shoulder and leaned out to take aim. Morgan Black was staggering back and forth, still shooting the Sixer he kept hidden on his body, but the weapon was out of power.

Travis stepped out from behind the cover. Morgan pointed the little pistol at him and pulled the trigger, but nothing happened. The assassin was in shock. He couldn't understand what was happening. Travis raised the butt of his rifle and slammed it into the side of Morgan's head. He dropped to the ground. Travis bent down and slid a plastic restraint over the severed wrist. He slid it up to just below Morgan's elbow and tightened it to make a tourniquet.

No one was concerned about him anymore. There were people moving in the street, rushing to find cover or try to escape. Travis saw his father's body, and that of Augustine Ward too. He needed to get to the ship, but it was two miles away, and Travis was in no shape to carry anyone anywhere. He turned, looking for Soto, but there was nobody. Travis had no idea how badly the avenger was hurt, but he didn't have the time to worry about it either.

Suddenly a horse appeared out of the dust. Hogan leaned forward in the saddle, looking at all the bodies in the street.

"You're a hell of a fighter," the older man said. "Throw them bodies on the spare horses and let's get out of here."

Travis lifted Morgan Black and flung him across one of the horses he had brought from Hogan ranch. Augustine went across the back of another. Travis was tired, hurting, and afraid that he was taking too long, but he went to his father. Leon lay face down on the street. Travis rolled him over. His head stayed twisted at an unnatural angle. It took all of Travis' strength to lift the dead man.

"Hurry, the natives are breaking past the defenses," Hogan said.

Travis hadn't seen the raiders, but he didn't doubt his friend. He flung his father onto a horse. The body hung off on either side. There was no time to secure it. Instead, Travis climbed into the saddle on the roan and followed Hogan through the compound.

"Can't just run," he said. "They'll have auto cannons set up. That's why the raiders hit the Strip instead of sneaking around the back of the compound."

"What are you saying? Are we trapped here?" Travis asked as

they led the horses through the stacks of stolen goods that were laid out in the center of the Incendius compound.

"No, but we need to hit the generators," Hogan said. "And take down at least one of the cannons."

"I don't suppose you've got explosives in the saddle bags."

"Don't need it," Hogan said. "Just stay close to me and watch my back."

Travis had left his Slinger and the Kicker behind. But he had his Ranger rifle with a full battery. It would be enough to keep anyone from getting close. Hogan was familiar with the camp. He didn't bother sabotaging the generators. It was enough just to shut them down. In the confusion of the attack by the natives, no one would care about the power station. What they didn't think of was that the auto cannons used the power from the generators to keep their battery supplies filled.

Travis saw several native warriors with their painted bodies running through the camp. Laser fire flashed from the Strip. Hogan got remounted, then hurried toward the edge of the camp. Somehow, the bodies stayed put on the horses. Travis had to climb up onto one of the shipping containers to deactivate one of the auto cannons, but had a moment of inspiration and turned the weapon around instead. He didn't deactivate it, but rather set it face into the compound. That would keep anyone from coming directly behind them. Not that anyone from the compound was even thinking about what Travis and Hogan were doing. It was a struggle, a desperate fight for survival along the Strip. If the entire camp hadn't been enthralled with the showdown between Travis and Augustine Ward, followed by the fight with his father, they would have seen the natives coming in time to mount a proper defense.

He climbed back down from the shipping container and mounted up. They got out of the compound and moved north. It was wide open country. They were several hundred yards from the compound when Morgan fell off his horse. Travis stopped long enough to get him back on the animal, and Hogan helped secure them.

"Think he'll live long enough to be worth messing with?" Hogan asked.

"Do you know who that is?" Travis asked.

"No clue," the older man said. "Looks sorta like a raccoon with them black eyes."

"That's Morgan Black," Travis said.

"That lump is the Man In Black?"

"One and the same," Travis said.

"Don't seem so scary to me," Hogan said.

"He was scary fast on the draw," Travis said. "But not fast enough."

"How'd you cut off his hand?"

"I didn't," Travis said. "Remember the avenger I told you about? A guy called Soto?"

"The one who took Grant Stevenson from your ship?"

"Yeah," Travis said. "He was here."

"What happened to him?"

"Got hit. I guess the impulse to pull the trigger still worked even with a severed hand."

"Ain't that something," Hogan said. "I've heard it said a viper will still bite you after its head is cut off."

"Must be true," Travis replied. "I'll take Morgan to the authorities, whether he lives or dies."

"With this passel of criminals, they'll have to back off that fine," Hogan said. "What'll you do now that you've caught the most wanted man in the galaxy?"

"Maybe I'll follow your lead and retire somewhere," Travis said.

"Ha! Somehow, I doubt that."

They reached the ship and got the criminals locked in the holding cells. Augustine Ward was locked in with Falisha Willcott. Travis didn't trust Morgan Black not to kill anyone he was locked up with. The prisoners were all unconscious, which made things a bit less stressful, but Ava was ready to leave immediately.

"I got your money box from the cabin before the natives raided it," Travis said. "It's in your saddlebag."

"Much obliged," Hogan said.

"You're welcome to come with us," Travis said. "You can set up a homestead on Expanse. They need good horses there too."

"Can't leave these behind," Hogan said. "Maybe I'll sell 'em and meet you out there on the fringe one of these days."

"We'd like that," Travis said.

They shook hands. "It's always an adventure when you come around, Travis."

"Thanks," Travis said. "Thank you for everything, Mack."

"Better get moving before Morgan Black bleeds out."

Travis walked up the rear hatch, turned and waved as he hit the controls to close the ramp. Hogan waved back, then turned his horses and rode away.

"Ava, let's get off this rock," Travis said.

"On our way," she replied.

Travis turned and looked at the body of his father laid out on the deck between the holding cells and the engineering section of the ship. It was a stark reminder of how close he had come to dying himself. And while he wanted nothing more than to clean himself up and go to sleep, he forced himself to get the medical kit and see to Morgan Black.

28

Soto limped to a narrow space between two shipping containers. The laser blast from Morgan's Ripper had blown a chunk of flesh from the outside of his thigh that was nearly as big as Soto's fist. He was sweating, his leg was pure agony. The laser had burned through muscle, cauterizing the wound, but leaving him in a pain so exquisite, Soto wasn't sure that he wouldn't pass out from it.

He leaned against one of the cargo containers. There was fighting all around him. He needed the chaos to wane a little before he tried to reach his ship. He looked down at the wound. It was nasty. Through a scorched hole in his breeches, he could see muscles and tissue. It was blackened and smelled terrible. A cloudy fluid was seeping from the wound too. Looking at it made Soto's stomach twist. He leaned over and threw up.

Part of being a warrior was understanding injuries, and how the human body reacted to trauma. Soto knew he was in shock. He had severed Morgan's gun hand cleanly, and it didn't make sense to him how it still pulled the trigger of the gun. But he was lucky it hadn't hit further over on his body. If it had blown a hole in the middle of his leg he wouldn't have been able to walk at all, not with his femur vaporized by the laser blast.

He straightened up, wiped his mouth with the sleeve of his coat, and then flung his hat away. His jacket was next, although he cut it into strips and tied one around his leg. It wasn't bleeding, so that wasn't an issue, but the counter pressure helped ease his agony a tiny bit. A desperate man rushed into the narrow alley with Soto, his face covered with dust and sweat.

"I'm out of ammo," the man said, looking at Soto for help.

Soto lashed out with his Kodachi, slashing the desperado's throat so fast the man never knew what happened. He topped back into the street, his head nearly severed from his body, and bled to death.

Limping out after the man, Soto saw bodies everywhere. It was a pitched battle between the Incendius Organization's people and the natives. Some of the locals pitched in, but most were just looking for a way to escape. There was movement in the camp, and then explosions as one of the big auto cannons opened fire back in toward the compound. Soto had a transport. It was a wheeled vehicle that he had parked at the end of the strip. He just had to get there without getting himself killed.

A native warrior rushed at him through the clouds of dust. The man was tall and lean, with red and blue paint across his bare chest and shoulders. He carried a lance with a wicked-looking metal spearhead. Soto bent his knees as he started to go into a fighting stance, but the pain in his left leg made it give out beneath him. He fell to the ground. The native suddenly loomed over Soto and rammed the spear towards his face. Soto dodged to the side, but didn't quite escape the attack. He felt a fiery thread burn down his cheek from the spear blade. And at the same time Soto drew his Kodachi and thrust it upward into the native's stomach. Blood poured over him for a second, and then the man stumbled back. Soto held onto his sword as the man backed away, freeing himself from the blade as blood and entrails poured out of the hole in his stomach.

Soto sat up, then used the native's spear to help him get to his feet. He pulled the weapon out of the ground, and turned it so that the point was facing the sky. Then he leaned on the lance as he hobbled toward the edge of the strip. More people raced past him. Another warrior in red and blue tried to club Soto with the butt of an old rifle. But Soto ducked under the attack and cut a deep gash across the warrior's side. The man stumbled away, trying to hold himself together.

Soto never saw who shot him. The bullet was hot as it punched into his chest on the right side. He fell. Part of him wanted to close his eyes and let the pain wash him away into the darkness. Breathing was difficult and each breath sent waves of pain through his body. It was so intense that he forgot about his leg. There was a fire in his chest that couldn't be quenched. Yet somehow he got back up, and kept moving.

Perhaps because he was covered in blood, or maybe because he could barely stay on his feet, no one else accosted him. He staggered past the last of the shipping containers and saw his vehicle. The doors were open, but otherwise it looked intact. He had the fob in his pocket that allowed the vehicle to start. He got to the vehicle, let the spear fall to the ground, and leaned on the engine compartment as he shuffled to the driver's door. The seats had been cut, and the digital instrument display was shattered. But there wasn't much of value in the vehicle. Soto dropped into the driver's seat and reached forward with a trembling hand to push the activation button. He didn't bother to close the doors. He shifted the vehicle into drive and pressed the accelerator. It shot forward. He could barely steer, and every bound was agonizing. Eventually, Soto got clear of the fighting. And then he passed out.

When he woke up, he was out of the vehicle and on the ground. There was a saddle under his head, and he could see the glow of the smog layer in the night sky, lit by stars and the light from a full moon on the far side of the pollution. He reached up toward his chest. There was a bandage covering it, but no shirt.

"You're lucky it was a small caliber bullet," a stranger said.

"Who are you?" Soto managed to say, his voice cracking as if he hadn't had anything to drink in ages.

The stranger put a canteen to his lips and let some tepid water flow across his tongue and down his throat.

"I'm Mack Hogan," the stranger said. "Found you out here bleeding to death."

"The bullet?"

"I got it out," Hogan said. "I figured it was only fair since you saved Travis' life."

"You know him?"

"I do," the stranger said. "For a long time now. Good man."

"Hai," Soto said. "He is honorable."

"That's a good word for it," Hogan said. "You know killing people is against the law."

Soto didn't respond.

"Not that I care," Hogan continued. "Seems to me like you're killing the right people."

He gave Soto some more water. Everything hurt. His chest was still on fire, and his thigh too, but he was alive, and his mind seemed to be clearing. But he knew he needed more rest. There was no way he was going to get up and find a way back to his ship in the condition he was in.

"Go ahead and get some sleep," Hogan urged him. "I ain't going nowhere. The horses will warn us if anyone comes around."

"How can I repay your kindness?" Soto asked.

"No need to," Hogan replied.

"Must," Soto replied, thinking that he didn't want to be in anyone's debt. Nor did he want to create bad karma for himself by taking the stranger's actions for granted.

"Well, I'm planning to sell these horses and get off this shaky rock before it comes apart. I'm guessing you've got a ship here somewhere."

"Hai," Soto acknowledged.

"Well, I wouldn't say no to lift to someplace a little more civilized. I'm getting too old to be fighting for my life all the time."

Soto turned his head and saw three horses on leads that were tied to the rear bumper of the vehicle that Soto had been in. There were three more on the other side. He froze when he heard the whisper of steel on the wooden scabbard.

"Hell of a sword you've got here," the older man said. "I did my best to clean it up for you. Your clothes are drying, but might still be a few hours after sunup before they're ready to wear. I figure you need that much time to recover anyhow."

The sword hissed as it slid back into the scabbard. The guard clacked against the wood as it seated home. The stranger put it beside Soto, who closed his hand around it. It felt good to have the weapon, as if some strength from the Kodachi flowed into Soto's broken body. He would live, that was good. And he wasn't alone. Fortune had smiled on Soto. He could have been found by outlaws or some of the natives. Or just forgotten and left to die all alone. Instead, he had been discovered by someone who was friendly, and who had helped him. That was more than he could have hoped for. It meant his task in the galaxy wasn't finished. He would live to fight another day, and that was the thought he focused on as he drifted off to sleep.

29

Travis gave Morgan a dose of morphine before he used the surgical laser to cauterize his stump. He still screamed in pain and passed out. But Travis got it bandaged up, then made his way to the cockpit.

"We're in orbit," Ava said.

"Smooth," Travis said. "I didn't even notice the transition."

"You look like you wouldn't notice it if you were run over by a train," she said. "What happened."

"Set the autopilot and I'll tell you all about it."

He stumbled to the bathroom and got his filthy clothes off. He was sore, his throat bruised, the eye under the gash was blackened. Ava came in and disinfected his wound. She sealed it with flesh glue again, and after he showered she covered it with a bandage.

Travis told her about the fight. He cried as he told her about killing his father.

"I'm sure you didn't have a choice," she said. "It's a miracle you survived at all."

"Everything happened so fast," Travis told her.

"And now it's over," she said. "You can sleep. I've already set a course for New Salem. We'll be there in six hours. You want some-thing to eat?"

"No," Travis said.

She helped him to the bunk and stayed beside him for a while as he slept. Eventually Kaylee needed to eat. Then she checked on the prisoners. Some were waking up from being stunned. They were sick from the stun blast hangover, and complained about their treatment, especially Falisha Willcott. She didn't like being in a cell with a man. Augustine Ward was out cold, and Ava wasn't going to try and move anyone without Travis' help.

They arrived in the Francisco system low on fuel, but without any incidents. She woke Travis, who messaged the GCIB. When the ship docked at the station there was an entire squad of law enforcement waiting, along with EMTs with a hover gurney.

"Is it true," Logan Brand asked when Travis and Ava opened the airlock. "Did you really get Morgan Black?"

"He's in there," Travis said. "He would have gunned me down but I got some help. He lost his hand."

"Man, I don't know how you're still standing here," Logan said. "It's unbelievable."

"Yeah, tell me about it," Travis said.

He led the EMTs in. They took Morgan Black away on the gurney. The other prisoners were led out by the law enforcement officials. Travis and Ava were taken down to the GCIB level where they were questioned individually. After telling the entire story three times, to three separate officials, Travis was tired. The little interrogation room was spotless, but it felt like a prison cell to Travis. And that only got worse when the door opened and Logan led Special Prosecutor Sabrina Astor inside.

"What is it now?" Travis asked.

"I have questions about Leon Hurts," Astor said.

"He's dead," Travis said.

Logan leaned against the wall behind Astor and didn't say anything.

"Yes, that's been confirmed. Initial report is that he died from a broken neck," she said. "Can you explain how that happened?"

"I already have," Travis said. "Three times."

"You really expect us to believe you murdered your father?"

"I didn't murder him," Travis said. "We fought. He was trying to kill me. I was afraid for my life and did what I had to do to survive."

"Convenient," she said. "We're just supposed to take your word for it?"

"You can go to Dur Rohstoff and see for yourself. There's bound to be a person or two who survived the raid that can corroborate my story."

"Don't get cute with me, Hurts. You're looking at a murder charge."

"I believe there was a reward for Leon Hurts," Travis said. "Dead, or alive. You have no grounds to accuse me of anything."

"He was your father. I think you killed him out of spite."

"Lady, you don't know what the hell you're talking about," Travis said.

"He was a fugitive from justice," Logan said quietly. "The report on him said he was considered extremely dangerous."

"That doesn't give a Recovery Specialist the right to administer whatever justice they see fit," the special prosecutor snapped. "I should yank your license right now."

"But he repaid his fine," Logan said. "We've confirmed Morgan Black's identity. He's wanted for multiple homicides on several systems. And he carried the biggest reward I've ever seen. A full million credits, which more than satisfies the fine you levied."

"I want him held for questioning," the Special Prosecutor said.

"That's outside the limits of your office," Logan said. "I've already spoken to the criminal prosecutor. He has no interest in charging Travis Hurts with a crime."

"Then I'll charge him with obstructing my investigation," she snarled, turning against Logan. "And that goes for anyone who tries to help him."

"Word already leaked to the press," Logan said. "They know he captured The Man In Black."

"Then you'll be charged for leaking that information."

"Wasn't me," Logan said. "I haven't spoken to anyone. But the medical staff doesn't have the same protocols as we do. The EMTs probably started posting about it online the minute they dropped him at the medical ward. You charge Travis with a crime, especially some bogus charge that won't stick, and you'll lose whatever political backing got you to this position."

"This isn't over," she snarled, turning back to Travis. "You're a lucky man, Travis Hurts. But no one stays lucky forever."

"That mean I'm free to go?"

She didn't answer. Instead, she stormed out of the room, and Logan waved for Travis to leave as well. They walked toward the bank of elevators.

"Ava was sent back to the ship with little Kaylee a couple of hours ago," Logan said. "And I saw to the reward confirmations myself. The money should be in your account by now."

"That's good," Travis said. "I didn't know how I was going to pay the docking fee, much less refuel the ship."

"Well, you've got plenty of credits in the bank now. Nearly a million all told. You can do whatever you want. Know where you're headed?"

"Scye Primary, in the Toothsbury system," Travis said. "I owe Eduardo Hernandez for some work he's doing for us."

"And after that?"

"After that I honestly have no idea," Travis said.

"Well, stay out of trouble. There's going to be plenty of people who want to buy you a drink for bringing in Morgan Black."

"And plenty of outlaws who want to pad their reputation by saying they killed the man who took down the Wraith."

"Yeah," Logan said. "Better watch your back. And, there's just one last question."

"What?" Travis asked.

"Your father's body. We've confirmed his identity, the Galactic Coalition is through with him. Do you want to see about his final arrangements?"

Travis didn't answer right away. It felt terrible to have lost the last thread of his past. He was an orphan again. Leon Hurts had been a terrible father, and there was no love in Travis' heart for the man, but he still felt a little untethered knowing he was dead. But then he thought about Ava, and Kaylee. He had no connections to his past remaining, but he had good things in his future.

"No," he said. "He's your problem now."

"You sure about that?"

"Absolutely," Travis said. "I'm moving on."

"Glad to hear it," Logan said.

They shook hands and Travis got on the elevator. When he reached the ship he found that it was already refueled and ready to go.

"I was beginning to wonder what else that witch might conjure up against you," Ava said when she saw him. "She came to question me. Special Prosecutor Sabrina Astor, like that's supposed to intimidate me."

"She saw me too," Travis said. "Threatened to charge me with murder."

"Are you serious?"

"Yep," Travis said. "Logan backed her down, but who knows for how long."

"She's out of her mind. They need to lock her up."

"Some people aren't happy unless they're making other people miserable. On the other hand, did you hear about the reward?"

"What reward?"

"Morgan Black was wanted for a million credits," Travis said.

"But no one knows who he is," Ava said. "How can they be sure?"

"DNA evidence is enough. They'll want to charge him. It'll be a circus, for sure, but Logan pushed through the reward."

"So, we're free?"

"We are and we've got money."

"How much money?"

"Enough to get the ship extension thing you talked about. Or to build a big, pretty house on Expanse. Whatever you want after we repay Eduardo Hernandez."

"All I want is you, Travis," she said, wrapping her arms around his neck.

"We're free, Ava," he said, kissing her gently. "We can go where we want, and do what we want. I say we take our time deciding."

"I think that sounds wonderful," she said. "No one is trying to kill us anymore?"

"No," Travis said. "That's all in the past."

Epilogue

"I want him dead!" Dice Jester shouted. He pounded the table with his fist. "Nobody insults this organization and walks away. Who the hell does this guy think he is?"

"He captured Morgan Black," Sid Ott said.

"And destroyed the compound on Dur Rohstoff," Lucious Grieves added.

"How much?" Jester asked. "How much did this prick cost us?"

"Hard to say," Sid replied. "Billions on DR. Plus the millions you already paid Black."

"And Iona Freeze failed," Harv Butler said. "She spent millions getting the bounty hunter's old man out of Lucerine."

"And burned our contacts there in the process," Lucious added.

"It's a disaster," Dice said. "I want him here. I want him alive. I'm going to carve him up myself. I want it to last days, weeks maybe. Nothing else matters. We send everything, no matter what it costs. Travis Hurts is a dead man. No matter where he goes, we'll have people waiting. There ain't no place safe for that bastard anywhere in the galaxy."

"We'll make it happen boss," Sid said.

"Then why are sitting here?" Dice shouted. "Go! Do it. Get me that bounty hunter and bring me Freeze too!"

Author's Note

It's not often a writer gets to tell an epic story like the Travis Hurts novels. There's always a reason to write something else. If you've made it this far, thank you so much for reading. I hope you have loved the stories as much as I have.

Please leave a rating or a review on Amazon or Goodreads.

Read on for an (unedited) sample of the fourth and final book in the Travis Hurts series, *Lingering Threat*.

Lingering Threat Prologue

She didn't have to wait long. The attack came from one of her lieutenants. Iona Freeze had known it was coming, just not from who, and not when.

Failure was not something she was accustomed to. But she had failed to ensure that Travis Hurts was killed. That was the task Dice Jester had given her. It didn't matter that Morgan Black had been captured without completing the job. Or that her own plan of springing Leon Hurts had been a bust either. It was all on her head, and the Incendius Organization didn't accept failure, either real or perceived.

She had just finished working out. Iona Freeze was a purist in the gym who enjoyed lifting heavy weights. Unlike most women who focused on body sculpting, Iona was fully devoted to strength training. And after years of daily workouts, she could outfit most men. But that wasn't why she did it. Iona liked being strong. And she like the message it sent to the people around her. She wore a snug fitting leather vest with nothing underneath it. She liked showing off her arms and shoulders, and even the muscle striations across her upper chest. It wasn't the type of beauty that many women aspired to, and to many people it was a turn off. But Iona wasn't interested in winning a beauty competition or finding a husband. Fear was her goal, and with her muscular physique, and angular features, just one look at her made most people uncomfortable.

Meesha Tate had always claimed to have a similar interest. Not in strength training, but in gaining respect through fear. She was in many ways the opposite of Iona, a woman who looked completely harmless. But in reality, she was a ruthless killer, especially with a knife. While Iona trained with weights, Meesha trained in Kali martial arts. It was a weapons based fighting system, and she could twirl her custom blades in a beautiful display. Iona had seen her slash a man's throat before he knew she was a threat. Since then, Iona had always kept her distance from Meesha, which was what saved her when the inevitable betrayal happened.

They were on the Putnam Exchange, a large space station that was located on one of the galaxy's most often used trade routes. It was Iona's second home, and she kept a small apartment on Putnam. Her best people ran a few rackets on the exchange. It was the perfect place to move stolen goods, partly because of the amount of trade that took place on Putnam, and partly because she was bribing most of the Transit Authority officers on the exchange to look the other way.

Iona came out of the gym with a towel around her neck. Meesha approached holding her data slate in one hand. Iona knew that sooner or later Dice would want her dead. She was paranoid, but she knew how the game was played. Word had gotten out that the boss of the Incendius Organization wanted Travis Hurts dead. But the bounty hunter was still alive, and had recently apprehended the most feared assassin in the galaxy. It was a bad look for the crime boss. He appeared weak. In fact, if Iona hadn't been his target she would have been plotting to have him killed so she could take his place. But she had become his scape goat, and he would have her killed to restore his reputation.

"I just got word from on high," Meesha said as she approached Iona. "They've got a new plan."

"What is it?" Iona asked, pretending to wipe the sweat from her forehead.

"They want you dead!" Meesha snarled.

The blade was fast. It cut through half the towel that Iona used to block the slash at her throat. But it wasn't an unexpected attack. Meesha hadn't caught her boss unprepared. Iona wrapped Meesha's hand, and the blade, in the towel, then kicked Meesha's knee. It was a simple, stomping action, but with her heavy, lace up boots, the blow was powerful. The strike came down and forced Meesha's leg to bend the wrong way. She screamed and stumbled back, limping from the pain in her leg.

"It didn't take them long to turn you," Iona said, stalking down her associate.

"They didn't have to," Meesha said, waving her curved knife blade in a menacing fashion. "You've lost touch. It's time for new leadership."

It was the way the gangsters to always be testing the limits of the person above them. It took ambition to break the law. People who were risk adverse didn't become outlaws. And those that did were always looking for their next target, a better con. Iona had risen through the ranks because she could get things done, often better than her male counterparts. And she was an earner too, with schemes on a dozen worlds. Each scheme was run by teams of hand picked people, many were made men and women with strong ties to the Incendius Organization.

Iona feinted one way, then lunged the other. It wasn't an unexpected move, but with one leg throbbing in pain from being kicked in the knee, Meesha wasn't agile enough to dodge out of the way. She tried to stab Iona, but the stronger woman caught her wrist with one hand, and punched her straight in the face with the other.

Iona stumbled backward, her head hitting a metal wall. She groaned, bent double, then straightened with a laser pistol in her hand. It was a tiny, one shot, laser weapon called a Stinger, but one powerful enough to kill. But before she could point the weapon at her boss, Iona grabbed the hand with the knife and twisted it hard. He wrist bent backward and Iona shoved it into Meesha's stomach. The Stinger fell from her hand, and she looked up with fear in her eyes.

"You shoulda had my back," Iona said.

"You killed me."

"You're lucky I can't kill you twice, because I would," Iona said.

She backhanded her association hard enough to send her sprawling on the deck. Then she picked up the Stinger and looked at the tiny weapon. It was made of some fancy material, maybe carbon fiber, or some exotic polymer. It probably wouldn't get pinged by a metal detector, the perfect self defense weapon for a criminal who always needed to protect herself.

"Did the boss really order a hit?"

"No," Meesha said in a weak voice that was barely more than a whisper. "I thought..."

"You thought you would be proactive and bring the boss my head," Iona said. "Did you really think I wouldn't see you coming a mile away."

"You've been slipping."

"No, I've been trusting the wrong people," Iona said, pointing the Stinger at Meesha.

The woman had once been a close confident, but that relationship was forever shattered by Meesha's betrayal.

"And I'm correcting that mistake," Iona continued, just before she pulled the trigger.

The laser beam wasn't powerful, but a close range it was deadly. It hit Meesha in the left side of her chest, the focused light vaporizing skin, muscle, and bone, before burning through her heart. She died instantly, and Iona began making plans to get off Putnam and track down Travis Hurts. The only way she survived was to kill the bounty hunter herself. And she had an idea of how she might pull it off.

Lingering Threat Chapter 1

"It's used," Ava said, "but's made for a Econo Freighter 228, just like the *Purgatory*."

"You're kidding," Travis said, not quiet believing she had done it.

"No, it's only four hundred and ninety-nine thousand."

"Half a million credits?"

She shrugged. "It's pretty nice. A full galley. A bigger bathroom."

"And it fits our ship?"

"Yes, it's made for it, Travis. It's got storage, real closets, the rec space is twice the size of our total living area now."

"And it won't slow the ship down?"

"No, it stays in space," she explained. "When we're in orbit, or between systems, it's locked onto the *Purgatory*. You go through the airlock, up a set of stairs, and you're in a real crew quarters. We can turn this living space into an office. And when you go down to a planet, it disengages from the ship and stays in orbit."

"Where is this incredible wonder?" Travis asked.

"It's isn't far," she said. "It's in the Hyburnum system."

Travis knew the system. He had done some work there. Hybur Four was a highly populated planet. The system had a thick astroid belt. There were several mining operations. And a major refinery station, as well as a ship yard. Several of the planets in the system had outposts, although Hybur Four was the only habitable world with a breathable atmosphere.

"I've been there," Travis said. "I picked up a fugitive that was working for a mining company harvesting the belt.

"We could go and see it," she said. "As soon as we're done on Scye Primary."

"I don't suppose it could hurt. I just can't help but think we could use that money to build out the house on Expanse, or make a down payment on a condo somewhere."

"Why spend money on a place we're only going to visit from time to time?" She argued.

"You really want to keep doing this?"

"We both do. Don't deny it," she told him. "Let's just agree that we're going to be honest about every job, and we're going to live with a certain level of danger."

Travis looked over at Kaylee and couldn't help but smile. She was asleep in her bassinet and looked so peaceful and innocent. He probably could have given up chasing down outlaws for her, but Ava wasn't asking him too, despite the fact that they had nearly been killed numerous times. In fact, in his entire career he had never come so close to dying even once. But with Morgan Black in custody, Travis felt a little less worried about their safety.

"Yeah, okay," he said. "We'll get our new safety clothing from Edwardo, and go check it out."

"I'm going to message the owner. I don't want him selling it to someone else," she said.

Travis sighed, but it was a sigh of contentment. They had planned to spend a few days in Capree taking in the sun and surf along the coast, but he knew that after they paid Edwardo, she would want to leave immediately. And to be honest, he was pretty excited about the prospect too. A real bedroom would be nice, he had to admit it. Two would be even better. And if Ava could do so much with the tiny kitchen in their tiny living quarters on the *Purgatory* he couldn't help but wonder what she could create in a full sized galley.

They reached the Toothsbury system an hour later. By that time they were both very excited about the prospect of expanding their ship. Ava took the controls. Flying the *Purgatory* had become her passion. Somehow she managed to take care of a newborn baby, make Travis' life wonderful, and fly the ship. All he did was catch outlaws and desperados.

He was nursing a few bruises from his fight with his father. Leon Hurts was an escaped felon that Travis had tracked down on Dur Rohstoff. Seeing him again, after over twenty years was difficult. Time in the penal colony on Lucerne had not been kind to the old man. He was still strong and cruel, but not as tough as he once had been. Yet somehow, even in death, the old felon still found a way to torment Travis. Not an hour went by that he didn't question the fact that he could have found a way to bring his father in alive. Guilt was like a knife in his back. It plagued him, and there was no cure, no way to stop the painful memories. He knew time would ease the feeling of hurt, and regret, but there was no way to speed the process. And there was no guarantee that he wouldn't carry the scar of having to kill his own father for the rest of his life.

They landed in an airfield on the edge of Capree and took Kaylee out into the fresh air. She was a happy baby. Travis wondered how different his life would be if Kaylee were fussy and cried all the time. He had heard horror stories about infants that never stopped crying, and parents who never got any rest. But Kaylee was a calm, happy baby. And she had stolen his heart.

They were flush with money too. They had returned from Dur Rohstoff with a ship full of fugitives. The reward money, even after repaying his fine to the GCIB was nearly a million credits. He had insisted that Ava put two hundred thousand into a private account for her and Kaylee. She swore that she wasn't going anywhere, and they were even talking about marriage, but he wanted to have options. Especially if something were to happen to him, which in his line of work was a very real possibility.

Edwardo Hernandez was one only a handful of tailors in the galaxy that wove laser absorbing fibers into clothing to create a barrier that could stop a laser blast, or at least reduce the damage it would do to his body. Travis had ordered a new coat and shirt. His last outfit had been ruined by Morgan Black, but he didn't like thinking of that terrible night on Expanse either. He even wondered if they would ever return and finish the homestead on Expanse. It held a lot of bad memories for Travis and for Ava.

"Welcome, my friends," Edwardo said when they reached his workshop. "Come and see what I have for you."

They followed him inside and found a holographic display running the news story about the capture of Morgan Black. The news anchor was going on and on about The Man In Black, the dreaded Ghost Gun assassin that was more myth than man. The newscaster even mentioned Travis, but thankfully he didn't have a photo of the lawman responsible for bringing down the most infamous outlaw in the galaxy.

"You are famous!" Edwardo said.

"I was lucky," Travis said. "I didn't stop Black. I just took him into custody."

"They say you saved his life," Edwardo said. "Not this clown. He is bought and paid for by the Galactic Coalition. But there are better stories out there. They say you cut off his gun hand."

"I didn't," Travis said. "That was someone else. I just took an injured man into custody."

"But he was there, to kill you, no?" Edwardo asked. "Did you face him down, Travis?"

"I saw him," Travis said, not mentioning that it was just after he had killed his own father.

"You are brave. And you did it without my clothing," Edwardo said. "We must change it. In fact, I have an offer for you. I think you'll like it. First, let us try on the clothes, yes? It will be fun. Ava, let me hold the baby for you!"

Edwardo took Kaylee. Travis put on the shirt that Edwardo had made. It was a simple garment, gunmetal gray, long sleeves with button cuffs, and buttons up the front. Travis put it on and found it to be a perfect fit. It wasn't stiff. There was stretch to it. And onto of the shirt went new, knee length coat. It was thicker that the shirt and made to be worn open so the could get to his weapons, but it could be buttoned up too.

"I did some experiments," Edwardo said. "The shirt has one way fibers, enough to absorb fifty to sixty percent of a normal laser. But the coat has a fibers woven into the wool in two directions, overlapping. It's not body armor, but my experiments show an increase in the efficacy of up to ninety percent, depending on the power and range of the weapon."

"You're saying this will stop a laser blast?" Travis said.

"Not the kinetic energy, but the heat, yes," Edward said. "As well as the body armor you gave me."

"Mine too?" Ava asked.

Edwardo nodded. He had made her garment that was more cloak than an actual coat, although it had sleeves. It was big enough she could wear it over herself and Kaylee, if they were in a dangerous place.

"Yes, it should save you," he said. "At least from the initial shot. Don't go waltzing through a war zone and expect to live. But you shouldn't be killed by a laser shot in the back."

"That's all we could ask for," Travis said. "This is great."

"You look handsome," Ava told him.

"You look great too," Travis said, silently chiding himself that he hadn't told her how beautiful she was first.

"Yes, you're both picture prefect," Edwardo said. "Which brings me to my proposition. Would you allow me to share that I have made these garments for you? Perhaps get a picture with you, and a small endorsement from the man who captured Morgan Black?"

"Of course you can," Travis said.

"You haven't even heard what I'm offering in return?" Edwardo said.

"Doesn't matter," Travis said.

"You sir, should not go into business. You are a terrible negotiator."

"We're just pleased," Ava said. "We appreciate you letting us pay you in installments."

"We have the other hundred, and ten thousand we owe you," Travis said.

"That's just it, my friend. Give me the endorsement, and I'll wave the rest of what you owe. Is that fair?"

"More than fair," Ava said.

"Yeah, we can't do that."

"Yes, you can. I'll more than make up the difference in what I make in future work," he insisted. And if you ever need more, I will ensure that you have it."

"But we'll pay for it," Travis said. "I'm not sure how much my endorsement is going to help you."

"You let me worry about that, my friend. Come, let us get some pictures in your new clothes. And if anyone asks, you tell them that Eduardo is your personal tailor."

Lingering Threat Chapter 2

Morgan was on powerful pain medication, but not so befuddled that he didn't know he was locked to the hospital bed. His left hand, and both ankles were strapped down with metal shackles. His right hand was missing. There was a medical device on the stump of his left arm, and the pain of the amputation was stronger than the medication. His brain knew it hurt, but it was confused about the searing ache.

Medical staff were in and out of the room. They had humiliated him. He was stripped naked and clothed with a paper thin medical gown. He had only a scratchy blanket to keep him warm, but it wasn't doing the job. He had a tube inserted in a very sensitive area of his body to capture his urine. And there was a needle in his arm delivering fluids, medications, and the powerful pain killers. The doctors and med techs came in with scanners. They poked and prodded him. There was no privacy. The lights were always one. He slept only because of the pain medication, and then it was barely more than doze. The hospital was a noisy place. Morgan Black, the most feared man in the galaxy, didn't even know for certain where he was.

But he had contingency plans for exactly the situation he found himself in. And it all began with a med tech who didn't belong in his room. He pretended to be checking on one of the monitors that was displaying his vital signs. Morgan wasn't talking, and neither did the med tech, but he did slip a laser cutter into Morgan's hand and cover it with the thin blanket. He left without saying a word.

Morgan didn't immediately cut himself free. There would be a time for that. But first he needed to clear his head and prepare himself to take advantage of the moment when the time for escape was upon him. It took time. Another person came in with a doctor's long, white coat. He looked official, but he wasn't. He was an imposter, one that had been well paid to deliver him a message.

He lifted Morgan's right arm, pretending to inspect the device that covered the stump of his wrist.

"They've got people everywhere," the man said softly. "Outside the door, at all the elevators. But they're planning to move you the day after tomorrow. My people will be on that ship."

"Good," Morgan Black said.

"We'll have a doctor, and pilot. We'll take out the crew, but you have to neutralize the guards."

"With pleasure" Morgan said.

"Very well, I'll see you in two days. Be sure you have the money ready, or we'll kill you ourselves."

Morgan wasn't afraid. He had planned for his inevitable capture. He wouldn't go to jail, but he was no longer a free man. Even if he escaped he would be forced into hiding. The legend had fallen, and he was just a criminal. The galaxy, once wide open to him, had narrowed significantly. There were only a handful of worlds on the fringe of the galaxy where he could go to hide. But he had made plans for that too. He would miss his ship. The *Dymtr* was a custom build vessel, with a small fortune in custom weapons and clothing, not to mention plenty of hard currency. Maybe someday he could got back to Dur Rohstoff and retrieve it. He wasn't sure. All he knew for certain was that the day after tomorrow he had to be ready to act. Which meant less medication and more pain. But Morgan Black didn't fear death, and he didn't shy away from pain. He was a killer, an experienced death dealer, and he could face whatever it took to escape from the people who were set on bringing him down.

The doctors and techs didn't ask his permission. He couldn't simply request more pain medication. He would have to shut off the spigot himself, and make sure he was ready when his moment came. It all started with the little laser cutter. It was small, which meant it didn't have much battery life. He couldn't waste it. And it wasn't exactly easy to operate with just one hand. The shackle on his left hand was connected to the bed rail. He could slide it up in order to scratch his nose, and back down again, but he only had about eight inches of play in the small, metal links of chain. He took his time, angling the device and getting it right onto the chain where he wanted it. The cutter was small, and wouldn't damage anything that wasn't up close to it, but he didn't want to scorch the bed clothes or the bed frame. He got the cutter under his chain, with the device point upward, before he activated it. It took two seconds to cut through a single link of the chain that had him confined to the bed. As soon as his hand was free he slide the cutter under him to hide it, then made sure the break in the links wasn't obvious.

The doctors weren't law enforcement officers. They didn't inspect his shackles. Likewise, the medical technicians looked after the scanners and devices used in the room and rarely paid him much attention at all. One had taken a self with him using a little camera he kept on a device in his tool pouch. Morgan wasn't bothered by such banal acts. In the past he had worked hard to keep his identity a secret. But even though he didn't have access to a television, holoprojector, or data slate, he knew that word was out about him. He had heard the doctors talking. One had been on a news reports and the others mentioned the pictures of the patient looking graphic.

He supposed he had looked graphic coming in covered in his own blood. The assassin who nearly killed him had been a complete surprise to Morgan. He had wrongly assumed that his escape from the Luxor Resort and subsequent flight to Dur Rohstoff had been enough to throw off the attacker. It didn't make a lot of sense why the strange man was trying to kill him. Yes, Morgan had injured the Asian assassin on Expanse, but only in self defense. The man had attacked him on Travis Hurts' homestead. And he had done his fair share of damage to Morgan too, nearly blinding him in one eye.

But the attack on Dur Rohstoff had been a shock, and it had happened so fast. The only thing that Morgan could remember, other than the terrible jolt of pain when his hand was severed, was that the assassin had been wounded. Morgan could only hope it was a mortal wound. If not, the man might show up again. And while Morgan normally insured that he remembered anyone who slighted him, and vowed to track them down to exact revenge, he genuinely hoped he never saw the silent assassin again.

His only other memory from the fight on Dur Rohstoff was of Travis Hurts slipping a simple little plastic restraint onto his arm and tightening it painfully. But he supposed that Travis had saved his life. There weren't many medical facilities on Dur Rohstoff. And there's no telling if anyone would have bothered to help him. He had a vague memory of the compound being attacked. He wondered if Mallorie McSwain had survived, and if she knew who he really was? If so, she probably hated his guts and it surprised him to find that thought uncomfortable. He was used to fear, to insecurity, and disgust from his victims. They had every right to hate him, but Mallorie was different. Not that Morgan felt anything like love for her. But he preferred not to think that she hated him. It seemed unseemly to him for some reason.

A doctor came in, looked at the vitals on the bank of machines behind Morgan, then gave him another dose of the pain medication. He would have to do something to keep his mind clear soon, but he still had time, he reasoned. And the pain was truly terrible. The medication hit his system quickly, and while it only dulled the searing pain in his arm, and befuddled his brain, it did help him to sleep. And as he drifted off to where the pain couldn't hurt him anymore, he felt more at ease knowing that steps were being taken to ensure he escaped. A few more days he would get proper care, and that made all the difference.